Hemo Sapiens

Hemo Sapiens

EMILY A. WEEDON

DUNDURN PRESS

Publisher: Meghan Macdonald | Acquiring editor: Russell Smith
Cover designer: Laura Boyle
Cover image: Valeriya Simantovskaya

Library and Archives Canada Cataloguing in Publication

Title: Hemo sapiens / Emily A. Weedon.
Names: Weedon, Emily A., author.
Identifiers: Canadiana (print) 20250160579 | Canadiana (ebook) 20250160668 | ISBN 9781459755673 (softcover) | ISBN 9781459755697 (EPUB) | ISBN 9781459755680 (PDF)
Subjects: LCGFT: Thrillers (Fiction) | LCGFT: Paranormal fiction. | LCGFT: Detective and mystery fiction. | LCGFT: Novels.
Classification: LCC PS8645.E33 H46 2025 | DDC C813/.6—dc23

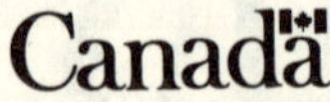

Canada Council for the Arts Conseil des arts du Canada

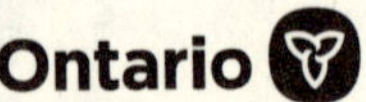

We acknowledge the support of the Canada Council for the Arts and the Ontario Arts Council for our publishing program. We also acknowledge the financial support of the Government of Ontario, through the Ontario Book Publishing Tax Credit and Ontario Creates, and the Government of Canada.

Printed and bound in Canada.

Dundurn Press
1382 Queen Street East
Toronto, Ontario, Canada M4L 1C9
dundurn.com, @dundurnpress

To Willem. Ride or die.
To Ginger. Proof of evolution in humans.

Chapter 1

HELOISE

Heloise drove, hands gripping the wheel, pondering the haplessness of men. She was driven by her hunger for one man. Enclosed in the capsule of a rental car, she went without sustenance while her car devoured miles.

She was aware as she drove that her pulse was up. She thought of him and felt her heart flip. That old catch always got her, despite herself. She should have been better than that. She *was* better than that.

Even so, the thought of silver stubble studding the cliff of his jaw made her ache and sent shimmers of want from her gullet through her spine straight down between her legs. She was pinned to a moment in time by the clear grey of his eye under an arched brow. They held hands across a starched linen tablecloth, for the first time. Heat from his long fingers had warmed her cool palm that evening. As the waiter approached, he pulled his hands away. They slid back to his side of the table like guilty snakes. They would go on to finish the meal, and their eyes would be the only contact between them because it was a popular Chicago restaurant where many other lawyers ate, where many clients ate. Where friends of his wife ate.

Later she would grind her tender cheek against that stubble, in the parking lot, in his car. Over time, the sight of that sandpaper stubble would come to trigger a Pavlovian response in her and the mere sight of it would be the overture to being taken to his bed. But never to his heart.

And so, she was hungry.

He had kept her on a diet, all these months. For years now.

Her heart was ravenous for him. Her body too. She wanted him for herself. She wanted him for his genetics. She wanted, after all the other accomplishments in her life, to procreate with him the way other people wanted to complete marathons or land on the moon. She had a destiny to fulfill, via her body, via him, via their alchemical fusion.

He knew precisely what she wanted. He knew how deeply it clawed at her, from within, her want that had become a bloated need. And he kept her hooked to him, enthralled, hoping, month after month, cycle after cycle, knowing how deep the hormones had dug grooves into her brain. And he knew most of all — when she could easily have had anyone, made a brilliant match with any number of young hustling partners to be — that she wanted him. And he delayed her gratification to the *nth* degree. Neither of them admitted it openly, but that was the dry tinder between them. Her insatiable want, his coy ambiguity, his dangling of the faintly possible.

When they lay entwined together after fucking for hours, he would praise her long flanks, her lean muscles, her titanium bones, her *Übermensch* athleticism. What fine children she would make, he would say, seemingly without guile. He knew that every thrust, every climax was ferocious and hungry and wild and natural and voracious and welcome because they were driven by her baby need. They would fall against each other, flesh long against flesh, and right at the moment when she fell apart under him with want, he would pause for a jarring moment and conspicuously put on a condom.

The thin sheath stank of chemicals and power. It was his cruel, knowing denial. They would then rake each other's flesh and inside she would die with want and hunger for what should be. But she would say nothing, with a fierce contempt for showing weakness.

He knew she was hooked, practically addicted to the hope of him and the day that he would deign to give her a baby. If they had kids, he would tease her with his gravel voice, of course they would be lawyers, *super* lawyers like them.

"Supreme court judges," she would correct. "Presidents." Provoking laughter. Later he would untangle from the hot, damp sheets, stride naked to the bathroom, and then casually say, "It's just not in the cards, though, Babe," as though he and he alone were the arbiter of everything that would or could be.

But her kind were rulers.

His kind were sheep.

How dare he dodge her, play with her, breadcrumb her with promises of month-long vacations, midnight invitations to his lake house, his endless fucking deferments of *one day, really, I promise I will get divorced*?

She would lie awake at nights, one hand across the pulse in his throat, thinking all this, when he had yielded to sleep, but, yet again, not succumbed to her will.

In the old days, her kind would have selected him, based on his strength and genes and smarts. They would couple and then she'd feed. The blood meal was critical to conception. Devoured, seeds and all. His husk would be discarded.

Of course, the old days were old for a good reason. Civilization had moved on from barbarism to tolerance. But in those lusty old days, those at the apex had walked tall, taken whatever they wanted, and kept the flocks enthralled through a delicious and unpredictable application of fear.

She had wished none of that for him. She'd wanted him at her side. He had foolishly thought all this time that he'd raised her — from college to the bar to associate to partner to pause here, at sex toy. She was perfectly content to allow him to continue to think that was so. And she was prepared because of the heat of his kisses and the hone of his thoughts and the shape of his cock and the meat of his muscles to raise him up to sit for a time by *her* side, her chosen equal. Her mate.

Her mind ferreted through remembrance of the taut texts that made him ever unavailable to her while she drove past the belching flames of the Hamilton refineries, speeding south toward the border. And that one text of his:

Babe, I just can't see myself starting a new family. Ever.

She drove too quickly over the St. Catharines bridge, her gorge rising while she thought of how often he'd promised to finalize that divorce. She smiled sweetly at the border guards who kept their words professional but couldn't keep from drinking in her brushed glossy hair, her perfect teeth, and her understated perfume. She dazzled them with tactical flirtation and enjoyed their dumbfounded gaze. They permitted her quick passage. They regretted doing so when she was reduced to taillights and memory. She knew how to cultivate hunger in others: she was herself always hungry.

In Buffalo she parked. She hailed a cab to a different car rental place and slipped behind the wheel of a plain grey Toyota. Under the murky orange of sodium vapour highway lights along the I-90, she permitted herself a few tears. This *was* a momentous trip. Everything would soon change. There would be regrets. But things had to be forced to a point. Change had to occur. As she drove she worried her tongue piercing, twirling the head against the roof of her mouth. He'd always loved it. Got so excited when he bore into her mouth with his tongue. Admitted how hot it made him to know that she always had it there, under the conservative navy-pearl-strand regulation-hem-and-neckline corporate shell she projected.

The whole drive was just over eleven hours. She had to stop in Toledo where she stayed in a roadside motel. She could not arrive before 9:00 a.m. In the hotel she checked her basal temperature. She was entering the release day window. She checked again before leaving at 4:30 a.m. She was wearing the stockings he always said he liked. He'd promised to buy them for her, many times. Ultimately, she bought them herself.

She left the car on the side of the road, up above his sprawling lake house. Her heels crunched grit against the glistening asphalt. The air was fresh here. So fragrant. She could read the scent like a newspaper, just like any predator. There were snails moving up a tree trunk, beside her. A rabbit had urinated somewhere nearby. A hawk circled overhead, tracking the phosphorescence on the rabbit's pelt. Internally, she could feel the way her own hormones were synchronizing with flesh and fluids.

His Modern Tudor mansion towered, peaks and stone cladding, over the sweep of the drive. Several of his vehicles peeped out of glass garages like mannequins on display. She let herself in the glass double doors, her face turned away from the security camera, using the key he'd given her with such ceremony. As if coming by to have wild, no-strings-attached sex whenever it pleased *him* was somehow a gift to her. It was still before 9:00 a.m., which meant he would be drilling figure eights in his private underground squash court. She descended flights of concrete and redwood steps to his home gym thinking about his sweat. His ragged breaths. The blood and oxygen streaming through his body. Despite herself, despite her anger, she was stirred. She loved the feeling of his sweat-slick skin.

At the foot of the stairs, the landing was littered with exercise machines and crossfit toys he never used. The Naugahyde benches, however, had frequently hosted intimate athletics between them.

He looked genuinely happy when he saw her framed in the glass doorway. And his grey eyes flashed with such warmth, the edge came off her hunger a little. She let him nourish her with it.

He certainly didn't complain when she straddled him. At first he didn't complain just because he was happy to give in to her. But mere moments later, he didn't complain, because he wasn't able to. She covered his mouth with Olympian hands. And soon, the only ragged breaths in the echoing glass and drywall and wood of the squash court were hers.

She had never overpowered him before, though the strength had always been there. He was surprised when she resisted. He wanted to turn her over, get back into one or another of his favourite dominant positions. They both liked it when he flipped her around so. He was surprised that she countered his force. At first he thought it was a frisky novelty.

"Feisty!" he grinned and then got up to flip her for real this time. Except that he couldn't. Under his squash clothes, his abs and obliques rallied in union but may well have surged against a steel door. She would not be moved. She could not be moved.

"Heloise. What is this?" He said it when she bent to look at him closely and allowed her laced fingers to slip from his mouth.

"You know I wanted a baby."

He scoffed a little, letting her be aware of his full scorn, and turned his head, calculating whatever phrases he thought might calm her down.

"I came hunting," she said before any words occured to him. He turned back to her. She kept him pressed down and gave a knowing, conscious tilt of her pelvis against his, while holding his gaze. "You've been avoiding me. You've been keeping me on a shelf. On tap. At arm's length. You've been keeping yourself from me, trying to make me crazy. Trying to control what I feel. What I want." In between her words, she pressed hard kisses to his neck, his face.

She could feel his uncertainty. But she felt him responding. She breathed in through her nose and she knew many things about him from what she sensed. His fear was there too, which had always been absent before. But not because he was some great, brave thing — it was because he'd been ignorant about her. Underestimated her.

She pressed his hands, their backs against the polished wood floor of the court, and rode against him, pressed into him through her dress and his shorts. He was blocky and hard under her.

She pulled at his shorts, she pulled at her dress. She grasped him, directed him, and sank onto him. They both gasped at this foreign feeling: unsanctioned flesh against flesh.

"Oh my god," he uttered, pressing his head against the boards, and arching up. She released his hands, and he grabbed her hips to keep their contact sealed.

She felt somewhat disembodied, which disappointed her. She'd always thought the moment would be all about keener senses, being more sharply there. But a calm directedness took her over. She moved with purpose, finally tending to the hungers she'd nursed. He smiled and she smiled in return. She was sorry it had taken him so long to come to this point of giving himself over to her. And she was sorry that, in the very moment that they finally found fusion, they would also find their end.

He would be consumed.

He wrapped his arms around her as their breaths and cries subsided and for a moment, she gave into the sweetness of that. She let the momentousness of what she had done exist there in the same space as him.

"I ovulated this morning," she whispered into his ear, while she stroked sweat along his neck. She felt his body stiffen when she said that. And she twined her fingers deeper into his hair.

"Ohhh, god. This was not a good idea," he said. She let her fingers curl into his hair and gripped it. She kissed him, open-mouthed, running the stud of her tongue piercing along the inside of his lip. He'd often played with it, had it in his mouth while they rode each other, playfully. She put it in his mouth now. And he finally learned its real purpose.

She stayed on him, mounted, feeling his pulses weaken and she sealed his sounds with her kisses.

"I thank you for this sacrifice," she whispered to him. She spoke the old, traditional words, the ones that had always been a lie, to cover her theft. The *s* was slurred through his thick blood. She was still gripping him with her body, her whole being, while she accepted her harvest. First his semen. And then his blood would seal everything, create the future she'd longed for. Without the blood meal, there could be no child.

She thought of all the herds, running, sleek in the sun, sun-dappled, feet pounding the earth, salt tang of sweat thickening the air. Salt tang of blood. Blood in her mouth. And the hunger of decades finally, sweetly, fully slaked. He slipped from her, a damp empty pod. He had given everything. She petted his hide, overwhelmed by his gifts, his great sacrifice. She was deeply thankful. Somewhere, deep within, she was slightly regretful.

Chapter 2

LUKE

Bloodball. Luke knew that was the direct translation of "hemoglobin" from Greek, provided one had a sense of humour about these things. A little ball of blood. All humans, in fact all vertebrates, they just teemed with bloodballs. And crammed inside those little balls were the metalloproteins that take crucial oxygen throughout a living body, metabolizing all the processes of life. Like sleeping or digesting. Procreating. Fighting, fawning, fleeing, or fucking. It occurred to Luke that it could have been zinc, maybe, in some mixed-up version of the world and universe. He tried that one out on Beatrice once, when they were lying around after sex.

"Can you imagine if we had different chemicals — you know, compounds? Elements, I guess. Like that we weren't mostly made of carbon? Or maybe we needed zinc instead of iron?" The last few words died on his lips as he uttered them to her. She was scowling at him over the edge of the sheet. So much for post-sex glow.

"We *don't.*" She turned over with a hard shoulder and dropped like a payload into sleep. That was early on. Luke got wise to sharing whimsical thoughts as they popped into his head.

And Beatrice was right: for *Homo sapiens* and all vertebrates, blood was iron-based.

Common knowledge is that it is iron in the heme that gives blood its characteristic ruddiness. Common knowledge, Luke knew, was too common and very often wrong. Porphyrin moiety was the real reason for the colour of blood. "Compounds connected by carbon, in a functional group." This was how that cute toxicologist with the utterly perfect heart-shaped ass once put it to Luke. That was right before he put it to her, with gusto, over an entire long weekend in a ritzy hotel she'd begged him to book. Her hair was long and chestnut-coloured. Her fingers were strong, and her sensible nails still had a little bite to them. Her techno-science talk was intoxicatingly hot. And she made sure he was fully aware how much she had to dumb everything down for him. Somehow even having things dumbed down for him was hot. She was the brain. He was the hunky cop. She was also the last woman he had touched, before he'd got married.

Sometimes he liked to wander through the memory of her body compared to his wife's form. Not in a weird way. Not in a longing way. Well, maybe a little, since his wife's body had become just a memory too. He used to like remembering his wife's solid body, which at times seemed cut from stone. No, the comparison was simply an … *appreciation* of biodiversity. He didn't think the toxicologist was better. She was just different. Slacker in places, cushiony. Curvy. She had a different quality of flesh that could be understood only by comparison, like a designer weighing different fabrics in his two hands. A swell of lip on one, a hollow of collarbone in the other, a plump handle of a hip, a lush, overflowing handful of breast. Freckled. Unfreckled. Living flesh, alive under his hands and mouth.

All that was academic now. Abstract. The toxicologist got filed with the other useless science stuff along with Grade 5 science fair projects in his brain and rarely called up for re-examination.

He was at a time of change in his life. He'd gone from stranger to lover, lover to suitor, suitor to provider and had lodged here at stabilizer. Cheque signer. Visa-bill payer. On the rights and obligations spectrum, he was listing hard now into the obligations end. At the moment he was currently obliged to sit on a wobbly plastic chair in a chilly exam room, holding his wife's purse on his lap.

The blood he professionally observed in his line of work was typically directly splattered on or immediately adjacent to corpses. It was in the process of breaking down. Hemoglobin into methemoglobin. In other words, old blood. Brown blood. Clotted, congealed. Certainly, all done moving around.

He glanced at his wife's body, crinkling in the paper gown, yet perky and alert on the exam table. The blood they were taking out of her was different. Vital and lively, vial after vial of the stuff, pooled thickly into lavender and goldenrod-topped tubes. His eye was drawn to the gravy-ish consistency streaming down the butterfly needle's bevel. His eye roved back to his wife's paper-clad body. How did she make a paper gown look good? And back up to her face. She was smiling at him broadly, with a smart-ass expression.

"I can't believe how much of a lame-o you are with this." She turned to the nurse and jerked her thumb toward Luke. "All day, this guy. Elbows-deep in blood and trauma and violence and then he's a total wuss when it comes to needles." The nurse who was drawing all the blood chuckled and released the final vial. She tossed Luke an extra glance, an appraising glance, which he noticed. He maintained a poker face. But he did ruffle his hand through the grey-shot full hank of his hair up top. It was nice to be noticed.

Luke kept his lips tight. His wife looked bright and cheery even. Making jokes in doctor's offices was her way of coping with the stress. That and making him the butt of her jokes. Deflect attention away from herself and her worries.

He was not a wuss. He worked with corpses. He dealt ably with corpses and killers and coroners. He dealt with corpse-like bureaucrats who dealt with actual corpses day in and day out. He saw things daily that would send other people blithering straight into therapy. He was not a wuss about blood. But she was the kind of person who needed to say he was, so that she felt better about herself. Her humble brag was how great she was with medical stuff and to seem better, he had to seem bad about it, whenever they were talking with others. One of those quirks about people you only discover when you've been with them for pushing three years.

"Most of the blood I see isn't sloshing around all over the place, Beatrice," he muttered. He wasn't mounting an argument. Gentle pushback to remind her he still possessed a fully intact backbone. "I deal with blood that's nice and still. And all I have to do is look at the patterns."

"Ugh. Please. Too much information." She held up her hand.

Okay, so that conversation was over now.

"All righty. You are free to go, Mrs. Stockton," said the nurse. Beatrice nodded, her hands were a nest in her lap, the knuckles white with pressure.

"I hate this place," she said to Luke as soon as the door closed.

He stiffened. Something was going on. Something was always going on, lately. He'd peeked at the *What to Expect When You're Expecting* disaster manuals. He'd come to expect everything and anything. *Women start laying down different neural pathways as soon as they become pregnant.*

"What's going on?" He had learned to keep his questions very open ended and to remove any hint of judgment or criticism.

"You moron. First, they kept us waiting for forty-five minutes. That idiot there read the wrong chart ..."

"That's a simple mistake."

"It said Mrs. Ramachandran. Do I *look* like I am East Indian? She was telling me about the test that was positive ..."

"It's okay, Bea—"

"Not okay. It was a negative. One second of not paying attention, Luke. That's how malpractice starts."

He breathed in sharply through his nose and clenched his molars together.

She leapt on his silence. "Anyway, I've already decided I want a different doctor. One who makes sure this baby gets born healthy." She pulled one arm of her sweater on. While she felt for the second sleeve, she was already shoving some brochures at him. He glanced at them while she crammed the rest of her clothes on without bothering to smooth them out.

The brochures were all for ob-gyns. Two of the utilitarian ones were way uptown with soothing, competent Jewish names. The fourth generation of doctor types.

"I don't think we should switch. Dr. Ko is great."

"Phht."

"It took a lot to get Dr. Ko." The clinic shown in the third brochure was slick. A gorgeous, competent-looking blond woman perched on the edge of a massive desk with a view of the city and the lake. He caught the words "exclusive" and "cutting edge." It reeked of money. He said, "And we can't afford to go to a private place. I already wiped out most of my RRSP for the mortgage. I can't afford this." He stabbed at the blond fantasy doctor lady with her slim crossed arms and her piercing look of über-intelligence.

Beatrice was already out the door so fast that her purse got caught in the jamb. He pulled her back gently to release her. And then suddenly she was crying and actually turned to him, *to* him, and hid her face against his chest and cried hot, hard tears that went straight through his shirt and found his skin. He grasped her trembling shoulders with his big mitts and leaned his mouth and nose over the crown of her head. He'd missed that scent.

"Okay, B. Okay, okay. We'll check them out." He heard a strangled cry in the folds of his shirt and felt her give a few hard nods. Okay.

"I just th—"

And then his phone went off, pinging and buzzing.

She pulled away. And gave him a stabbing look. The goddamn phone. And they both knew from the signature ping, a work text. The curtain went down over her eyes. For just a moment, they had been warm and limpid and needy of him. Now, iron curtain.

"I'll be in the car."

†

The seatbelt made a cold metallic snap as Luke strapped in. The brochures were between the seats. She'd twisted the three of them together, like wrung out cloths. He could still see parts of the blond superwoman with her intense gaze. He pushed them into the console. Tried to keep his tone light and non-confrontational.

"I'll drop you at the diner. I have to get over to the job site."

"Job site" was their couple term for crime scenes because to her it sounded more job-like. Less distasteful. She was wiggling in her seat.

"Oh god. I need to pee. I should have gone when I was still in the office." She messed around with the seatbelt, trying to get the pressure off her bladder.

"Do you want to go back?"

"No, I need to eat more than I need to go to the bathroom. Did those eggs this morning make you gassy? Like, more than normal? Maybe that's a pregnancy thing?"

She had become a detective in pursuit of the meaning of her collection of symptoms, the same way she'd been a beat cop chasing down a perp when it came to conceiving. She got her man, she pinned him down, extracted what she needed from him, and was now focused on incubating to the exclusion of everything else.

Of course, that wasn't really it. He'd always wanted kids. Wanted homemade Halloween costumes and snugglers on the couch. He was prepared for nighttime incursions into the marital bed. He got misty seeing men walk knee-high kids to daycare. He wanted the whole messy thing.

"Hey, it's Friday," he said, giving her knee a squeeze. Her one night per week that permitted a glass of vino. And maybe even a slim chance of friskiness.

"Yeah!" she said, absently. "Flew by. Drive faster. I really have to go."

Very slim chance.

A series of work texts came in, rattling his phone in its holder on the dash. Something big, apparently something grisly in an alley downtown. Beatrice sniffed, glancing at the texts crowding the screen, and then turned to look out the window.

Chapter 3

HELOISE

She lay in the long shallow dent of a hotel mattress in Toledo. A different motel from the one before, zigzagging her movements across the state. She knew she was colouring outside all the lines she'd ever been taught to respect. It was lonelier than she expected. But it also felt as though a noose had slackened against her neck.

A blade of light cut through the rusty textured blackout curtains. It fell warm and bright across her knees. She woke with a feeling of well-being, noticing that warmth. And then, with a sharp breath, she was suddenly fully awake and acutely aware of how fetid the motel air was.

Foul cigarette stench clung to every divot of the coverlet — the sheets, the walls, along every fibre on the lampshade, and into every dent of the cinder-block walls. She wanted to vomit. Not because of the life she carried. Instead, to protect it. She could feel herself folding around it, already, curled inward like petals. Here was the loneliness again. This was something she wanted to talk about with someone. A wise someone. Should she be able to feel this life already? Was that normal for their kind?

She guided a pointed toe down through the cling of brand-new tights and relished the grip of the synthetics as they clung to her. She felt strong. She felt the life within, also strong. And then, she sat down for a moment, stabbed in the belly with grief and guilt and realization because she also felt him. Diluted. Within. But unmistakably him. And she was thankful for it, though sick with the consequence of everything that had passed under her hands. He was bonded to her now.

It meant he would never again lie to her over a phone or across a starched linen tablecloth. He would never again push against her, his jaw sharp against her shoulder blade. He would never again call her "Babe." And yet … life. He would be within her. As long as this life was. The hugeness of it all was almost intolerable. For a moment she thought she was so sensitive that she could feel the grinding of the very earth on its axis, the low, deep rumble of the planets and the stars, particles of light stranded through her, connecting her to every moment of creation and destruction through time impenetrable, to now, and on to inexperienced future time impenetrable. She was the axis.

She was hungry — not hungry in her stomach; there was no peevish flip and gurgle of digestive chemicals making the glistening stomach wall heave. There was no sense of faintness and ebbing sugar. It was mechanical — no … animal. Obligate. It was a river, a geyser of hunger. She balled up stockings and lingerie and tied them into a white plastic bag along with her Prada dress and a Miu Miu blazer and dropped them into the wastebasket. Refuse from her cheese and biscuits she threw on top, along with the dregs of a strong coffee, to deter nosy cleaning staff.

The hunger propelled her from the room, on her heel, down the walk, out from under the overhang into a cascade of warm sunlight, into the rental car and up the highway, north. She could master the urge, wait to slake it. Until she was back across the border and back into darkness, she could wait. It didn't make her needy. It made her powerful. And the life, small and steady as a new candle flame, was the focus. She would use all that power for its sake.

Chapter 4

LUKE

Homicide. Homeless vic. Alley off St. Hebert @ Yonge.

Sometimes, in the flurry of a given day, a text like this stopped the world for a moment. Sure, Luke shrugged some of them off, the way he'd seen plenty of old hands do so. It was the job. Violence. Sudden death. Small crimes. Great crimes. Ugly crimes. But once in a while, a few characters in a little blue bubble on a screen re-arranged themselves back into *the* big picture. A life. A life someone had once anticipated. Birthdays. First steps. New shoes. First days of classes. First kiss. First job. First fight. Last breath.

It made Luke sigh. Made him wonder. Could he do this? He'd gone to school for it. He'd always told everyone he wanted to be a cop, become a detective. He'd borne the Dudley Do-Right jibes of friends and family. But there was always that sneaking suspicion that he, more than all the others who chose this path, let things in; allowed texts to become baby booties. Could see the horror through the jargon and acronyms. But an avalanche of details and procedure usually cured him of momentary lapses of total perspective. There was a method to the method. Crime was perpetrated on society, and he was a functionary of society connecting dots on many documents, drawing a line between them.

When he arrived there, the "job site" was indeed what his wife would consider distasteful. Not merely a homicide scene, St. Hebert was a grimy, foul, dark, and narrow place where things were dropped and hoped forgotten. St. Hebert was south of Bloor, where the glitz and glass and marble of Yorkville gave way to tacky liquidation shops built of crumbling bricks, fast food joints, towers of garbage bags, and a roving homeless population. They'd taken to calling them "unhoused" lately. Point was, they roamed, they slept in alleys. They were constantly threatened by disease and death and violence. They collected in the core here, pooling in the alleys off Yonge Street, forced into the cracks. Once the biggest artery in the biggest city, the main street of the city seemed anything but main anymore.

The alley was between two tall buildings. An overhang between them created a perfunctory shelter that drew homeless people in the area to it like a magnet. The brick and asphalt were permeated with the smell of urine, partly thanks to a complete lack of public toilets in the city. The waste had to go somewhere. Despite the thick stench, it made a place to shelter from the sun or rain or snow. Every night people bundled up behind recycling bins or unfurled a sleeping bag to attempt to sleep while the city buzzed by only steps away. It also served as an ideal place to do drugs before crashing and blocking out life with a little bit of merciful unconsciousness. All of the above was likely the case for the deceased he'd been called down to investigate.

Before Luke even got close to the yellow tape, a beat cop put out a stern hand and puffed out his chest.

"Careful. Lot of hypodermics in there."

"Thanks, New Kid." Luke lifted his foot to show off his sole. Steel-toe, steel-shank Doc Martens. Good for kicking in doors and/or faces. Good for not getting accidentally poked by hypodermic needles while walking sketchy crime scenes. The cop depuffed a little and took a half step back to let him through.

The asphalt had once covered the alley and led to a parking lot behind. Now potholes spread like an infection, exposing a gravel bottom that was rutted and covered with pools of muddy water from rain several days back. There was nowhere for the water to drain.

The kid's body was under the overhang. He was face up, serene, zipped into a forest-green sleeping bag. The bag was absolutely soaked through. On the top, where it was exposed to sunlight, caked mud had dried into white swirls. On the bottom, a sodden mess. He must have felt the moisture wicking up through the bag and right into his clothes as he was losing consciousness. Or maybe he was too far gone by then.

The kid had a messy ring of dark reddish-purple lining his mouth. Luke tugged up on his pants so he could squat down and look closer. On the way down to his haunches, he suppressed a little grunt. Truly, over forty years old and not getting out for a run three times a week anymore was starting to make everything creaky. He could feel the top of his pants bite into the flesh of his middle these days.

Up close, he realized right away that the dark colour around the kid's mouth wasn't blood, or even biological. Little telltale flecks of mica sparkled in the light. Lipstick. They were subtle flecks, though. This wasn't some teenager's bubblegum lip gloss. This was a high-end, sophisticated mouth paint with a little glam, a little sexy rev. Luke motioned for the SOCO, the Scene of Crime Officer, Tymika, to grab close-ups.

Tymika had arrived ahead of him, which was partly procedural and totally *her*. She had gotten straight to work. She was one of several SOCOs attached to his platoon who could process the Forensic Investigation of relatively uncomplicated scenes on her own if need be.

"Thank you, Trainee Detective Constable," she threw out and she leaned hard on the *trainee.*

"Fantastic. Great job," he said. He'd read the training and managerial manuals that emphasized it was everyone's job to "grow" the skills and talents of members of his team. The endless complimenting and handholding felt disingenuous to him. When he was coming up, it was all about "Yes sir, how high sir?" — none of this coddling "growing" business. He had never been complimented or encouraged or mentored his whole life. He had kept out of the way of some assholes, run afoul of some assholes, and done the bidding of some assholes until he got to be the trainee asshole himself, only to discover that no one "did" asshole anymore. It was all Mr. Rogers nicey-nice all the time now. The juniors and reports were all about being anxious and worried and traumatized. If anyone spent the mandated amount of time holding these kids' hands after a traumatic day, they were going to run out of time to actually do their jobs. Besides which, he happened to know Tymika was on a career fast track to become a Trainee Detective Constable herself. She'd be lapping him in no time.

By the odour of the kid, and the fact that his shoes were shucked off, he'd lived on the streets for some time. Just long enough for some mild trench foot to set in, with its distinctive, insistent smell. It was simple ignorance and naïveté: the kid hadn't figured out how to take care of himself on the streets. He was smart enough to be sleeping on top of his boots and not wearing them. He was young enough that he still needed a full set of parents to get him to take care of himself at home. He was old enough to shave but hadn't been doing so. He wasn't emaciated and had relatively neat fingernails. Slight sign of a struggle, by their colouration.

The kid wore Gap and J.Crew clothes, newish but torn. The boots were Brooks Brothers. Those cost at least five, maybe six hundred bucks. A recent runaway from a nice home who'd met with trouble? Maybe a bad drug deal? A fight over a dry place to sleep, which was why he was in the puddle at the end? The dental would reveal a lot. Luke expected to find a mouth full of neat teeth — regulation, expensively braced, well-lined-up teeth.

He did not expect to press down on the bottom lip with a gloved finger and find that the kid had almost completely lost his tongue.

Luke had seen tongues bitten off or nearly off, due to seizures and drugs and fights. This was a clean, practically surgical slice. But it was still hanging on by a segment.

"Exsanguination," Tymika remarked. Pointing her mouth toward her body camera mic, she noted how close to the wall the body was situated. She'd already worked the outside of the scene and was getting into her close-up shots. Her evidence markers peppered the ground. For newer kids like her, talking into the body camera and narrating everything they did was completely second nature. It still felt foreign to Luke, but he was catching up. Tymika liked to spice up a work session by spitballing potential causes of death. She treated it like a game that she was up or down on and jockeying for position with Luke. All of which gave Luke a real tension headache.

"Exsanguination. You *think*? You get twenty-seven thousand points," Luke told her dryly. He'd learned over time that him giving her "points" seemed to give her the attention and ego boost she needed to make her shut the fuck up.

"Awesome," she said, between the hot whines of her flashbulb's capacitor.

"Nice potholes here," he remarked to her. A few muddy potholes had no water standing in them. They were crisscrossed with grooves, divots, and partial footprints. One of them, readily noticeable: the kid's Brooks Brothers footwear with a distinct pattern of circles on the soles.

"You like those, do you?" What she really meant was: *I already noticed them. Stop micromanaging me.*

"Sure, like a Hallmark greeting card. Plus, you get to play with your plaster cast stuff."

"Oh yeah. My total fave." Her voice was fully dipped in sarcasm. It depressed him a little. He'd loved doing plaster casts. Loved the idea of powder and water congealing into something concrete, immortalizing tire or footprints into a matrix that made the crime an artifact. It used to make him feel like he could do something about all the chaos. He wasn't sure why Tymika was here, beyond hustling her way up, rung after rung, to some bright future. She was good, but she didn't seem to like it.

What he really wanted was space away from Tymika's constant banter to think his own thoughts. The kid was pale enough that he could have bled out. So where then was the pooled blood? Why was it such a neat wound, such a targeted one? Could the body have been moved after the fact? The mouth and the head were clean. His eyes were sunken. Pale, chalk, ghost white. Could he have swallowed his own blood? Drowned in it? Still couldn't account for all the missing blood.

The coroner van arrived, ninety minutes later, stymied by traffic. Luke overheard the team getting the rigamarole about the hypodermic needles from Mr. Super-Cop. Luke waved absently at them as they pulled their equipment out. Even Tymika was starting to pack up her crime scene kit, including her yellow evidence markers and camera bits — and she was famous in the platoon for being a stickler to the bitter end. Luke wondered with a slight ache in his chest how long it would be before he reported to her, and not the other way around.

The body was sealed into a black bag, and the bag was identified with time-and-date stamp, location. Tymika would stay with the boy, all the way to the morgue, waiting for the autopsy, in a kind of vigil. She would observe the sealing up of the body bag, and she would observe it being opened later, in the presence of the coroner, maintaining an utterly strict chain of custody. She would put a sticker on the cabinet where the body reposed after the autopsy. Time-and-date stamped also. That was procedure. It rationalized the process of understanding and documenting the crime scene. It depersonalized and systematized.

It tugged at Luke's feelings; this was more attention than the kid had likely had for a long time. Driven away from his family via whatever fights or forces, into homelessness and nameless obscurity. And from obscurity to the extremely, the overly intimate actions of the individual who had slain him. And now he rested under the watchful eye of Tymika, who left nothing unturned. Finally, the coroner who would wash and tend to the kid's remains, nurturing and protecting, coaxing, seeking.

Luke left Tymika to release the crime scene. The yellow plastic tape would be pulled down. In a matter of minutes after they'd all left, the stage would reset and the alley would revert to the people who made the street their home when no other home was there for them.

Chapter 5

LUKE

Luke sat on one of those twirly stools arrayed along the salmon-coloured melamine counter. Olympic Diner. A narrow little place on a street parallel with the train tracks. Under the restaurant name, the sign proclaimed its self-deprecating slogan: “Reliable since 1952.” The “reliable” part was thrown further into question by the quotation marks around it. He’d been coming there since he’d been in university. Best grilled cheese in the city, because for some reason cheese, butter, and grilled toast was something people could manage to cock up.

Luke was reliably the first one there. That way he could nab the one stool that sat level instead of orbiting its post in a drunken wobble.

Harry would have gladly moved the date over a terse “Scene’s still hot” text, wouldn’t have whined about it. Especially since it was Harry, with his TV looks and beaming smile, who frequently bailed because of a shoot, a meeting with a producer, an expert interview on CNN, a shave and a haircut.

Truth was, as Harry was Luke's only real friend, Luke put up with forever being put off. Luke held the thought in his mind at a distance without closely examining it, because it was one of those embarrassing facts one doesn't poke one's finger into.

Harry was a former work colleague who'd moved on from detective work to security consulting and lecturing and media appearances and big-shotdom as the host of a true crime show. He had become more acquaintance than friend, but they still went through the motions. They could still talk shop. When they worked together, years back as rookies, they used to talk about dating. Or, more accurately, they discussed Luke's lack of enthusiasm about it, or total refusal to get off his ass to go on dates about which he could later complain. Harry wouldn't have helped Luke move a couch or anything, though. They still had that kind of formality between them.

Luke also held the thought in his mind that maybe it was weird to not have a "real" friend, or even more outlandish … Friends. Plural. Who *were* all these people who had time to go to movies together, take strolls, chat about things? Lately, Harry had been even harder to catch for an after-work beer, so the last few years had settled into a fast lunch three or four times a year.

"Sorry, sorry!" Harry took up most of the space in the room as soon as he finally arrived, his smile entering the room before he did. The waitress noticed him as soon as he pulled the door open sharply. Luke saw the light in her eyes turn on. Fair enough: Harry's suit was cut to actually fit his body and he was in wicked shape.

"I'll have my regular," Harry told the waitress. His subtext was *I'm hot and we both know it and right now I'm focused on you.* She smiled and nodded, star-struck, like she'd been done a favour to take his order.

Harry would have what he always had not because he liked it, but because it cut to the chase. Plain hamburger, salad, black coffee.

He liked the bill to arrive at the same time as the meal. Harry liked to move through life with purpose and leave people always wanting more of his time.

"For Chrissakes. Did you go get your teeth whitened?" Luke wanted to know.

Harry flashed the super white teeth in question even wider. He smoothed out his long wool coat so it wouldn't crease as he sat.

"Heya. Thanks for squeezing me in." Luke moved an accordion folder already stuffed with paperwork for the Alley Vic to make room.

"Yeah, sorry, this is what we're reduced to — lunch between appointments. How you doing? Looks like a skinny file — new case?"

"Yeah, new one. Kid in an alley. Things are fine, great. Everything's great. I'm great. Everything is going great." Luke put down his spoon in his saucer with too much force. "It's shit. Everything feels like shit."

"Yeah. Just hold the great next time and skip straight to the shit. Saves us both a lot of time. How's Beatrice? Congrats by the way. Is she showing yet?"

"Not yet. Only eleven and a half weeks. She keeps checking in the mirror though."

"Oh god. You're documenting that, yeah? You know you need to be documenting that, right? I didn't do enough with our first kid, and I think we almost got divorced over it. Take pictures every day."

"Harry, I already take so many photos I should have taken Photography instead of Criminology."

"Beats working!"

Luke laughed at the inside joke. Harry was the original workaholic. "It's been hard in the husband department. She doesn't want to get close, things about her are changing … I feel totally …" He dropped his voice because he was going to say something that he knew he should not be feeling, or be allowed to feel, or admit to feeling. "Totally weirded out by the pregnancy."

"You'd better get over that right quick, boyo. For number one." Harry held out a finger. "You have to share her going forward from now on with at least one other person, so get used to that. You get used to taking care of things for yourself in the uh, husband department. And B," he added, counting out the second point on his finger, "no matter how you actually feel about it, you tell her she is the most beautiful goddess you've ever seen in your life, every day, multiple times. Trust me. Any less than that and you will have constant strafing to deal with."

"She never feels like it anymore. And on the rare occasions I do, she's been talking so much about her gums bleeding or her eyesight getting blurry or her back or boobs aching that I'm honestly finding it hard to keep interested."

"Yeah, I know, it's super hot. But you stare at the ceiling and think of Victoria's Secret and you tell her she's a goddamned goddess and you work your ass off at making her believe it. It does get better, man."

"Yeah, really? When?"

"In your sixties. Aha, kidding. Around age six. When the kids start having sleepovers. Or can at least get up and fix some cereal. Morning nookie is what saved us."

"I dunno."

"What?" Harry's tone was openly frustrated. Normally, he had more patience for Luke's meandering neuroses.

"Sometimes I almost feel like I got taken for a ride. Like she got what she needed. And now I'm … extra. Dressing. Maybe not even that."

"She needs you, man. More than ever. Hang in there. It's the most amazing ride of your life. But no one said you're gonna like all of it. Besides, Beatrice is hot. Total catch. Incredible. You're lucky to have her."

Luke sat with that last bit in silence. Harry had never stated it quite that bluntly before. In Luke's world a guy didn't outright state that to another guy.

Sensing the temperature drop, Harry stabbed his spoon in the direction of the skinny file with his coffee spoon. "So, what's the deal with your Alley Kid?"

"Near total exsanguination."

Harry wrinkled his nose. "So. Homicide."

"Ya think? At first I thought: straightforward. A runaway, probably an overdose. There's enough of them, god knows. But turns out, there are a few more kinks in the details."

"Like?" Harry sounded unimpressed.

"Like a slashed tongue. Almost clean through."

Harry rewarded him with a raised eyebrow. He peeked at Luke's cellphone screen. "Busy alleyway. That kid's right out in the open. You'd think a person would want to hide it a little."

"Yeah, no effort to even cover him up."

"Shows the perp feels contempt for the victim. Have you considered who your perp could be? Maybe a trick gone wrong? I'd be looking at your regular john types who like to recruit street kids. Someone with a punitive streak."

Luke made a noncommittal sound. He pulled up another photo. "Maybe not John. Lipstick all over him."

"Come on. Gender's got nothing to do with lipstick."

Luke felt his back go up at the grating sound of Harry being right. And using that "School's in Session" tone of his. "Yeah. 'Course. I didn't rush to assume the lipstick meant female. Anyway, it's ringed right around his mouth. Signs of defence. And found these prints on the ground ..." With a hand partially cupping the screen to shield a casual glance from traumatizing someone, he showed shots of the lipstick on the kid's mouth and the markings in the puddle. "Still think it's just a bad trick?"

Harry blew out a slow puff of air. "Looks like he was just chucked away. Like so much take-out food. If that's a trick, someone was really slumming it. Those shoeprints there — the shoes are Givenchy."

"Huh?"

Harry pointed out the heel and toe pattern embossed in the mud to him.

"The boots. One of the many ways I continue to prove myself a model husband: thousands of dollars spent on shoes."

"Thousands, Harry? Come on." Luke added the sound of a marital cat-o-nine-tails landing on Harry's flesh.

"Listen, you know damn well I hang out with extremely good-looking co-hosts. My hair and makeup hotties flirt with me constantly." Harry outlined their shapes in the air with his hands. "My wife knows exactly what figure I make, and I therefore make good with the presents. I think of it as marital insurance. And those, boy, those are some super pricey ones. See the cross-shaped heel?" He produced his cellphone and after a few taps, pinched open a photo to show Luke. He'd zoomed in on the sole, which had a diagonal pattern of repeating letters. "Check out those little *G* logos?"

Now Luke saw the little *G*'s and resented Mr. Hot Shot for it.

Harry sat back, hooking a thumb into his waistband, looking all superior. "Those are some very fancy boots. Definitely not some streetwalker or alley drug–type. Unless they have one hell of a pimp to keep them well heeled. Lunch is on me." Harry started reaching for his wallet, but Luke stopped him.

"It's all right, bud. I don't need a TV star sugar daddy paying my way for me."

Harry just shot him a pained look and pulled his wallet out regardless.

Chapter 6

LUKE

The boots were, indeed, some fancy ones. Luke picked up the right shoe from a Plexiglas plinth where it was displayed like a museum object. He turned it over in his palm. As soon as he held it, he had the impression he was handling something precious and bespoke like a violin or a vase. The sudden curves on the thing … the sprung tension of the arch roller-coasted along the heel, and twined inward to a fine point on the toe. Sweeping up and along the racy swell of the pump, the leather was strong, yet butter soft. The height of the spike defied logic and shot electric messages straight to his amygdala. Every millimetre was engineered, purpose-built, to elevate the pulse and the senses.

They were certainly not meant for speed, at least not the moving along the ground from point-A-to-point-B kind of speed. The supple leather cladding the body made him think of late summer-warmed skin. The tiny pyramid-shaped studs at each precise axis where the fine-stitched quilting and the leather met were a toothy juxtaposition. These weren't boots that a knowing woman wore just to raise an eyebrow, just to raise a pulse. The studs said, *I know what I'm doing. I'm not a pushover. And I'm in complete control of my own sexuality.*

He'd always personally thought heels were a ludicrous thing. Other men waxed on about the way they thrust out an ass, lifted the calves, lengthened the legs. There was something so contrived about them to Luke. They broadcast at once a puzzling helplessness and a cunning knowingness. They rendered the wearer incapable of fleeing, yet suggested violence with their sharply pointed heels and toes. They'd always made him think of sharp teeth. He was more of a bare-feet-and-jean-cut-offs guy. Jean cut-offs cut way too high up the thigh, with those little threads that got caught on your nails on the way in …

"Can I help you?" Luke put down the shoe like it was hot.

He'd been standing there in the glossy white marble luxury department store for perhaps thirty seconds before "Help" had come. The Help was coming for the boots, since they were almost two thousand dollars and Luke looked scruffy. He detected curiosity on the face of the Help, as in, *What the fuck is a guy like you doing presuming to handle merchandise like this?* Then again, chances were, creepy guys likely came in to handle shoes like this from time to time, because it was as close to a woman as they would ever get.

"I'm looking for shoes that have these." He held up his cellphone with photos of the heel shape and the toe print. He could feel the judgment seething out of the shop guy and took some pleasure in him being surprised by the image.

"Givenchy." The guy made a suppressed little laugh. Appreciation? Derision? "Those are very exclusive."

"More exclusive than these Givenchys?" He showed a screenshot of the instrument of sex-slash-death on his phone.

"Those ones are an older model. A few years ago. And a limited edition. Are you looking for a gift, perhaps?" The tone he used said, You can't possibly be able to afford these. Luke considered purchasing them for Beatrice for a wild moment just *because*, but, no, heels and pregnancy seemed like a bad combo. And Beatrice would likely tear him a new one for spending the money. That was her domain.

"No," he said, and decided he disliked this guy enough to go for full shock value. "I'm a homicide detective. Looking for some leads on a particularly grisly murder. You take good care, now." The chastened look on the Help's face was well worth it.

Even though the glossy white luxury spaceship vibe of the store made him want to chew his arm off, he made use of the stop to buy a moisturizer and grab a perfume sample. Beatrice didn't need to know the stop had originally been work-related.

On the way home, Luke took the twists and turns of his Mississauga suburb sedately. There were always kids on bikes or building plywood ramps out here. Years he'd lived here and for years he knew he would still have to squint to be sure he was pulling into the beige brick semi-detached that was actually his.

"Sage green garage door, sage green garage door," he'd whisper to himself to avoid parking in front of his neighbour's place. Yet again.

The basement and garage were already crammed full of future-baby furniture, so he parked in the driveway and took the long way through the front of the house. He pulled off his shoes wearily. His sock feet on the tile and hardwood were silent as he wound his way through to the back of the house. The place was dark except for an inviting oblong of orange light cast by the stove hood.

Luke deposited a shiny little bag with rope handles on the speckled granite counter next to Beatrice. He got a little warm buzz as he leaned over her shoulder to place it on the counter. He was anticipating her pleasure. He hadn't been giving Beatrice treats much at all, lately.

He got a scalding whiff of garlic and frying organ meat when he leaned in to kiss her neck. And an eyeful of hot grease when one of the kidneys heaved in the pan and lobbed hot oil straight into his eye.

"Beatrice, ow, Jesus!"

He didn't expect she'd be cooking kidneys. A pair of them, fat and greasy, sat spitting in the pan.

"Oh god, you okay?" She slid the pan off the flame and whirled around to him fluidly.

"Yeah, yeah. Fine. Since when do you eat kidneys?"

She looked sheepish. "I had a craving." She was already back to it, cutting straight into the rare meat.

"Whoa, whoa, babe, aren't you supposed to cook it all the way through? You know, listeriosis and all?"

She laughed at him, showing her teeth, and tilted her head back. She popped a steaming, glossy piece into her mouth.

"Stop being such a wuss, Luke."

"I'm not. Soft cheeses, rare meat, c'mon — you were there when the doctor was talking about listeriosis."

She shrugged and attacked a second piece. "Personally, I'm listening to what the baby wants. I trust the wisdom of that. And I trust my body. More than that idiot doctor."

"Great, so we're already caving into the kid's demands?"

She was rummaging in the pretty baggie he'd brought. Her greasy fingers were staining and sticking to the tissue paper.

"What's all this?" At first she sounded pleased, verging on delighted, as she tore through and pulled out the moisturizer. She frowned. "Luke. You know I don't have combination skin. Is this supposed to be some kind of diss?" She had one greasy, balled-up hand on her hip and wore a look of angry disappointment.

"Oh. Sorry. I just thought that one would cover the most … possibilities. The perfume is nice?" It was a question, and he knew it. She glanced at it. She nodded curtly. Okay, maybe not so nice.

She took in a sharp breath then turned to him with a smile. It was like the sun came out.

"I'm sorry, honey. I'm being ungrateful. You bought me something and that's sweet of you. Thank you for trying." He accepted her firm hug and mentally forced himself to let it go. Letting the faint praise get under his skin would only make things worse.

"We'll take it back together and you can pick out a better one," he told her. The hug and her whole body softened against him. Things were back up a titch.

"I don't know what's with me today. I'm all over the place. Up down, grouchy. Hopeful. Worried about the whole autism thing."

"Yeah. It's a thing." He'd learned to agree without casting aspersions. He thought it was a bunch of tripe. Seemed like everyone in the world had autism these days and it was frankly one of the last things he was worried about. But worry had become one of her hobbies.

They both sat at the counter while she kept cutting bites from the kidneys. He avoided looking at the gooey, rare meat. Around the food in her mouth, she asked, "Luke, don't you sometimes wish for … I don't know, a little more?"

Luke looked around the kitchen. The kitchen was a cavernous space, with an eating counter and an empty dining table that could hold six people. There was a whole other *formal* dining table in another room reserved for the day they would eventually entertain royalty. They tended to live around this counter in the kitchen, despite all the unused space in the rest of the house. The study, the living room, the family room. Who used studies, anyway? Yet they had one. And four bedrooms. Beatrice wanted more. More of everything. Space. And stuff to put in the space. Accomplishments. That had always been clear. And one baby was definitely only the start. From Luke's perspective, they were already in the lap of luxury.

"I think we're doing pretty great, Boo. This place is so big I have to text you to find you sometimes. Look — we even have a double-door fridge — it makes ice cubes — for us!"

She made an annoyed sound. A short, puffy sigh.

"Not that. I mean with your life. You know, you could be lecturing. Like Harry does. He makes a great living. He wears those sexy suits. He doesn't crawl around filthy crime scenes. He has regular hours. Fans! Luke, he has *book* deals."

It wasn't enough that Harry had sexy suits. Now Luke was supposed to compete with book deals. It was a slippery slope he was always climbing. In the beginning Beatrice had been all about the cop thing, about him hustling up to detective. Now she wanted him to do something more that would make her feel better about him. He started to regret everything. He should have worked harder in school. Put in longer hours. Put in for the trainee position sooner. Levelled up faster.

"Ah right, here we go … Beatrice, I happen to *like* my job. I get a rush out of attending the crime scenes. It's what I went to school for. It's what I get up for."

"But you're so cute —"

"Don't butter me —"

"— and with a nice suit, a properly tailored suit, you could —"

"— up … I happen to like being the guy crawling around dirty crime scenes, catching the real live bad guys …"

"— you could even be one of those guys they interview on CNN when the really interesting cases come up."

Their words fell on top of each other.

"Oh, right. I know the drill. Go out, and date. Meet someone nice …"

"No, Luke. Come on. I have to be allowed to say what —"

"Yeah. Meet someone perfectly nice and then spend the rest of your life trying to change them into something completely different."

"I'm thinking about us, Luke. I'm trying to share my —"

"Just change everything about them."

"— hopes and dreams."

It was a script, a scene they'd finessed and mastered. The groove at the bottom of their particular rut. We all have them, his mother had always said. Work through it. Get up and out of the rut. Let the small things go. Never let yourself go to bed angry. And all the other things people said. They bought those sayings stitched onto expensive little pillows you can't ever lean on to decorate couches you can't sit on.

He lightened up.

"Come on, baby. We're doing great. I love you. And I'm still bringing home the bacon. Even if you'd rather have … organ meats."

Beatrice smiled despite herself.

"You're my workaday guy, aren't you?" She said it a little wistfully.

"Old faithful." He winked at her, and the mood lightened, like the sun had come out.

Up and out of the rut.

She turned to her meal, playing with a grisly looking piece, smearing it around the plate. Without looking up, she murmured to him.

"I found a new clinic," she said. "For the baby."

Chapter 7

LUKE

Another medical appointment, another trip downtown. As Luke navigated the valleys of glass down Bay Street, he was consumed with thoughts of where to park. Beatrice was talking to him, at him, but he was wondering if he should risk a left turn at Charles or go all the way around, making consecutive right turns at College to go back north. They were late, so he let Beatrice out to find her way in first.

As soon as he arrived on foot outside, he had a shudder. The Medspa had huge letters that lit up at night, like a beacon, visible all the way down by Dundas. Those things cost money. Expensive signage was a great predictor of expensive invoices. The building looked like a huge, transparent glass block had been floated on a steel skeleton. According to the monolithic chrome directory in the lobby, the Medspa took up several floors of the place — at street level and others throughout the building. It came as little surprise to him — he'd learned that the women's beauty industrial complex was massive and sprawling and dedicated to doling out hope and expanding credit card debt. He'd had the negative balances to show for it. Figuring out which floor was going to be a challenge.

The reception was all hard lines and spotless, gloss finishes. Two modern leather-and-metal chairs hulked in a corner. These were chairs for buying, showing, looking at, not chairs for sitting in. A wall of shiny white panels dominated the space. A long white reception counter merged with this wall. If it weren't for the receptionist sitting in her Eames chair, with only her head and shoulders visible above the counter like some kind of glamorous puppet show, the reception would have looked like a continuous wall. It made him think of the Death Star.

The receptionist wore a snug burgundy cardigan and had a riotous mane of artificially red hair pulled into a ponytail on the top of her head. She was the lone swatch of colour in that sere space. She smiled a red-and-white smile as he entered.

"How can I help you?" She may as well have been a stormtrooper, complete with fibreglass armour. She was less greeter than she was gatekeeper. Because what Luke distinctly heard instead was *what the hell are you doing here*? It was that high-end department store all over again.

"My wife is here for an interview. An info session. We're deciding." He fumbled the last bit because he wanted someone to think he had some say in this whole thing, though he knew damn well he didn't.

"Welcome! New intakes are on the fifteenth floor." She lifted from her seat to reach over the tall counter and point him toward a bank of elevators.

He crossed the lobby at a clip but before he could touch the Up button, a French manicured nail reached past him and the button bloomed into life. The elevator sprang open immediately and he allowed the woman to enter first. The door closed on them and sealed in the bitter aroma of her dark coffee and the tannic blue notes of her perfume. She was unmistakably the woman from the brochure Beatrice had shown him.

"Which floor, ma'am?" he asked. After years on the force, those "ma'am's" always sprang out, respectfully. She made a noise in the back of her throat and leaned against the handrail.

"How pleasant. No one ever asks, anymore. Fifteen, please." He nodded and stood with his hands behind his back. A cool blond, she looked like one of those airbrushed poster girls from the 1980s — all sharp corners, clean lines, and racing stripes. She wore her hair cut crisply right at the jawline. It came to expressive points near her mouth, and she'd coloured it a luminescent pale silver. Her eyes were a hot blue, as though independently powered, with hard, sharp pupils. He had the urge to duck out of their aim. He reminded himself a little irrationally that she was not his "type." Absolutely not at all his type.

"Have you been in the military?" She was still leaning on the handrail, arms easy over her abdomen, hands cradling her coffee. Her off-white skirt suit hung off angular shoulders and clung to her legs. With a shock, he realized the tone, the warmth in her tone, hot and sugared like a cup of coffee, was flirting. He felt like someone had opened a curtain and let a blast of warm sunlight fall on him, from her side. He turned his head, slightly.

"No, ma'am." He could feel her look him over, sweeping from head to toe and back. And he heard her laugh, to herself, in the back of her mouth. Something self-satisfied.

"Ma'am," she teased. "Strange. I'm usually right with my guesses."

The elevator dinged and the doors parted on fifteen. He pivoted and held his arm across the threshold to bar the door and allow her to pass first.

As she walked on sure, heeled feet, she spoke, only barely tossing her words back to him over her shoulder.

"You must be my one o'clock. I gather that's your wife in my office already."

"You gathered right." He held the door again, a little formal, and made a show of a big kiss on Beatrice's cheek.

"Hello, Beauty." He said it for the benefit of all three of them. He spoke it like a shield, erecting protection between her cool-blue scent and her scalding glance. Beatrice gave him a sharpish look.

"I'm Cleo Drover. Beatrice, thank you for contacting me. I was happy to set up this appointment … and congratulations. I'm always thrilled by the thought of a new life."

"Detective Luke Stockton."

She gripped his hand like a man. Like she wanted him to back down. He didn't fawn. He gripped back. And then resumed his seat. Beatrice just gave a little wave.

"We've met." The two women exchanged a knowing laugh.

From this point on, Cleo spoke directing herself toward Beatrice who sat forward in her chair. Only once in a while, in a practised way, did Cleo cast her eyes toward Luke, as a sort of token gesture of acknowledgement. No more internal noises.

"From our material and website, I'm sure you know we have procedure rooms, recovery rooms. We have a veritable army of in-house doulas and midwives, though we are extremely exclusive about who we take on as clients. We do ask that you sign up exclusively with our services, which are comprehensive. Every labour room is fully equipped for water births and to create a welcoming environment. Unlike the public health care system, the sacred significance of birth is not lost here."

Beatrice squeezed Luke's forearm hard at this. "See, Luke? I just wish hospitals understood that."

Cleo nodded. "For a broader clientele, we do laser treatments through there. Minor day surgery is on another floor. For more comprehensive procedures, we have four operating theatres that run full time. Overall, though, I think we're most famous for our vampire facials." She leaned into the word "vampire," enjoying the hype.

"Vampires get facials?" Most people hated his jokes. But Luke couldn't help himself.

"Not funny, Luke. Vampire facials are super common."

Luke noticed Cleo clocked their exchange.

"PMP is the official name. Platelet Rich Plasma. It has incredible properties for youthful looking skin. Regenerative. Come try one. It's on me, Beatrice." Cleo handed her a silver card, which Beatrice readily took.

"Where exactly do you get the plasma?" said Luke.

"Do forgive me, I shouldn't banter with a detective about such things. It's nowhere near as exciting as you're making it out to be. We store quite a bit of plasma here in various forms. For the PMP facial, it comes directly from the client. Few people are aware, that we also offer a number of gynecological medical procedures, all the way up to obstetrics. For a very exclusive clientele. And, of course, a price."

"Your facility looks a lot higher-end than our ob-gyn," Luke remarked.

"I'm also very competitive, Mr. Stockton. I want your business. I want to be the place your wife has her miraculous child. I think you'll find we have many financing options that will make you comfortable."

†

"I am not comfortable with this, Bea," he told her as soon as she hopped in the car. She'd already found a roast beef sandwich in the time he'd taken to fetch the car and pick her up.

"I am, Luke. That place is amazing." Her mouth was full of beef, tomato, and sourdough. "God these are good. They're like, twenty-five dollars per sandwich but they're just *so* worth it."

Luke gripped the wheel, white-knuckled as they nosed along. *Just put it on the tab.*

Chapter 8

RENARD

Halfway around the world from Canada, he'd crossed into the Balkans under cover of night and abandoned his identity as Martin Lévesque.

He had left Rimouski, where nothing was left for him, on a bus. He needed supplies in Montreal for his forward journey.

In a dusty checkerboard-floored Comptant outlet, he pawned the useless engagement ring but kept the box. A little old man looked at him with watery eyes and wanted to know if he was sure, maybe she'd change her mind?

"I don't need the romance," he'd said. "I just need the cash." The old man passed over the paper money.

Later he found *Surplus Global*, between the delis and record shops and *boites de nuit*. The old guy behind the counter gave him some respect, because he still wore a military buzzcut and stood up straight. He didn't need much from the surplus guy: they would give him arms and clothes on the other side.

He landed in Budapest, boarded the 200 bus bound for the metro. After studying the various subway lines, he set out for Békásmegyer district. He'd booked a flat online, one of many former communist apartments turned rooming flat on the Pest side of the river. The neighbourhood was littered with broken glass, dog droppings, and blood. It suited him fine.

The next morning, a coffee at a dreary Keleti train station, and a cheap ticket to ride through the flat pan of Southern Hungary. He rode, watching grey fields against grey skies pass, thinking dully: if someone had had more use for him — the army, his girlfriend, the hotel, *someone* — he could have been pouring a beer and having a laugh on a patio with other guys while the sun set over the St. Laurent. Instead, he was here, skin feeling crepey with jet lag in a country where he couldn't speak a damn word to anyone.

Agnus Dei, he'd sung once upon a time as a boy in church. He never could think of the lamb of God without thinking of the green plastic runner down the aisle of the church. How many times had he watched sun motes dance on that carpet while listening to sermons about sacrifice, about lambs to slaughter, sins washed away, the great gift, the willing sacrifice of the risen god? All that BS. He'd been Josée's lamb, once. Follow her skirts, suck up, make nice, get a job, be square, lamby-hubby, led to the altar to sacrifice his crazy youth for a paradise of togetherness. Not now.

In Pécs, a bus took him over the border into Croatia. In Požega he bought puny fruit, a wrinkled sausage, and crusty bread. He walked out of town and headed straight for the trees.

In the forest he stripped off his jeans, T-shirt, and Tevas. He shoved them with his identification into a garbage bag. His passport, birth certificate, health card, and, because he was lovelorn, the ring box … all went in. He used a folding trowel to dig, brushing worms and beetles out of the way. Soil stuck to the pine sap on his palms and made a film of grit against the handle. Standing there, naked, he marked the place with a red zip tie on a stout pine branch. Martin Lévesque was laid to rest.

Outside of Požega, wearing fatigues he'd bought in Montreal, he took a bearing almost directly south for twelve kilometres, cutting through fields, forest, and small streams. Up hill and over fucking dale, still dazed from jet lag, and hot in the sun. He hiked until he met up with the Sava River. He waited for nightfall, sitting under cover of bush and branches. He ate the sausage that was chiefly balls of grease and gristle and rinsed his mouth out with the salty-tasting fizzy water. He dozed until nightfall when the cool air woke him and he sat up. He stood at the river and listened to its courses rippling along the shore. With his pack on both shoulders, he walked in and accepted the feeling of the water seeping into his boots, his socks, prickling at his flesh through his ancient fatigues. No point even trying to stay dry.

He'd been a Wolf Cub, way back. Stood to attention. Whittled the right things. Learned how to fold his clothes, make a hospital tuck on a bed. He was a good soldier by the time he was ten and so fucking eager to please. He would puff his scrawny chest out when they'd brought the embroidered badge around, ruffle his hair, tell him he was a good boy for being of service.

Once upon a time, he thought he would have a few little ones with Josée. And then he'd show them how to be Cubs too. Take them out into the woods on weekends. Show them how to pack, pitch a tent, knock a stake into the ground, start a fire with dryer lint. He set fire to that nostalgic thought. He was a company of one. So be it.

It was her choice, ultimately. He could have been lying tangled up in the biggest suite of the *auberge* with her, tasting coffee on her mouth. And later they would have drunk a bottle or more of Asti Spumante. His *maman* loved that stuff, and he'd developed a taste for the sickly sweet stuff at celebrations. He could have been lying in a marital bed, he could have been feeling her nails grazing up his calves, across his kneecaps, sweeping around to the inside of his thighs, and teasingly, squeezingly, upward. Instead, she chose Patrice and so for him it was cold Sava River water leaching into his briefs and making his balls squeeze. Weirdly, he welcomed the cold stab. If it wasn't going to be a life of pleasure and love, it might as well be a life of hardship and pain, he thought, with the self-deprecation that was typical of his whole family. Fuck everything. Across that river was Bosnia and Herzegovina, and war.

War was the only thing that wanted him now.

Chapter 9

HELOISE

Heloise tracked the runner as he came down her street, locked on his passage. The runner was semi-famous in Summerhill for his outings along the tony side streets. As an ultra-marathoner, he regularly put in sixty-mile weeks. Almost never went a day without putting in at least one mile. Heloise's narrowed eyes followed him along the street — taking in his gait, the sure fall of his feet on the pavement, his exquisitely balanced, perfect, pronation. She drank in the unavoidable fact that even in the cool weather, he ran wearing nothing but shoes, socks, and fluttering, brief shorts. He pounded the streets of Summerhill, the Beltline Trail, wove through all the side streets up to Lawrence and beyond, and down to Lakeshore or else threaded his way through the labyrinth of Rosedale.

Of course Heloise clocked him. She'd watched him, running up Russell Hill, or down, skin slick in a downpour, in sticky humidity, dappled in crisp fall sunlight over the years. She'd even seen him in various corporate boardrooms, almost unrecognizable in Italian wool and French cuffs, but for his mane of ashy black hair and his sun-browned skin.

She wasn't even sure what his slant was. Did he prefer men or women? But she knew on some deep level that he was not for her. She was not for him either. They were both spectacular specimens. They would have fit well together physically. But in those days, she'd been jailed by her love of the lawyer.

But she had always been content to observe him, enjoy his form as he passed by, chest muscles taut across his intercostals, nipples brown and flat, lean as a skinned chicken breast. As he passed by her window, she enjoyed the sight the way one enjoys someone else's lilacs or a European master's painting behind a plate of Plexiglas. Flawlessly beautiful, untouchable.

Days were speeding by for her. Changes had begun within her that she could not count, much less name. Life grew in her at an alarming rate. Cleo had warned her long ago that the placenta tended to be aggressive. Some days she regretted her course of actions. Not the baby, of course. The life was everything. She was born to do this. But the surrounding events, specifically striking out on her own. She could have had a safety net with Cleo and the other selected sisters. She could have had regular medical checkups under Cleo's protection. She could have let herself be enfolded by the others, drawn into ancient ceremonies and rites expecting a girl child of the elites. Her hunger would have been kept at bay, tamed by readily available injections of blood. Cleo had offered injections. The idea was insulting to her. Heloise wanted to drink.

Hunger gnawed at her day and night. She sought the usual items, of course. Fresh meats, fresh fish, fresh fruits, especially peaches, greens of all sorts, supplements of all sorts. And iron supplements. Her constant urge for iron took her by surprise. She found herself fantasizing about metal, even. As though dragging her tongue over a raw, rusty I-beam might allow her to leach a few more molecules. She had gone on a kick, felt like she'd spent all day acquiring food, preparing food, bolting the food, while dropping crumbs over the sink. She was hoping she could take the edge off the need. Mitigate the need. Control and master it. She had withdrawn from anything other than sleeping and eating anymore. She napped and shopped and ate by day. She was becoming crepuscular. Pre-dawn and post-dusk, she was most alive. Most sleek, most alert and agile.

Something about the feeling of cool air on her skin was starting to feel better. And she knew, when the time was right, she would want to be in a dark cave, away from the light, away from people, with crisp dead leaves underfoot and cool limestone at her back. She would make a fire and she would gorge on iron, swallowing down the element while her body bore down. This life would be fed in the old ways. Would start, steeped in the old ways. When realizations like this washed over her, she knew she'd done the right thing. Supplements were modern nonsense. They were for the sheep who were built to graze, built to be penned. Built to be easily caught, shorn, and chewed.

She was drawn out to the streets, into the fading heat of early evening. She was thinking about the runner and the fuel within him. Wandering on quiet feet, to the dead end of a street that funnelled down into the ravine system, she saw instead a boy. Once upon a time it had been a milkman's path, according to the street sign. At night there was a steady stream of people, many of them boys, wandering up from the busy dirty streets in Boy's Town, or the flashing lights of Yonge, flowing away from fixes and meals and tricks or dangers, seeking quiet, with a piece of cardboard under the trees and a back leaned up against a bit of wall or rock. Coming or going, the people who passed were oblivious to the world around them. Instinctively, she knew to loiter there, like a spider.

As she waited, invisible between the branches, breath stilled, the boy shuffled past. What had alerted her to him first was not the squelching of his running shoes, it was his rank adolescence, like a barnyard animal, an acrid, sharp tang that hung around him in a veil — a miasma of hormone, pheromone, sweat, fight, flight, life. Coupled with it, a heavy, oily, funky stink of smoky cannabis, which made her quail a little. But she wanted his life for her life. It was a fair request, to her. No less sensible than a trip to a grocery store or farmer's market. She could feel the shape of need in her mouth, she could sense the individual components she needed, molecularly, with her tongue. And chief among them, iron. Heme.

She followed him in the tunnel of trees where the streetlight was swallowed up. She could feel the glands in her mouth start in, and she clicked the tongue piercing against her lower left molar. A bolt of awareness went through her, and then she heard a laugh. And several more.

A gaggle of young people. Girls and boys. He was not alone. He was merely the first of the group. He pulled faces with them, made odd little dances. There were too many of them. Disappointed, she turned on her heel and strode away, just some well-dressed woman out getting evening air.

As soon as they were gone, she turned again and merged with a twiggy spirea bush, unconcerned by the way the fresh-trimmed branches dug at her bare arms. She went down on her knees and felt the compact dirt there sift through the net of her tights. She spanned her belly with long fingers, as though it might soothe her.

She felt an acid hunger from her lower abdomen reaching up to her breastbone. She was crouched outside a house. From inside the house, her sharpened ears detected the rustling of a person shifting in their bedclothes in an upstairs room. She lifted her chin and breathed in, seeking more information. It was an old man. When he scratched the nape of his neck, she heard his long nails scrape against his flesh.

From elsewhere she could sense the rise and fall of a sleeping dog's breath some sixty yards away. She knew there were birds huddled together on a branch above her. It felt like there was no longer any barrier between herself and the world around her, that she was swimming in senses. The smell of the runner's clean sweat was what washed over her first, and she knew him by his signature scent. Not adolescent. Not rank. A perfect brew of electrolytes, and balanced salts and sugars. His fluids, his proteins, his carbohydrates, everything in peak balance. They needed to be, to feed the machine of his body.

He came powerfully up the hill, out of a tunnel of darkness, cresting easily, his footfalls light and springy, favouring his toes. Without thinking, her hand darted out and grasped him by the ankle, quick as a shot. She dragged him to her in a swift, fell motion. She was almost as surprised as he was to be there.

He lay on his back, flat, arms cocked at the elbow, winded by the fall. His hands fanned out, asking the question that he couldn't articulate. He searched her face, which he did not know, with wide, squared eyes. She put a long cool hand against his heated cheek, felt his stubble.

"Thank you for your sacrifice," she told him, wistfully, before the hunger drove her on.

Chapter 10

LUKE

Luke sat at the kitchen counter with photos of the boy in the alley spread out. He was cross-referencing the numbers on the photos with an Excel spreadsheet he'd built to connect items, and to try to keep track of a spiralling to-do list.

"Can't you use the study instead?" Beatrice asked from behind him.

"Jesus."

"Good morning." Her kiss was dry.

"You startled me."

"I can see that." She looked down at the photos and paperwork. He shuffled them into a pile, sheepishly. But he resented it. No, it wasn't nice for her to sometimes have to see such things. But normally, she was still asleep at this hour. And these "things" were what kept a roof over their heads.

"I saw that Harry is going to be on TV tonight."

"Yeah?"

"Yeah. Don't you care?"

"I mean, sure, that's great. I'm kinda snowed under here."

"Well, it's on *The National* and I'm planning to watch. He's doing a juicy serial killer segment."

"I work with killers."

"Regular ones. Hardly serial."

"Still."

"And Harry is always so cute on air. Those tailored shirts …"

"I'm cute."

She paused and looked at him. "Got something there. Little bit of your breakfast. Right there." She wiped at the corner of his mouth. "Got it."

Which was weird because he hadn't had any breakfast.

"Why up so early?"

"I told you."

"Okay, Bea, refresh me." He knocked against the side of his head like a chimp, their little love language for *I'm so stupid*. But it was only ever Luke who did it.

"Eight-thirty a.m. intake assessment meeting with the ob-gyn. Then interviewing the doulas."

"I thought you already had an intake assessment?" he asked while swivelling to the calendar. Huh. There it was, written down on the date: 8:30.

"Well, this is another one." She smiled with a broad smile that reminded him she sometimes worked very, very hard to barely tolerate him. "Love you." And was gone.

He'd just gathered up the papers when his phone almost buzzed itself right off the counter.

Another homicide. At the top of a ravine in the heart of Rosedale. It was going to be a headache just cordoning it off, dealing with the locals and their short bursts of curiosity tempered by long bouts of irate homeowners. *Just how long is this investigation going to block entry to my heated garage?*

He was going to have to come up with another numbering system to keep track of everything.

Chapter 11

LAUREN

Lauren always got a kick out of giving her Rosedale address. In shades and a ballcap with Lululemon pants, she could easily have convinced someone she was a monied maven slumming it during the day. For all the shopkeepers or delivery services she gave her address to knew, she lived in a sprawling four-story with peaked roofs, brick driveways, and a coach house out back. She could be heading home to meet her private hairdresser and slipping into a gown for a big gala to raise money for Babies with Zika Virus–Caused Encephalitis.

It was instead a basement apartment with a view of a cement block retaining wall at the base of a squat yellow brick infill apartment. Today it was an apartment with an entryway nearly blocked off. She'd come home from shopping to find scrolls of yellow tape and four cruisers and a bunch of cops directing traffic. She managed to wander down toward the bottom edge of the yellow tape, where a walking path led into the forest. And tantalizingly close, but out of proper sight, they'd erected a small tent. There had been a crime in there. They were combing the ground everywhere. The buzz of energy was intoxicating. Everyone had such a special job. It put a little band of hurt around Lauren's heart to look at it.

Lauren knew she could have been a cop. A CSI just like the people on various shows. She obviously wouldn't wear as much lipstick or padded bras as the television liked to suggest they did. But it could easily have been an option after studying Anthro and Biology.

"What's going on? Is everyone okay? Did someone … die?"

"Ma'am, I'm sorry, but we need you to keep the perimeter clear."

"You know, I'm an archeologist. I know exactly what they are doing over there."

"That so." The cop didn't even bother to look at her.

Normally when she told people that, they were duly impressed. *An archeologist, really!* people would normally say with big eyes. But this cop did not register interest.

"More of an anthropologist, really, but yeah," Lauren added, in case the cop had not heard her. "Digging up bones. Just like Indiana Jones and all."

It was not actually true. It had been remotely true, once. It could have been her life. And it always felt so good to get the charge of recognition and amazement from regular pedestrians, lesser people who were never going to be more than data-entry types. People like the cop in front of her with his thumbs in his belt.

"I'm trying to get into my residence. Over there."

"No problem — there's an officer over there who will help you get around the tape. The secondary entrance to the building is open to accommodate residents at the moment. Ma'am." The "Ma'am" was a period at the end of his sentence. He set his eyes on the horizon, far above her head. Lauren huffed at him, to herself.

These guys were always such idiots. Bungling everything. Full of themselves. Couldn't solve a crime if a murderer walked up to them and said they'd done it.

Chapter 12

LUKE

"So, what do you think we should do with the placenta?"

Luke hadn't even closed their front door yet, before he heard — misheard? — her question. *Placenta?* Was that really something he had to think about?

"Huh?"

"The placenta. We have to figure it out. Unless, of course, you're too squeamish to talk about it."

He frowned but let it pass. She was sitting on the couch, feet tucked under her. Books about expecting and magazines that appeared to be about the entire Pregnancy Lifestyle were strewn all over the coffee table.

"I'm not too squeamish. What do other people do with it? Throw it away? Burn it? With fire?"

"A lot of people plant it."

"Plant it? For fuck's sake. Are they hoping to harvest more babies?"

"Luke. I am serious about this."

"Okay. Fine. Plant it. We'll buy a special trowel. From Pottery Barn." He picked up one of the pregnancy magazines with a woman dressed in magenta holding up baby booties festooned with silk flowers. "An engraved, silver trowel. We'll cover it with ribbons. It will be so cute. And so expensive. It'll become a family heirloom."

"Well, some people do it. And then they plant a tree. They bring the kid there later to see it grow. Life feeds on life stuff."

"Yeah, life's a rich tapestry. People increasingly do a *lot* of really weird shit." Luke wondered if anyone was better for knowing about all the weird things people did. Wasn't it better back in the day when people did all their weird shit, wrapped in guilt, wracked with shame, but mercilessly secret?

"It's actually an ancient tradition."

"Great. Ancient wizards and druids. When it comes to babies, Beatrice, I guess I'm sort of all about modern traditions. And popping something gross like a placenta into an incinerator and going home to a house filled with working plumbing and electricity." He was in the kitchen and tried a honed tactic that usually dissipated a fight. "Are you hungry? I picked up some of that Ethiopian kitfo stuff. I won't even complain about watching you eat it."

"Yeah, well some people eat the placenta."

He couldn't help the disgusted sound he made, hearing that. "Ugh. Beatrice. Come on!"

"Oh, I thought you said you weren't squeamish."

"That sounds like cannibalism to me, for Chrissakes."

"Christ. There's some cannibalism for you. 'Eat the body of Christ,' much? It's perfectly natural, Luke, and I wish you would at least pretend to entertain something I say, for once. Most animals do it, right away. Gobble it up. It's an excellent source of iron. Which postpartum nursing women need."

"Your spleen is natural too. You gonna eat that if you get it removed?"

"Well, probably not, since removing it means something was wrong with it. But why not? It's not like it's someone else's. Isn't that technically what makes a person a cannibal — eating someone else?"

"Are we going to get into a fight over the semantics of the word 'cannibal' now?" It was an attempt at a joke, but it squeezed out of him tight and defensive. "Look, I don't want to be a killjoy, but Bea, for God's sake, please count me out of the whole placenta-eating thing."

"I wasn't offering you any. Iron loss is a serious thing, you know." She rubbed her tummy even though there wasn't a sign of anything there yet, in a gesture that Luke was starting to clock as *whatever it is that we are talking about, with regards to the baby, I am right, and you are not part of the decision*. "Luke, iron is what makes our brains grow. Over the centuries it made babies' heads larger. Made humans smarter. Which in turn makes labour so dangerous for women."

"Which is why I guess they always talked about men bringing home the bacon in the olden days. I figure, take an iron supplement, and maybe leave the placenta to the pros? And have some of this. I'm told rare Ethiopian beef is chock full of iron." He dangled the baggie, which dripped an orangey grease from the bottom corner onto the tile floor. "See, positively gruesome. Should be right up yours and the baby's iron-crazed alley."

"*The* baby." She said it with scorn.

"What?"

"Don't just call it 'the.' It's a *him*."

Luke was intrigued. She looked a little vulnerable. A little hopeful. He approached and she let him slide both hands around her waist.

"So, it's a him, now? Is that what you want, a boy?"

"Mm-hmm. I think I can feel him. He's sitting high. They say that's for sure a sign it's a boy."

"Did the ultrasound tech tell you something?"

She shook her head at his question.

"I was kinda holding out for a little girl." Luke said.

"No way. Not me," she snapped.

He was floored by how quickly that came out of her. And how firmly.

"Whoa, why not? Aren't we just happy for a healthy baby?"

"Yeah, yeah, no. It's just …" Beatrice was stammering. "I really think it's probably a boy. I read stuff online about cravings. And the way they sit in the belly. High up means it's a boy."

"Right. Same place you read about eating placentas?"

"Very funny. Call it intuition."

"You still wanna get an ultrasound or do you want it to be a surprise? We talked about it being a surprise. I was hoping for the surprise."

"No. I have to know."

He withdrew his hands. There was a warning waver in her tone that he'd learned to respect. Instead, he busied himself with bringing her kitfo to the couch on a plate and curating a night full of sitcoms. The laugh track was a blessing. The bleating of the audience filled up the room so there was no need to come up with something stupid to say.

Chapter 13

LUKE

"I would like to make a report. I found a boy in the park on Royal Road."

David Yang stood in front of the long desk at 14 Division. Even brushed and washed, he appeared to those who didn't know him as a street person. Disorganized and deranged. Cagey. But whenever he spoke, it was with an impeccable accent. The contours of his speech were clipped and tinged with bygone British dominance. Mr. Yang was well known to the staff at 14. He had a mania for bottle collecting and was known to snarl traffic on College St. while pushing his rickety cart along. His wife, in one of her knock-off Chanel suits, inevitably came along to take him home to the house they owned together. The desk officer showed Mr. Yang to a room and brought him tea.

Luke found David there, sometime later that evening. The old man was small in the molded plastic chair pulled close to the melamine table. He appeared endlessly patient. The room was a little funky with the mothballs and stale beer that permeated the old man's jacket.

Luke clicked on his camera.

"Hello there. I'm Luke. I'm a detective. I'll be recording this interview." He offered a hand and took Mr. Yang's cool, loose fingers in his. He left out the bit about trainee because it would only sound confusing.

"Good evening, Detective, a pleasure. I am Mr. Yang."

"Nice to meet you, Mr. Yang. I'd like to thank you for coming to us with your report. I have read what the constable took down, but I'd just like to hear some of it from you, if that's all right?" Mr. Yang bobbed his head while Luke settled in. "So, tell me where you were earlier tonight?"

"I was in Smith Simpson Park on Royal Road."

"You were out late?"

"I don't like to be in the house at night. It makes me restless."

"Okay, sir. You were there at about eleven-thirty p.m. and …?"

"I saw a very beautiful woman. I should say, first I heard her."

"Heard?"

"She wore very nice shoes, tall. Very loud on the pavement. Tic tic tic."

"Mm-hmm. Can you describe her?"

"Very, very tall. Elegant. Dark clothes. Smooth skin. Asian, like me, but I think perhaps mixed descent."

"And what did this woman do when she walked near you?"

"She walked by me, and she stopped a little distance away —"

"How far?"

"Perhaps fifteen feet, at another bench."

"You can see okay that far?"

"I require glasses for close up, not distance."

"Good. And you saw?"

"There was a boy on the bench. He was sleeping. She woke him, and I thought, she is kind."

"Why?"

"He is a homeless person. Quite a scruffy look. I have observed him in the alleys taking food from restaurant bins. It's very sad. Very young."

"Yeah, it's getting to be a real problem, all these young kids on the street. She woke him up and ..."

"I thought she was going to give the boy something. But instead, she sat down. And put her arm around him. Then she started to kiss him."

Luke felt a little crawl of revulsion hearing this. "Really? Did it seem like the kid wanted that?"

"At first they became passionate. And I looked away for a bit because I didn't want to pry. But I could hear them. This ear is the best one." He pointed to his left ear. "They kept kissing. Then I heard the boy make a sound, a cry."

"A cry like, good? Bad?"

"As though hurt. So, I looked again and saw that she was sitting on top of him, over his lap. He was trying to get up and she wouldn't allow him to. They began to struggle in earnest, and he was able to get away and run. He ran right past me, and I saw that his mouth, his face was bleeding very heavily. He was holding his mouth, and the blood was coming through his fingers."

"What did she do?"

"She ran after him, and I was rather impressed at how powerfully she could run in those tiny shoes. Very fast. Very powerful. He ran away from her, and I saw her follow. And I heard him shouting, 'No, no, leave me alone' like this. But she caught him and took his shoulder and turned him and then hup! She put him on her shoulder and went deeper into the park. And I remember thinking, 'Oh, this woman is very, very strong.' After that, I came straight here."

Up until the last bit, everything seemed nice and clear. But a woman lifting what he knew to be a grown-ass man-boy and then throwing him over her shoulder? Luke began to wonder if they could be dealing with a man dressed in women's clothing. Running at a strong clip in tall heels was impressive though, regardless of who was wearing them.

For now Mr. Yang's account was the only one they had, because the boy himself had been found alive, barely, and unconscious.

When officers attended the scene, he was a few hundred yards away from the path in dense hedges. They'd found him lying on his back, blood around his mouth. Unconscious. Even awake though, the wound he'd sustained would prove to make talking difficult. She'd bitten his tongue, according to EMS who found him. Luke knew, when the kid woke, *if* the kid woke up, getting a story out of him would require some extra supports.

Chapter 14

HELOISE

She came to in a shop, standing near baby onesies. The first thing she noticed was the metallic click of her tongue piercing. She'd been tapping it against her back molars, but she could not say for how long. Someone addressed her, and she swivelled to look. A shop woman was approaching with a tissue held out cautiously at the end of her arm, like someone attempting to feed a bear.

"Miss?"

Heloise inhaled. Wiped something dark brown from her mouth. Found matter on her fingers, and then walked out of the shop.

She was miserable.

She thought the pregnancy was going to make her feel better. Powerful. She thought a return to the old ways would make her feel an infinite connectedness with everything. She thought ascending to her proper role as apex would have made her feel as though the world was hers. Instead, she felt hunger, again, like an unwelcome house-guest. She was not its host. She was its slave. And for the first time, she allowed herself to have second thoughts.

She could change her mind. She could go back. She could do things the sanitized way with Cleo's help. One of the chosen sisters who were allowed to have a daughter. She could go back to all of them, cry some tears, be folded into welcoming embraces, and let her body, herself and her baby, be taken care of. She could feed as often as she liked, under Cleo's sanitized regime. She could carry on like normal, dressed in a workaday suit, take on clients, disappear into the normal world, while safely feeding her needs.

It surprised her to say the word, "baby," to herself, in her inner voice. That made everything more real.

And then suddenly, she was gripped inside by a wild, feral, explosion of indignation.

She would not.

She would do this her way.

This was her young and her life.

She'd rather give birth in the bracken and tear apart any creature that came near her and her child.

She was done with being socialized out of her true nature.

She was through with tidy, clean, quiet, invisible.

She re-examined the hunger, her insistent house guest. She was forced to admit it was not alien. It was an integral part of her. And she would own it. She would feed it, take care of it.

She was entitled to whatever she needed to take care of it.

Chapter 15

LUKE

Extra communication supports for the victim found in the park were not needed. Before he could even start lining up an appointment with the sketch artist, or an interpreter to get a statement from the boy, Luke got a message on his cell that the kid was being discharged. He was clinically brain-dead. A transfusion had not come soon enough. Such an end seemed, in a modern day and age, utterly sad and senseless.

Luke made it to the hospital just in time to see the kid being wheeled out, along with a grim mother. So, he had one.

The woman was stone-faced. Spoke in single-word answers. She was just there to sign him over to a long-term hospital where he was going to live as a vegetable, she said. Not much different from how he was at home before, she said. Which made Luke's belly churn. He watched her sign over papers and stand there while orderlies loaded her child up into a non-emergency ambulance and cart him away. The kid's hair had been washed. His face had a spray of freckles. Looked like a nice kid. They all did when they were asleep, or dead.

In the past, sure, he would have felt bad for the kid, bad for the kid's parent, sad that a young life had got fucked up to the point where he'd found himself living on the street and never got the chance to turn things back around. But now he found himself ruminating over it. At what point before dying, in a park, at the hands of some psycho-strong woman, or possibly man, could the kid have been caught? Adjusted? Put back on track? Housed somewhere?

The thought that a child of his own could one day grow up to be roaming back alleys looking for something to eat out of a dumpster made him feel ill. Ditto the thought of them passed out alone in a sopping wet sleeping bag at the mercies of the quick and wily. Having his own kid was making him more acutely aware that everyone who walked the earth was someone's kid. Everyone had a mother.

Two boys, street kids, with similar injuries over the course of several weeks were automatically connected. The alley kid's tongue was deeply lacerated, the park kid's was bitten. Despite the difference in approach, they were connected. It reminded him of those young East Asian men who'd disappeared in The Village a few years back. Their disappearance had elicited a cold shrug from a world morbidly fascinated by the deaths of young white women. All at the hands of a white serial killer who looked like Santa Claus and left their remains callously scattered in gardens throughout the city. God forbid this case could ever reach those proportions.

He walked the park on consecutive evenings, long after the police tape was down. At night streetlight sparkled off stones in the asphalt. His hard heels clicked where the ground was bare and thudded where wet leaves stuck to the pavement. Mr. Yang remained the only witness. Houses encroached on the park from all sides, but it was dense with trees and late fall had not yet stripped the trees of concealing leaf cover.

He imagined himself as the boy on the bench, and mentally walked through how the kid might have reacted. The old man had seen him returning the assailant's kiss. People did contradictory things when they were assaulted, and often felt guilty about them when recounting events. And fawning was an overlooked response but often more likely than fighting or fleeing. Women and men alike were further traumatized when their bodies reacted physiologically to assaults. The idea that their body might stir and respond to the attack drove them to despair and guilt and shame.

Luke thought through the moments that would have come after. Eyes coming into focus. The dreaded realization that a stranger hung over him. The mind and the body spinning gears, grinding against each other.

He tried to imagine what the woman must have been thinking as well. Had she seen Mr. Yang? If she had, did she carry on with her attack supposing he'd do nothing? Or had she been so hell-bent on the boy and what she hunted from him that she hadn't noticed him on the bench? Mr. Yang's bench at this hour stood in dappled shadow. A streetlight cast a powdery orange light down on it, but its head was haloed by thick leaves from branches that stood untrimmed all around it.

†

Luke spent late nights walking in the park. His early mornings therefore became gruelling. When Beatrice left for doctor appointments, she found him still rolled up in blankets. But he would dutifully drag himself out and go through the motions of dressing, brushing teeth, and knocking back forgotten cups of cold coffee on autopilot.

One hazy sleep-deprived morning, they were moving along Bloor Street in a light patter of rain. The sound of it falling on the car roof had further hypnotized him and made the creeping fog of sleepiness close tighter around him. He blinked and blinked, hoping she wouldn't notice how wiped he was, hoping that keeping his lids moving would keep him awake. They were going to be late for a medical appointment. The four-month pregnancy checkup was a big deal, especially when a woman was over thirty-five and considered "geriatric." Some nurses liked to lean on the word "geriatric" and they received hot glares from Beatrice as a result.

"Get me a little farther down the street. I see a spot." She was pointing at a parking space, and she was opening the door before he'd even brought the car to a complete stop.

"Whoa, whoa! Beatrice!" he protested. But she was a blur, unbuckling and throwing the door open and swinging out onto the curb dangerously in a fluid motion.

"Sukiyaki!" she yelled, just as the door slammed shut again. She was sprinting down the street toward a Japanese place they'd eaten at once before. More cravings. He was relieved to pull over. The instant he killed the ignition, he fell asleep, chin to chest, dropping out of consciousness like a stone.

He had one of those semi-lucid dreams while he was down. He and Beatrice were in the restaurant they'd first met in. Curiously, in dream logic, she had the baby with her, somehow already born, in a bassinet, on the seat. But he couldn't see the baby. She was ignoring him and cooing into the bassinet. The baby morphed into a man. She was holding her shirt open to a strange man who was kissing her neck and chest and breasts while she arched her head backward in ecstasy.

Luke started awake.

It was the car door opening. Beatrice dropped into the seat, already halfway through eating an order of sukiyaki in a Styrofoam container. She was eating it with her fingers. Through a full mouth she remarked: "Next thing I want to eat is that kitfo stuff again. Remember, the Ethiopian stuff?"

"Wow. Onto the next craving before you've finished this one?" He hoped he sounded wry, yet warm.

"Mm-hmm," she sounded around the beef in her mouth.

"Maybe take it easy on the raw?"

"If I want it, *he* wants it," she said. And popped a final morsel in her mouth.

Luke had to fight off a strange feeling of resentment creeping into his body via the dream. Silly. Ludicrous. Yet he felt shreds of anger at her. How could she? Right in front of his nose? And getting into it? And then he felt guilty for dreaming about her doing things that made him jealous. He commandeered his thoughts. Remembered he loved her. The *real* her.

Though he stared at rain on the windshield, he was looking back in time. They'd met at the Old York, a scuffed, narrow brick bar with slanting floors squeezed between row houses. He'd chosen it *because* it was scuffed. Dates sometimes picked way upscale, only to lay waste to his wallet. A good sign that she hadn't put up a fuss about the so-so locale.

She'd come in wearing a plaid dress and blouse and cute little boots and the second he'd laid eyes on her he'd felt relief.

Just a total wash of relief. They'd joked about it plenty of times when telling people who wanted to know how their internet date became the *last* first date they'd have to suffer through. "It was relief at first sight!" they used to say, almost in union, which always got a laugh.

He'd been actively dating, grimly, self-punishingly dating, for nearly four years by the time they'd finally met. He had frequently and genuinely thought that none of it was ever going to work. Gold diggers; crazed divorcees who got drunk and castigated their exes; sex maniacs who wanted to take him home halfway through the date; the indigent; the snooty wealthy who disdained his shoes and lack of disposable income; the ingenues who wanted to move to Tibet or Thailand; the drunks who wanted to move into the bar … he hadn't seen everything, but he'd seen more than enough.

It was sweet vindication that this date finally worked out, given how down his mother was on the whole thing.

"Meeting strangers online? Luke, it seems so dangerous. You just never know who people really are." She would complain whenever he told her that he had a new prospect.

"You do remember I am a police officer, right?"

"That doesn't mean you can't be harmed."

"Mom, *everyone* is a stranger before they meet. Not everyone on the internet is evil." He stopped telling her about dates. They never got past date four before ghosting or revealing a cult membership, or half stripping in a nice restaurant.

With Beatrice, right after relief, the next thing that washed over Luke, melting and hot, was actual attraction. She was cute. Cute in a way that made her seem both approachable and a "get" at the same time. Her glossy, dark hair cut sleek around a sweetheart face, her enormous fluttering eyes. Not too made up. Just … so cute. And maybe, best of all, tall. Nothing outrageous, but almost shoulder to shoulder with him. He'd dated pixies and Reubens alike. He enjoyed a nice round flank; he'd enjoyed the fun of a tiny woman tossing around in his bed. But Beatrice was just right, for him. And as soon as she sat down, she said a few things that sealed the deal.

"Oh, sorry. No alcohol. This is a very serious date," she told the waiter. Inwardly, Luke had swooned a little over that … fantastic, no excessive booze tab or sloppy weirdness, right out of the gate. "Okay, listen," she said. "I have a few codes. No matter how cute you are, I will *not* sleep with you until we've had at least three good dates." She leaned forward, her cotton blouse straining a little at her throat. She splayed her fingertips on the tabletop for emphasis. "And I am for certain looking for someone who can be faithful and wants the whole committed Actual Relationship thing too. Oh, sorry. I think I meant to say: 'Hi. I'm Beatrice.'" She took a sip of water. "You sure are a lot handsomer in person."

He'd suppressed the urge to ask her to marry him right then and there. But he'd learned over time that phrase didn't play well as a joke on a first date. It was no joke though. In his head he thought it. A year and a half later, he told her so. Two years after their first date, they married. The two of them, Harry, Harry's wife, and a Justice of the Peace at city hall.

When they first met, she was dating two other guys and she let him know that on the first night. Hence the no-sleeping-around rule.

"That's cool," he told her, about those two guys. It totally wasn't but he would knuckle through until they were history.

They closed the place down talking. She didn't ask once about the police work. She seemed genuinely uninterested in it, a total win in a world of tourists who wanted to see badges, ask about seamy details and ultimately get frisky with cuffs. She was more normal than anyone he'd met. He lived in a twilight world of abnormal, criminal, weird. Normal was a relief.

Outside the bar they made out, heavily, leaning against his car. She whispered in his ear how insanely hot she found the idea of conceiving during sex. He'd had to break away from the cling of her lips then to catch his breath.

"Have I said something bad?" she wanted to know. He shook his head. The combination of relief with her terminal cuteness and his raging erection nearly felled him.

"Just book dates two, three, and especially four, right now," he said, grabbing her hand and pressing it to his chest, just inside his leather jacket.

"I'm clearing my schedule," she said.

And that was that.

Things had moved quickly from their meeting to exclusive dating, engaged to married to pregnant. Unlike other people he knew of, they never had to spend an aching, agonizing amount of time trying to have a baby. No IVF, no angst. They tried and got pregnant fast.

The pace didn't bother him — he was a late starter on the family thing, already into his forties. He often found himself musing *when the baby's five, I'll be forty-seven; when they graduate high school, I'll be sixty-five* … But what had bothered him lately was that there was a straight arrow from distinct relief to silly infatuation to love and togetherness and marriage and pregnancy and then an almost complete and total stop. Terminal station for the Happily Ever After. He'd noted she often brushed his hand away when he reached for her. When he bent for a kiss, he got a cheek. Sex was a distant memory.

Right now, Beatrice was sitting in the passenger seat, scrolling through her phone. Without looking up she said to him absently, "Just drop me up here on the corner. I can go in on my own this time."

"To the appointment?"

"Yeah. I got this." When he made an unsure noise, she looked at him for the first time on the drive. "Luke. I don't require a chaperone." She was already out the door again, the second the car had come to a stop.

"What time later?" he asked through the window as it motored down. He tried to sound upbeat and not too needy.

He was planning to beat her home. Make dinner. Draw a bath. Make love.

"You too!" she said absently and blew him an air kiss. She slammed the door and winnowed into pedestrian traffic and was lost to sight.

Chapter 16

HELOISE

How did she get here? A dark place. A stink. Garbage. Cigarette butts. Laundry. Hash resin. A boy, in his underwear, chest heaving. He had a head of curls. And a flat belly. Naked fluorescents hanging from the ceiling. She could taste someone's blood in her mouth. She was faint. Blood sugar, blood iron, she felt like she'd been tapped and drained. Her muscles felt slack. There were more boys. It was supposed to be simpler.

He could have just come with her and then she could have fed properly. Instead, careening all over the city, cabs, yelling, chaos. It would have been better the other way. She was creating an ugly, visible scene when she knew she should have been discreet. But her wild side protested: an apex didn't stoop to being discreet. Apex took. Apex ate first, when hungry. Sheep scattered. Now she was penned. The sheep, the curly haired sheep with their vacant eyes and their slack mouths and their bleating words had cornered her. She inhaled the stink of him, read the information encoded in it as the one behind her approached. His blood was up. He was terrified, amygdala flooding him with endorphins. These idiot sheep. Had they figured out how to harness their chemical soup, they could have been more than dumb stock.

Her blood was not up. She felt a weakness in her knees.

Her hands gripped her belly over the baby, as if her fingers could protect it.

But it was not her belly they went after. It was her skull. She did not feel it. All she felt was anger. At herself. For leaving the fold. For striking out alone. *I am sorry for not doing it better*, she thought as the world tilted.

Chapter 17

LUKE

A few weeks after the park boy, a kitchen worker down in the club district made a discovery. His discovery made screaming headlines. Behind the Nausea club complex, shoved behind a hulking, filthy, industrial-sized garbage bin, he found two bodies. A man and a woman. A woman and a boy, really, but the media would report the deceased as a man.

Nausea was a sprawling warehouse-sized nightclub complex with multiple floors and hundreds of nightly visitors. There were smaller themed bars on different floors, with variously themed music and lifestyle choices. There was even a complete hair salon in one of the main women's bathrooms. One section was done up with a tropical vibe. It sold signature drinks made with house-toasted coconut and island-spiced meat skewers. A whole other floor went for a Studio 54 revival scene. A grotty, funky-smelling basement offered a kinky dungeon flavour and patrons could grind to Madonna and Nine Inch Nails while go-go dancers in candy-coloured pleather mimed getting whipped on padded furniture.

The metal bins were out in the alley, thirty feet from the entrance to the club, concealed by latticework and plastic faux boxwood shrubs. Neither the lattice nor the bins could cover the smell, which was different from the usual garbage and vomit.

Commercial waste removers came daily, so the bodies had to be from the previous night. Workers from the nightclub, day shifters, kitchen-prep workers, were traumatized by the find; they remained at the scene with a remarkable stoicism. A scrawny busboy hugged one elbow from behind his back and kept his eyes on the ground. The club owner arrived shortly after. He was greying on top, thick in the middle, and wearing clothes that had been edgy twenty years ago. His bedazzled patchwork sport jacket was stained at cuff and collar. The points of his shoes were long enough to be a serious trip hazard. He was concerned that the stressed kitchen staff would affect the club opening on time that night. Show must go on and all. His seedy concern made Luke all too happy to let him know there was absolutely no way he was opening the club that night. Too big a scene, too much detail to gather and document before the next horde of nighttime partiers planned to come dropping a fresh load of cigarette butts, glitter, sequins, condoms, and vomit all over the place.

The deceased boy had a slim nylon wallet on him. It opened and closed with velcro. It made Luke's stomach lurch to think how young this kid was. This was a baby's wallet. No loyalty coupons counting down to free coffee, no credit cards, no receipts. A few twenties and a condom. He should have had a license, as any club would have ID'd the guy before letting him inside.

The woman had no wallet or purse whatsoever. A few scraps of paper in her pockets. But one look at her long glossy black hair and her racy shoes made her familiar to Luke. She was almost without question the suspect from the park, and, he was confident, the perp behind the alleyway murder. All he had to do now was work the evidence to establish the link.

Tymika was already working away, her camera popping and whining.

"I'm guessing they were moved." The challenge in her voice suggested she wanted to play their usual one-upmanship game.

"Okay. How many points do I owe you now?" Luke sighed.

"Fifty at least. Rained last night around midnight. But they're completely dry."

"Okay, points. Also, no blood splatter present despite obvious trauma is a giveaway too."

"No fair. I was gonna say so, but you didn't even let me get the chance." She always shimmied the camera just a little before she pressed the button. "Ugh. God. I hate these places."

"Garbage alleys?"

"No, nightclubs. Same difference as garbage alleys though. Full of garbage people and pricey, watered-down drinks. Reeking with bad cologne and desperate hormones."

"It's not the watered-down drinks you should worry about; it's the ones with the questionable additives," Luke muttered, as he got down to look closely.

"Ech. I know. I wouldn't come within a hundred feet of a place like this. Imagine being drunk *and* having to fight off grabby guys? I'll take a joint and a deserted beach over that noise any day."

"If it's a girl I'm having, nightclubs are gonna be out of the question," he said. "Too stupid. Too expensive. Too dangerous."

"If it's a girl you're having, I'm pretty sure you don't get a say in the matter."

Luke was looking at the face of the Jane Doe.

The victim was posed with her wrists crossed over one another, and her legs crossed at the ankles. She bent forward slightly, a lock of hair falling over her face, which had perfect poreless skin. She looked as though she was deep in thought. Despite the tragedy of a life lost, the hideous body count this represented, and the avalanche of processing it would require in order to do justice for the dead, finding her came as a relief. Obviously, there was some connection to the other two boys. Maybe more. And quite likely she was the perp they sought. The tsunami of evidence and documentation would slow to a trickle eventually and the whole thing would be sealed in paper envelopes, wrapped in baggies, tossed in cardboard, and buried in a warehouse full of records. But it would be done.

The woman was dressed to impress a higher class than a tacky nightclub crowd. She wore a deeply plunging v-neck, angel-hair-thin spaghetti straps on the top. A slit in her pencil skirt zigged up her thigh. Knee-high boots with needle-fine heels. The kitchen workers had found her with a jacket tossed over her head to conceal her. It was the sparkle of sunlight glancing off a jewelled buckle on the boots that had caught the busboy's eye. They thought they'd found tossed-away jewellery. Instead, a tossed-away woman.

She'd been killed elsewhere and brought here. Yet her hand was stamped with the nightclub logo. So, she had actually attended the club. Killed elsewhere. Inside here? Brought outside? With only one way into the alley, and crowds until the wee hours of the morning, it would have had to be after club hours, and that narrowed down the window.

Luke felt a headache coming on just thinking about the list of patrons and staff that would have to be interviewed. He unfolded the papers he'd found crumpled in her pocket. A taxi receipt with spidery writing and a receipt for a spa. For a moment he peered at it, not making sense of the name or the address. Until it sorted itself out into the realization that this was Beatrice's Medspa. Well, the victim looked like she could easily afford the place. Far better than he could.

The boy was nearby, laid with his back against the wall. Sneakers — name-brand suede high-tops; strategically ripped jeans;

a standard-issue, untucked, "sexy" club shirt with the buttons undone just so. A good-looking kid, out on a Friday night, trying to get laid. If he and Beatrice had a girl, boys like this would be hunting her in the future. Well, then again if they had a boy, maybe boys like this were in his future … Boys he would teach them to avoid, kick in the crotch, refuse drinks from, join a religious order over. The kid sported one of those aviator haircuts Brad Pitt had made famous. And, looking closer, there was blood around his mouth.

Chapter 18

LUKE

Luke waited in the parking lot at the coroner's, leaning against the back of his car, waiting for Gertie to pull in. Even before she parked in her space, he could hear the sound of a strident voice booming out of her Bluetooth car speaker. Gertie sat in her slightly beat-up Honda, listening to that voice with a pained expression until they ended the call. Once parked, she had to shimmy out between the cars, which were too tightly packed together. Her reward was a smear from the offending car on her nice trench coat. This elicited a groan from her.

When she saw Luke had caught her dramatic entry, she waved her hands around and pantomimed having a nervous breakdown.

"Tough morning," he said, with sympathy.

"According to the school secretary, I'm the worst parent ever."

"Is that right?" Luke liked Gertie. She moved quickly with a balled-up energy, she spoke fast and unvarnished. Her hair always looked like it was escaping her ponytails.

"Oh yeah, second time I forgot my kid's lunch. This year. I imagine I'm going to be arrested. Actually, jail sound likes a vacation. I could sleep in until five a.m."

"No lunch. That is a pretty serious crime. Stiffer penalty for women, I believe."

"Oh brother, tell me about it. I still have to bake cookies for some damn thing." She shifted a heavy bag to her other arm. "Can you believe I'm supposed to put in a full-time job on top of all that? Maybe I should quit my job so I can keep the secretary happy."

"So, I should skip the whole parent thing?" Luke had to move fast to keep up with the slight woman as she power-walked through the front doors and into the coroner's facility.

"No, no. It's the best time you'll never get to enjoy yourself. It's fantastic. Wonderful. But yeah, skip town and get out while you can. But then you'd miss all the excitement of your Jane Doe. See you down in bay twenty?"

†

Bay twenty was Gertie's workspace. A long, low room with yellowish subway tiles. The tiles were placed upright, which always made Luke think oddly of teeth. He'd spent a fair bit of time standing around this room, counting those tiles while Gertie plied her trade.

"The date is November thirteenth. Subject is female. Jane Doe." Gertie spoke aloud, aiming for the mic that hung over the table. Speaking much of her inner dialogue aloud and consciously speaking clearly were forced habit.

"Jane's something," she said to Luke, off the mic. "She trumps all the other cases waiting to be processed."

"Processed," said Luke thoughtfully.

"I know, I know. Ms. Clinical. Sounds better than 'dissecting.' You know?"

"Sure, Spock."

"Please, you are no Captain Kirk."

"Why — I'm not heroic, romantic, impulsive?"

"No, because I hate *Star Trek* and all that space shit. Live on this planet." She looked at the woman on the table. Luke liked *Star Trek*, but decided to keep it to himself. "Okay. This is interesting. I'm awake now," said Gertie. With a gloved finger, she tapped the metal table Jane lay on with two sharp raps. "First day of school, amazing textbook cases, capital-*I* Interesting."

"Glad you think so." Luke was smiling. Nothing patronizing in his tone. He meant it. Gertie had a good brain. He liked to see her turn the high beams on.

"Subject is five-foot-eleven, quite tall, weight one seventy-five. Subject appears healthy, mid-thirties, fit, muscular, *very* well manicured, groomed, made up. The subject is unusually powerful. Fabulously dressed." Gertie sniffed, behind her mask.

"Warm scent. A spicy rose. Subtle. Expensive. Tom Ford maybe." She circled the table, with a sort of sideways walk, eyes on Jane. "You know, I often get people here still smelling of perfume." Gertie worked the details, forever open to curiosity. "Lot of the car accidents especially. Folks dressed in their best. Night out on the town. Nice clothes. Nice perfume. Death doesn't have to be all about unpleasant smells."

Luke rocked on his heels a little.

"The cause of death is most likely the obvious massive head trauma, blunt force. But we'll get into that as we go. I'm so curious about this sheer size. Subject is in no way overweight. An athlete's body." Gertie's hand passed near the long, powerful legs still clad in dark hose. "Italian hose with a fine denier. Thickly muscled legs. Oh ho … wow, Louboutin boots. Plunging-neck Hugo Boss dress, custom tailored. Chanel jacket. Hermès scarf. None of it flashy. This is a racy night-on-the-town look for a woman who must make a CEO's salary."

"I never thought I'd get a fashion education out of this. *Coroner Eye for the Dead Guy*?"

"Ugh." Gertie continued her walk about the body. "Biological female. Eye colour, dark brown. Hair chestnut, shoulder-length, straight. Eurasian. Estimate age at … thirty-five. Fingers, manicured. Wow are they manicured. She's wearing Pirate by Chanel on her nails."

"How can you tell?"

"Because I *know*. Hmm. Age. I don't know about the thirty-five. Her face is perfect. Taut. Dewy skin, even now. No visible lines. If the clothes were anything to go by, she had plenty of money for facials and other work. But everything, the skin on the backs of the hands, the nice firm snap of the flesh, seems to add up to perhaps thirty-five. I'm calling it thirty-five."

She catalogued and packaged the clothing, one item at a time, along with skin and hair samples into sealed tubes. She dug carefully under those perfect nails with their high-gloss finish. Next to nothing came out from under them, but she and Luke both knew all too well how often someone else's DNA wound up under nails …

Gertie removed the lipstick with a swab to make sure forensics could run samples.

"This is a nice lip colour she's wearing."

"I thought so too," offered Luke. "I thought it looked, uhm, well-bred. Not flashy."

"Hmm! Aren't you full of increasing sensitivity? I agree. Wealthy. People who wear lipstick this nice usually have nice country homes to match." Gertie smiled. "Subject has several non-practical black metallic buttons sewed to the front of her evening dress. Spherical buttons. Third one down has been torn off. There's a slight tear where it got pulled off. Probable struggle. Subject is wearing a single string of real pearls." She snaked it into a bag. "The clasp is nice and heavy. Gold. What's this?" She was off the mic with that last rhetorical question, out loud to herself. She had reached the subject's feet and twisted the right foot one way, and then the next.

"Something?" asked Luke.

"I thought I spied some dirt between the large toe and the second toe. But a closer look reveals …" Gertie bent closer. "Subject has a small tattoo. Between left big toe and second big toe. A small circle …" She took out her metal ruler. "A circle. With a cross, make that a plus sign. Seven millimetres in diameter. Black ink. Odd place for a tattoo. Seems meant to be unobtrusive. Okay. I'm going to send some stuff for sampling, give the room to the X-ray and UV techs."

Luke lingered professionally as Gertie worked through the autopsy. Calm and unhurried. While Luke moved digits around on his phone, she compared notes with the techs.

"Weird," Luke heard the tech say.

"Yeah," she agreed. "Dense." They were talking about the bones. "The woman is built like a Mack truck. Made out of titanium. So strong."

"Anything I should know?" Luke asked.

"Don't worry, handsome. You'll get my full report."

Some hours later Luke had a sore back from working while bent over a counter. His phone was almost dead, and he was leashed by a short charging cable. He realized Gertie had been nattering at him.

"So, you know, my kid has this goddamned geography project …"

Luke sometimes thought she talked about her kids to distract him from her work. Lately, he was thinking she was preparing him for the future.

"That was the other thing that didn't make it to school today." She worked the rubber block into place under Jane's shoulders, placing the body into position. "It's on the card table in the basement.

For some reason it's my job to clock these things. I must've put at least six hours into that project." She selected her favourite scalpel. "How did I become the one gluing toothpicks onto a map, after my kid went to bed? Helicopter parenting at its finest, I tell you, Luke. I'm more worried about getting a bad mark than he is." She started the incision where the underarm met the torso and pivoted along, arcing under the breast toward the sternum. "You know, I should be the one to get a gold st— Shit!!"

Gertie and the tech both leapt a little in surprise when the deep cut released a gush of blood.

"What's going on?" Luke had seen enough autopsies to know this wasn't standard.

"Well, that's not normal. With no heart to pump, there's no blood circulating in the body. It should be pooled on the back. Where it belongs on a corpse. But not this one."

The table had gutters, but nevertheless, it had come out in enough of a flood to make a small spill. Instinctively, Gertie stepped away. "Oh jeez. That freaked me out. There's always that little pinch of fear when contaminants get out of a body." Gertie and the tech were already cleaning it up and as she did, Gertie made sure to collect some in specimen tubes.

"How much blood?" Luke wanted to know later. Jane Doe was covered on the table.

"Like a lot. A *lot* a lot."

"Right. Is that a scientific amount I'm not familiar with?"

"Yeah, cute. It was enough to be suspicious and to note it and take samples. Approximately five hundred cc's. There's something like five litres total in a grown adult. Seems that our Jane here ingested it right before she died of blunt force trauma to the back of the head. The object was a brick. Got a sample baggie of fragments we collected along with skull fragments. That part was at least straightforward. But along with all the other anomalies, Jane didn't have a meal in the conventional way. Seems she had a meal of blood, and just to make things really fun, it wasn't filling up her stomach by the time I got to it."

Luke rubbed the small of his back.

"I feel like you're drawing this out for drama or something. What's the deal here?"

"This … person was full of blood. And it wasn't hers."

"Oh." This didn't come as a massive surprise to Luke. Unlike Gertie, he'd been to the crime scenes, and knew that several victims had been more or less exsanguinated.

"Yeah, 'oh.' She consumed a whole pile of blood and that was what came out of her when I started the autopsy."

Consumed.

The word hung there in the air. For a moment Gertie and Luke just met eyes. There weren't any words that matched how either of them were feeling. Both of them knew about that Interpol case with the Cannibal Guy from Austria years back. But this was here, in boring Toronto. On the table right in front of them. Gertie shook her head.

"She's really big," Luke noted, breaking the spell. "Like, unusually so."

"I know, right? To be honest, at first I wondered if this was someone who might have transitioned to female. But she's not. She's cis female."

"Oh, you mean original parts?"

"That's so sensitive of you," she drawled. "Yeah. Just an incredibly athletic and tall cis female. In fact, since everything else was so weird, and because I have so much extra time on my hands, I weighed the brain as well. The skull was caved, blunt force COD. But the matter was all there. At least twenty percent more weight than you'd expect, even given the overall size."

"Unusual?"

"Enough that I plan to keep Jane a few extra days, so I can make sure I've taken lots of notes. This is seriously one for the textbooks.

I could get some pretty life-changing career advancements out of this."

"And she's beautiful. Eerily so," Luke mused. Gertie registered this. She bent to look closer.

"Weird. Sometimes I feel like I don't see the person for looking at all the people. But you're right. She was a knockout. Makes me sad. I hope she enjoyed herself. Her beauty. Her life." Her words hung there for a moment. "There's more."

"Huh?"

"None of the blood went to the stomach. It went here." She pulled over a small metal table, also covered. A quick flip of a cloth revealed a small, unexpected shape.

"Pregnant?"

"Yes. Jane Doe was pregnant. And the uterus and placenta … not normal. I mean, placentas are weird as is. Like alien-technology weird. You know, it's the only organ in the human body that is temporary? A purpose-built sub-plant for baby feeding and baby waste. And they can go wrong. Looks like Jane had an extreme case of vigorous, invasive placentation. Placentas should constantly balance between the requirements of the fetus and the needs of the mother. A weak one means baby won't grow. Too strong and mother is at mortal risk. Jane shouldn't have been physically capable of sustaining a pregnancy. That placenta should have killed her."

"How is that even possible?"

"I wish I could say, but I haven't worked it out. So, short strokes, lots of blood, not hers, that she ate, but it didn't go to her stomach. Instead, it went to the fetus who did have it in its stomach."

Luke just stared. This was a lot.

"It looks like the umbilical connects farther up. Does not make sense, but since the whole thing is a bit of a carnival sideshow, what the hell. Look: these structures should be all contained within the uterus, but instead it's like a secondary conduit. Rerouted and connected straight to the esophagus."

"Come on."

"Jane here has so many anomalies, I'll be honest, I'm not even really sure how she was alive. How's all that for first-thing Monday?"

"It's enough."

"Hey — you're expecting a baby soon, aren't you?"

"Yeah. And today was positively enlightening."

"Mazel tov."

"Can you say that even if you aren't Jewish?"

"Okay, fine, neutral congratulations, Detecting Unit Comrade Stockton. Oh, and here." She brandished a paper baggie. "One last surprise. I got you some jewellery." She dropped the piece out into her gloved hand to show him.

It was a small silver piece. Sharply pointed on one end, with a round ball at the other, connected by a silver rod.

"Her tongue was pierced with this. Wicked looking thing." Gertie shook her head. "I honestly never understood how people could stand having something like that sitting in their mouth all the time. It drives me crazy if I have something stuck between my teeth. I'm always sticking my tongue in there. A piercing would drive me nuts."

Luke nodded and subconsciously ran his tongue over his own teeth. He'd forgotten to brush. Monday. Indeed.

In fact, it was only the start of his Monday, because he had to swing across town, through traffic, to make it in time to pick Beatrice up from her appointment. He was thankful that the traffic was choked all across the lakeshore and right up into the core. It gave him time to switch gears from a fetus on a gurney to the life growing in his wife and what a joy that was. By instinct, he plied through a few one-way streets and cut through a few alleys to get himself past where it always clogged on Front at that same left-hand turn. In fact, he wound up being early for the pickup.

"I hate these appointments," she said when she got in.

"Hi, I love you too. I thought you liked the new doctor."

"I do, I do. They're great. I'm spending time with lots of interesting women there too. Feels like a kind of club. I just hate being told what to do all the time. I'm not a child! I'm having one."

"I'm getting pretty nervous about getting a bill from them," Luke said.

"Oh, don't worry. Cleo said they'll give us a bit of a break."

"Really? Why?"

"Because. I sweet-talked that woman Cleo. God. Can you believe, they want me back there in a couple of days? More tests, more paperwork. I wish I could play hooky from it all."

"I don't know if that's a good idea, Bea."

"Oh, relax. It's not like I have a choice anymore. Starting to show," she said, with both hands on her stomach. "Getting more real." She checked her lipstick in the mirror. She dressed up for doctor appointments now, the way she used to vamp it up for their dates in the early days.

Chapter 19

LUKE

The receipt from Jane's tailored inner pocket connected Luke to the familiar sleek glass-fronted building on Bay Street.

This time, to get past the stormtrooper redhead, he was compelled to use big-boy words like "murder" and "police investigation." He preferred to gain entry to places like this just on the strength of his occupation and title and being friendly. The big words tended to make people edgy. Overly helpful. Or worse, cheerfully curious about his job and its processes. *Do you see a lot of dead bodies?* The morbid ones always wanted to know the gory details.

Luke waited perched on one of those not-for-sitting chairs for almost half an hour and was kept amused and jittery by a constant flow of hot, sweet espresso served in minute space-age cups. The red-headed receptionist with the high ponytail chirped to inquire how he was doing and that she would "just be a few more minutes" every five minutes like a persistent alarm. Over the course of thirty minutes, she brought out three of those miniscule cups. He didn't mind being served those mini cups. He certainly didn't mind watching her come and go to do it.

When a tall woman in a business suit came in, switching shoulders with a tiny purse and swinging her hair, he noted that the receptionist didn't go into stormtrooper mode. She sat up even straighter, smiled wide, and spoke in honied tones with her. The woman placed a platinum-coloured plastic card on the counter, and the receptionist stood. She reached behind reception to where glossy panels cleverly hid a refrigerator. Puffs of air swirled out when she reached inside. She withdrew a stainless steel canister from the fridge and placed it into a glossy tote with rope handles, emblazoned with the Medspa's logo.

"Enjoy," she told the woman with a plush, flirty tone. Which made it sound like she'd just made the woman a cocktail. The woman looked pleased with her purchase, so clearly the receptionist knew something he didn't. *Women and their creams*, he thought, turning back to scroll through his phone.

After one more mini coffee, another glossy panel slid noiselessly open, and Cleo appeared on needle-thin heels. She strode across the concrete floor to grasp his hand her power grip.

"Mr. Stockton. So sorry to have kept you."

"Almost the biggest part of my job, waiting."

"Do you need an espresso? A latte? Genevieve?"

"No. I'm about to jump out of my skin with all the caffeine Genevieve here gave me."

"Well, we can't have that." She swivelled and looked at him, pertly, like a bird. "How is Beatrice enjoying her sessions with us?" This came as a surprise. As far as Luke knew, they hadn't decided yet to make the leap. Cleo gave him a flashing smile over her shoulder as he followed her through the glossy door and into the darkness.

They passed through a dim hallway clad in beaten, aged copper on one side with a dim mural on the other.

"Executive pass-through," she noted. Hushed music filtered through.

"Looks kind of like those old cave paintings." Luke snapped his fingers. "Lascotte?"

"Lascaux. Very good. But no, something else altogether."

"From where?"

"You wouldn't know it," she replied firmly, and closed the door on the subject.

The stone exuded coolness. The air felt chilly here. It was almost like being in a cave. Ochre and charcoal figures danced over the porous stone, bearing spears, their arms truncated and legs spindly like twigs. He peered closer, eyes getting used to the dark. Was it other humans they were chasing?

"It's not real, is it?"

She turned back to look at him and smiled an indulgent smile. "I have a passion for ancient things."

Another secret-looking door led into a busier hallway — less barren, but no less high-end. Glossy floors, frosted glass walls partitioned off rooms.

"How is Beatrice feeling?" she said.

"Well, we're at the endless insane food cravings stage, apparently."

"Ha!" she said, and her "ha" was a long, exhaled, throaty sound, rather than a conventional laugh. "Those cravings. Such a trial. You know, they've actually documented women eating handfuls of earth as a result of their pregnancy cravings."

"Is that a fact?"

She showed him to a large, white office that overlooked the lake on two sides. He took a white-and-chrome seat in front of the wide desk and was surprised that she joined him on that side of the table. She folded into long, taut angles as she sat, knees and shins and ankle bones sharp and strong.

"Oh yes. Pica, they call it. In some cases when women are

malnourished, they resort to eating earth, soil itself, because they are driven to get the minerals and metals in it. For the baby."

"Well, we're mid-Pica phase then, I suppose. Ms. Drover, I'm not here as an expectant father today. I'm here in an official capacity."

"Oh?" She arched a brow.

"Mm-hmm. I'm on a lead, investigating a homicide. I fear my visit includes gruesomeness. We unfortunately found an unidentified woman dead ..."

"And that led you here?"

"This led me here." He showed her the thermal receipt for a debit transaction. "Not one of your bigger clients, obviously. But I'm hoping someone might recognize her ..."

She took the receipt and fluidly moved to her desktop. She tapped at a few keys.

"Instant messaging my assistant with the date," she explained. "That will narrow it down to whichever of our clients we saw, or at least charged that day."

"Is that hundreds of possible clients?"

"Oh no, not that many. I mentioned we're quite exclusive. Not your typical pharmacy cosmetics customer. We'll narrow it down. Our clients are extremely loyal. We have treatments that some come from around the world for. Our leech treatment is booked two years in advance."

"You don't say. What do amazing leeches do?"

"A highly effective treatment for major bruising, for one. I've seen them turn major hematomas around in a single treatment. They are miracles of nature. There's an enzyme they secrete after they latch on to the skin. They break down the dead blood and their feeding encourages circulation."

"I'm guessing leeches cost more than" — he took back the receipt, mindful that he didn't leave without it, and referenced the amount — "two hundred and fifty-one dollars and twenty-five cents."

"It's true, we don't have any leech treatments that fall under that amount."

"What does?"

"It could have been any number of products we offer in our shop. Takeaway treatments, lotions, serums. Many possibilities. Here we are … fifty-five clients that day. Once we pull the files, you'll be able to see what she bought, cross-referenced with our record."

"I'd like to show you a photo, but I have to warn you, it's —" She put up a hand.

"I have been medically trained, Mr. Stockton." She said it swiftly, almost curtly.

He produced the photo in a file. He found it made it easier to allow civilians to open the folder themselves. They picked the timing. It softened the blow.

"I was hoping you'd find her familiar."

She peered at Jane's lifeless face impassively, her eyes roving mechanically over the features as though processing data. She shook her head in a slow no.

"We can go through the files and match the face. We have photos for all clients who have had treatments with us. Please …" She stood and indicated he should follow her out.

She took him back through the executive pass-through to an elevator. It opened immediately and they stepped into a muted leather space, where tanned hides and a cedar scent mingled. There was something primal about the space. She leaned over him to press a button and he stepped back quickly, but not before clocking that she'd pressed her breast against his forearm. She wore a thin cream wool jacket over a silk camisole. And he'd felt the heat of her body, through her clothes and the cotton sleeve of his shirt.

Without acknowledging the moment, she leaned back on the railing in the elevator, both arms casually slung across it. Head tilted. Giving him that assessing look again. He felt a prickle in the small of his back that crept along the base of his spine hugging his pelvis and deep into …

"Your partner …" She allowed the word to dangle there.

"Beatrice," Luke offered.

"Yes. Beatrice. Are you and she planning your family in a traditional … closed relationship?"

The question was so blunt it floored him.

He guppied at her for a moment, laughed awkwardly.

"Yeah, yeah, yeah. She was crystal clear about that on our first date. We are super traditional on that front."

"How wonderful. So many people are doing alternate arrangements these days. It is so refreshing to find those who stick to the old ways. You seem like a lovely man. A man's man. Great stock. If you'd pardon the pun."

He stared. He could have cut slices out of the air and eaten them, it was so thick in that small space.

"Sure. I do. Oh. Stockton. Ha," he finally responded, after what felt like an eternity of dead air. He was relieved to leave the confines of the elevator.

She showed him to a room where a stack of white folders sat on a white table with two black chairs and padded cloth walls. Aggressive lights held short fluorescent tubes just overhead.

"Genevieve at the front can help you should you find a match. She will run copies for you. I wish I could be more helpful than this … Good luck. I hope you find her."

He nodded, still a bit gobsmacked. She'd hit on him, he thought. At least, he was pretty sure. He felt a little giddy. He'd forgotten what it was like to get the blood flowing. He took a seat at the stack of folders. He was happy for the grounding activity of the work. Open file. Pull out photo. Compare. Close.

"And regarding your wife, Mr. Stockton …?"

"My wife?" He swore he almost had a voice crack.

"I've left an envelope for you there. It's for five hundred dollars at the spa. My compliments."

"I can't accept that. It's —" She leapt in before he could finish with a coolly raised palm.

"Oh, don't be silly. It's not for you. It's for her. Expectant mothers need all the support they can get, don't you think?"

"They sure do. It's a great thought. But I am most definitely not allowed to accept anything like that. Departmental policy."

"Sterling. Of course not," she murmured to herself, silkily. "But she was supposed to receive it at our previous appointment. You're just the errand boy, in this instance."

He desperately wanted her to leave. He also wanted her to stay. He also wanted her right there on the table. But he needed her to leave. He wanted to luxuriate for just a moment on an exhale about the insanity of her come-on. And then compose himself and then go home to his wife. And give her a back rub and then spend two point five minutes alone in the shower with a soapy hand.

As she closed the door, leaving him alone, she smiled one of those arch, patrician, European sort of smiles models had in Amaretto ads. He heaved a sigh of relief and felt his stomach muscles unclench for the first time since shaking her hand.

File. Open. Scan, photo, close. Next.

The rhythm of work calmed him down. Forty files into the pile, he found her.

Heloise Wu. 35. Born in April. Resident at number 5 Playter Place.

For a moment Luke put his head down on the table and let all the adrenaline seep out and subside. He had learned to pause and pivot on moments like these.

A good, solid lead. A good connection. Sometimes they were made. Sometimes they led to conclusions. Sometimes they were smoke. They had to be celebrated a little when they happened. Otherwise, in the wash of so many unknowns, little wins like this could get lost and overwhelmed by the low-grade anxiety that came with the job. Stopping and recognizing them as small victories made the job a tiny bit more satisfying.

He staggered out, feeling a little light-headed after the scanning, the fluorescents overhead. Oh right, and the near-complete lack of sleep lately. He was feeling foggy. And had a sticky sweat creeping between his shoulder blades and up his neck.

He found his way to the fancy elevator, managed to press the wrong floor, wandered the clinic aisle for a few moments before realizing his error and spinning back around to the elevator. He spun too fast: as he did, a clinician with a wheeled aluminum tray barrelled straight into him. The cart and several stainless steel containers and implements and blood-stained cotton pads went flying. As well as four slithering, writhing black leeches, bursting fat with blood. Luke was not squeamish. But those things were disgusting.

"I'm so sorry!" gasped the clinician, gathering them in gloved hands and clippers. "We don't like to show people the leeches," she added, as if that explained something.

"I can see why," he remarked and wobbled back to the elevator and the exit.

Chapter 20

RENARD

Once he'd forded the Sava River, Martin rolled up in a crinkly silver heat sheet under a thick copse of trees. His waterlogged clothes still clung to him, clammy. Columns of ants kept him awake nearly the whole night. He walked ten miles on an empty stomach to the muster point where the Croatians, dressed in cobbled-together combat gear, met him.

There were huge smiles all around and men gripping each other's forearms.

"What do we call you?" his new comrades wanted to know.

"Renard."

"Does it mean anything?"

"Fox," he told them. He received blank faces. Then someone in the back called out in Croatian.

"*Lisica*." The soldiers clapped him on the back. "Now you are our fox."

He joined a unit of other foreign fighters: Brits, French (from France), Dutch, Poles, Finns, Swedes, and even Russians made up the corps. Mercenaries made interesting bedfellows when shifting lines between states blurred and corroded. Some were criminals back home. This was hinted at darkly via meaningful glances when asked about their lives, followed by meaningfully looking away. Some were there for religious beliefs. Some out of boredom. Some, like him, were there because they'd been unlucky in life but competent in combat.

He was welcome.

His penchant for self-harm was especially welcome.

Some guys had pictures of girls, or kids. He had no one. No photo to pin up with a thumbtack near his cot.

They trained him for a time, and he gave training to small groups in return. They joined skirmishes and advances as opportunity allowed. They were accused of war crimes and atrocities against villagers. They themselves knew what they were guilty of, capable of, and what everyone else was guilty and capable of. It was a messy civil war of overlapping cultures and faiths. They all did the needful, unspeakable things that war demands on a regular basis.

After a few months of light action, he took part in the Summer Offensive.

His unit advanced on Grahovo in an area heavily controlled by hostiles. It was a checkerboard of holdings by all the different players. His splinter group of twelve men was sent forward, out from under cover, where pines grew thick and knobby, and the ground was slippery with needles. It was steeply pitched, racing down toward the town. While running he lost his footing, faltered, righted, turned, and was hit in the back of his skull with a shell fragment.

He landed on the ground with his face up and his feet pointing down the hill.

He heard someone call.

"Renard!"

Part of him, unreasonably, wanted to chuckle. He felt the laughter squirming up his throat like gleeful snakes. Everything seemed strangely amusing and surreal. Renard? That wasn't his name. Why were they calling him that? But he found he could neither respond nor correct them, and shortly he didn't care to. Eventually, the snakes subsided and there he lay.

They kept calling "Renard, Renard!" repeatedly, which he found annoying. But presently, they stopped. He lay on the hill and looked at a piece of sky that was strung between spiky pine boughs.

His sight went dark, like someone dimming a switch.

He thought about Rimouski and the *auberge* and Josée.

How fucking stupid it was that she'd taken up with that drip Patrice who had always been a stupid little shit with his stupid turned-up golf shirt collars.

And then he didn't think about anything.

Chapter 21

LUKE

The homicide unit set up a tip line through the media outreach department. Luke felt little would come of it, especially as far as some street boys were concerned. Just forgotten troubled kids to most people. He did wonder if tips would roll in on Jane Doe. Even if she didn't have friends or family, a beautiful, affluent woman like her was bound to have admirers. But there was only ever going to be a certain window, a matter of days for the new piece to get traction. It would play out on the nightly news cycle, perhaps be picked up in some papers, potentially get spun into some "weird but true" clips bit on YouTube and begin its long life as an internet curiosity, lost in a boundless, seething ocean of "information." It would take up residence on the police website — a pencil sketch of an odd, attractive woman. Info@ regarding Jane Doe XB71. If it was going to catch someone's attention, it would be in the first few days, hours even.

It was much more likely that they would catch a lead on the young John Doe found with her behind the dumpsters. He was a college-aged kid in nice clothes. Unlike the runaways, a family had bankrolled his life in the big city.

Luke was home in time to catch the eleven o'clock news on the national broadcaster. It was a big enough story to merit running during national and not just local city news. Third story of the day, after an international military incident in the South Sea and a doctor's strike. Luke poured a soda in the kitchen, watched the TV from across the kitchen counter as Gertie popped up jarringly on the screen. It was always weird to see her on television, features flattened by the harsh lights. She looked a little wary and tired. Still, the bright light brought out the planes of her face in an appealing way. She looked … diligent. Trustworthy. She spoke with lips tighter together than she seemed to in real life, and she seemed smaller, framed by the camera.

On the couch under a fuzzy blanket, Beatrice stirred.

"Oh hey. You're home."

"Hi," he said with his eyes, trying to seem as friendly as possible while pointing out the news segment.

The blazing red chyron blared about the Jane Doe public appeal and mentioned "coroner speaks" second. Beatrice sat up cross-legged under her blanket.

"So, this is the one that made all the fuss lately," she said. Luke sat on the couch with one hand on her knee.

"… the subject was noted to have an unusually robust bone structure for a female and certain … biological irregularities that might have meant she suffered a medical condition we don't yet understand. She was likely being followed by a doctor who might recognize her." It was unusual for Gertie to stumble while speaking. She hated talking to the press but she was always professional. Luke felt a slight squeeze of anxiety on her behalf.

The sketchy pencil approximation of Jane Doe flashed across the screen. It barely resembled her.

"Tragically, the subject was expecting, so authorities wonder if someone out there who was about to be a father knows of our missing person. Police ask that anyone with any information at all please come forward."

Beatrice grasped his hand fiercely.

"Poor woman! Expecting." She gasped. "Poor you, baby. I didn't realize. Oh, Luke, this must've been so tough for you." Luke gave a quick little sigh to himself and pulled her in close while they cut to the anchorwoman who gave additional contact details and the usual Police Podium Speech. *Commander Blah Blah from the Blah Blah Command, we appreciate the public's help, blah blah* and then into a segment about the importance of cleaning eaves before winter snow and a commercial about erectile dysfunction featuring old people in his-and-hers bathtubs, holding hands and smiling at each other a lot.

Chapter 22

LAUREN

Someone else did pay attention to the news story about Jane Doe.

In her basement apartment, Lauren Esteban was making a pre-packaged microwave chicken alfredo. She burnt her fingers with the steam coming out from under the plastic wrap.

She dropped the damn thing on her tile floor and sighed. The sauce had worked right into the grout between the tiles. She was brushing chunky half-frozen, half-hot bits of it out from between the tiles, and this got her spinning that old painful memory of brushing dirt off fossils in the field. She remembered being crouched at a dig, sweat at the back of her knees, her hiking boots biting into her metatarsals, sun blasting the back of her neck through the scarf she'd put on under her ballcap. All the grad students slaved at sites like that, getting their critical field experience, helping teams gather information. It was dirty, exhausting, back-breaking, and the best time she'd had in her life.

They'd spent late nights drinking bad wine from thermoses at fold-out tables. They'd played cards and laughed their asses off. Never before and never since had Lauren felt so much a part of something in her otherwise solitary life. Early mornings, crouching and brushing layers of dirt before the heat of the day and bugs and wind could really take their toll. It was dues-paying time. Those hours under the sun were always meant to be hours banked toward acclaim, recognition. She was working her way up the academic ladder to one day being a Someone with a position and a title.

But now she was unemployed, cast out, crouching with one hand splayed on the cold tile for balance in the fluorescent light of her stove hood in a chilly condo, making a frozen meal for one. Again.

When the image of the Jane Doe flashed on the screen, she inwardly groaned. Who had they gotten to make *that* hideous sketch? Of course, the public didn't want to see death mask photos of dead bodies in close-up. But couldn't the police at least find an artist with more anthropology chops to get the bone structure, right? This one looked like a kid had drawn it. A stoned kid, at that.

But something about it drew her in. The heavy-lidded eyes, the sharp, prominent cheekbones. The way the orbital bone swooped and flared. That jaw. There was something weirdly familiar about this face. Not like someone she knew, but familiar like an icon, like Lucy the hominid. Like a celebrity.

She rose. Crouching was something she couldn't do for long these days without pinching her sciatic nerve. That's when they said the bit about the strange bone structure. And the biological … irregularities, the coroner woman had said with a specific stress. It made Lauren butterfinger the plastic tray of chunky alfredo back down on the floor again. She knew the coroner was faffing something about the good details in order to make it better for public consumption.

She bent back down to flick her wrist and efficiently dislodge chunks from the grout with her well-practised hand.

Instead of sitting at the table, Lauren put her plastic alfredo tray on the desk, which was pushed against the far wall, crowding her kitchenette. She put her papers into piles. The computer fired up while she bent over to fluff her hair a little. Upright, she applied some lip gloss. Once the ring light was on, she peered at her image onscreen and smoothed out her eyebrows. She pulled down a rolling map she'd affixed to a backdrop screen and emblazoned with a logo: "Missing Link Found."

Her script was in front of her. She had a series of clips — photos of Olorgesailie in Kenya. The pictures, largely black-and-white shots with rulers next to them for scale, showed various ancient, flaked, stone hand tools. To the untrained eye, just rocks. To someone like Lauren, the height of high tech for ancient hominids.

Just before the green record light winked on in her viewer, Lauren pulled on her field hat. Her one-sided canvas French bush hat. Her lucky hat, given to her on a dig when she'd got a terrible sunburn. Later that day despite feeling nauseated and sun-sick, she'd found several finger-bone segments. After that she never dug without it. She always wore her lucky hat when she was recording episodes of *Missing Link Found.*

"Hi, guys! Lauren here at *Missing Link Found*, where we always bring the real, dirty truth behind archeology, opening up a world of secrets and lies, and bring the coolest and most up-to-date true archeological facts straight to you. I'm 'Professor' (wink wink) Lauren Esteban. And today, before I get started discussing the link between *Homo heidelbergensis* and the Acheulean industrial tradition — 'Hooray for hand axes!' — I have something really exciting I just saw on the news in my hometown that I want to share with all of you. Don't forget to like and subscribe, all my little arch-y fans!"

She recalled the day she'd seen several fossil fragments spread across the worktable. Taken as a whole, they sketched out an arching blade that suggested a right upper thigh, a hint of a pelvis, and a smattering of vertebrae with many, many blank spaces, which could only hint at the whole creature that once used the flesh on its bones to walk the earth.

Lauren was one of a half-dozen archaeology masters students working in the lab at the time, and eager as hell to prove herself. It was a quality that should have garnered her praise and encouragement from her advisor. In the movie version of her life, it would have. The deeply compassionate professor would lean forward, cocking his head to catch her every breathless word. His faltering professional ardour would be reignited by her drive, and together the two of them would take the archeology world by storm and celebrate with splashy rooftop parties doused with champagne and flashing cameras. The first fiction was that there would be parties. The second was that there would be champagne. The third was that the professor was handsome.

In the movie the professor would be played by a Liam Neeson–type and the student would be a wide-eyed, pert Latina actress in a career-defining breakout role.

In real, tedious life, Professor Joe Broady was no Liam Neeson.

He was a tall man, with a suit of flab hanging on a lanky frame. His nose was purple and his eyes swam behind his glasses like indolent fish. Lauren watched him curdle with hostility whenever she spoke.

On this particular day in the late 20-aughts, in the vast cool space of a brick building on Spadina Avenue, among the ceiling-high tall shelves and long drawers where hundreds of thousands of fossils and bones were kept in the Anthro archives, when Lauren piped up, Professor Joe looked like he might have an aneurysm.

But Lauren knew in her soul that the right thigh fragment didn't really a hundred percent jive with the rest of the bones in what had been used as an example of a Neanderthal juvenile female for teaching purposes. Joe, as usual, said nothing to support her. He looked through the middle of his dense trifocals at Lauren with a decided *will you please shut up* look and kept going with the thought in his head he was trying to hammer home to the rest of the students.

That was the beginning of *it*.

Lauren, with the exuberance of youth, was certain from that day forward that she, and for certain she alone, had spotted something different. Something improperly classified and overlooked by her doddering and indifferent "betters." Joe was clearly too much of an idiot to see how brilliant she was.

From that moment on, Lauren poured herself into proving Joe wrong and herself right at all costs.

She performed all the requisites required of a budding academic. Published the right stuff in the right amount and in the right places. She was on track to one day become a tenured professor herself, perhaps even earlier than her peers. She tried not to let the fact that she could have been, *would have been* one already fifty years ago if she'd been a man, if the funding were there, if there wasn't so much competition for spaces, if universities weren't all gripped in a fever of bums in seats, if … None of it mattered as much as what had become her pet project, her raison d'être. That one thigh bone.

That one thigh bone fragment that just didn't look right launched Lauren into a lifelong quest to prove that beyond *Homo sapiens*, and beyond the Neanderthals, beyond the Denisovans even, as there were rumoured to be, there were still other undiscovered species of hominids, humanlike creatures. They were beings who had lived at the same time as humans, fought with them for land and space, traded with them, exchanged culture with them, interbred with them even. When she woke in the morning, she made mental lists of other archives in the world that had tantalizing mounds and mounds of bones. There were potentially billions of fragments mislabelled all over the world, hiding in plain sight.

She sometimes still felt a little sick when she wound back through time in her thoughts and played out everything that had happened. Down in the archives, while doing some sketches and comparing pieces, she'd noticed that the one guy caretaking the place had shuffled out. Silence surged into the room as she worked, and she relished the fact that his rhythmic chair squeaks and gum snapping were missing. Then, something else had seized her. Without a further thought, she'd stuck that fossilized piece of bone in her book bag. Popped it in. Just like that.

At home she put it up on a shelf. Out in plain sight. Right next to some chicken bones she'd assembled into a joke of a fantasy creature. No one she knew was going to recognize it. When she passed by, it gave her a little existential jolt. And a reminder to keep on track. And then after a while, she forgot about it a little.

It had taken months for anyone else to even notice. There were literally hundreds of thousands of fossil fragments in the drawers of the Spadina facility and it's not like they searched people in and out. But one day, the empty place on a shelf was noticed. At Professor Broady's urging, a bunch of disgruntled teaching assistants went through security footage. They found a blurry image of Lauren shoving the bone in her bag. Under Broady's instructions again, they played it cool, rather than stage an inquisition.

One day there was a photocopied notice on goldenrod paper on a bulletin board: missing department property, no questions asked, yada yada.

Only it wasn't in the end just yada yada.

They waited for her to come out with it, of her own volition. They finally pointed the finger at Lauren, brought her in front of Broady himself. She never fessed up. Not even when they barred her from campus. Not when they sent an actual police officer to her grad housing, nor when the university pressed formal charges. She knew that taking the worst of a sentence would one day pale in comparison to being right. So, with the virtue of the just, and the strength of the sanctimonious, she went to court, pleaded not guilty.

Her gamble paid off — she only got a house arrest sentence for two years and community service; hours of cleaning up litter on the sides of highways. But she never handed over the bone. She was its keeper. She was the one who knew the true importance of the artifact and she was ready to suffer anything to protect it.

When she went to bed at night, she fought off the slings and arrows of being the crazy person with her batshit focus on that one bone. She was lulled by thoughts of what her creature, *her* people, *her* undiscovered species would be called in all the journals if, no, *when* they were finally recognized. Maybe they would name it after her in recognition of decades of doggedly piecing together evidence? Maybe after the archive on Spadina Avenue where the fossilized bone had come to rest after thousands of years?

Whatever they would name her, Lauren thought of her as Mina. It was Lauren's private joke, from the *Dracula* story. There was always a Lucy in that vampire story — and there was that other superstar of evolution: Lucy, hominin species *Australopithecus afarensis*. Lucy was a young female hominid found in the Awash Valley — an early link to humans. Lauren knew all the exciting swoops and curves of her acetabular distance, her pubic arch, her iliac flare, her anterior wrap.

In *Dracula* Mina was the ballsy one. Lucy was just the simp.

Mina was the one who went after what she wanted: the lusty, bloodthirsty one. She was the foil to Lucy. So, Lauren's hominid would be named for the nemesis to Lucy — her own "Mina."

And when she was finally able to prove Mina was a thing — a species — she would hand-deliver a framed photo of herself and the article to Professor Joe. Just to see the old man's papery face turn a darker shade of purple.

Chapter 23

LUKE

DNA from the original owner of the blood found inside Jane Doe led Luke back to Club Nausea. When no one answered his knocks, he tried the handle, and finding it unlocked, he cracked the door. Someone was blasting Ramones over the sound system. Luke tripped over his feet walking three steps down into the dark. He could smell bleach, funky beer, and fermenting lemon. His feet stuck to the floor as he walked.

Just when his eyes grew used to the dimness, and he started to make out the warehouse-sized shape of the place, the overhead lights were killed, plunging him for a moment into complete blackness. A second later a spray of dancing lasers and twirling spotlights bloomed, burning into his retinas. They flicked through various colour palettes, meant to be timed to the pulse of dance music. The music died. The motes continued to dance like disembodied will-o-the-wisps.

"*Hey!*" he shouted into the quiet. "Can I talk to someone?"

"Accounts payable are in the business office, not here," some guy replied smoothly over a hot microphone.

Turning around, Luke could see a few people in a lit box near the ceiling. The DJ booth. He held up his badge. It picked up and reflected glancing lasers like a shield.

"Stay put. Someone's coming down."

A second later the overheads came back on. It was a cavernous, murky space. The walls were all black, spattered with abstract splashes of UV-reactive paint. Luke figured the spray pattern was connected to the club's name. Under the harsh glare of fluorescents, the concrete floor was stained, and the bar stools and cruiser tables were chipped and scratched. The whole place stank of rancid alcohol and old limes. At night when it was packed, all you'd see would be bodies: sequined girls, lights dancing over thrashing limbs. Presumably, all you would smell was fog machine vapour, Axe body spray, sweat.

Luke met the two guys from the AV booth at the bar. One of them hadn't been working there the night Jane and friend were found, with a clear alibi of working at his side hustle at a hockey game. The other guy had DJ'd that night. He wore silver rings on all ten digits and fiddled with a rumpled pack of smokes. He tore into one when Luke gave him a nod.

"You're allowed to when the club isn't open?"

"Why? You a cigarette cop?"

"Whatever. Did you see anything weird happen here that night?"

"You wouldn't believe the shit I see every night. But nothing criminal that I saw. I'm too busy unless I'm on break. I took two smoke breaks on the rooftop. Left at dawn. Took the street entrance out."

"Okay. You hear anything weird from anyone about that night?"

"What's going on?" asked a beefy kid with a huge five-gallon bucket of ice. Right when Luke made to answer, the kid started pouring it, making a clatter no one could speak over. Luke gave him a strained smile. He passed over the photo of the woman, taken from a low angle under her chin so the features were fairly clear.

"This is what went on. Were you working here Thursday?"

The kid froze. He shook his head and dropped the pail straight to the floor.

Luke turned back to silver rings guy. "So, what can you see from the rooftop?"

"Chuck, man," the DJ said. "What's up? Can I get that pineapple juice? Chuck?"

The kid walked off.

"Rude. Just walking away mid-shift. Barbacks gotta learn manners."

Luke peered up. The kid was halfway across the room and walking stiffly but with purpose toward the door that led to the alley. His ass was tucked under his spine, like a guilty dog. Inwardly, Luke sighed. Sprinting was a pain in the ass. And the Achilles.

The kid heard him, broke into a run, smashed through the door.

"Kid. Stop," Luke shouted. The kid was halfway down the alley by the time Luke had made it to the door. That was when Luke called the beat cop parked nearby. Someone else could blow their Achilles out over this one.

It came out later, while Chuck inhaled dry supermarket sandwiches and knocked back station house coffee, that he had run because he'd freaked out. He had indeed "known" the Jane Doe. Unfortunately, only carnally, and hadn't gotten around to formalities like her name.

He and his roommates had all met her at the club. Based on a mutual attraction, so he said, Jane and the boys had decided together to move on from the club to another location, their shared warehouse space. Then Jane had taken off and they'd all passed out.

Given that drinks and other substances were likely part of the equation, Luke wondered how much of a collective decision any of this was. He prodded the kid for important details like "How conscious would you say Jane was?"

Images emerged of an insatiable Jane draped over their laps, definitely not strapped into her seatbelt, per the highway traffic act. Fellatio in the taxi en route. Chuck was very sketchy on whether her eyes were open at this stage or not. Their interview had to stop when he began bawling, unintelligible. He took a breath long enough to stutter out for a lawyer. Luke took this as a perfect opportunity to step back. Time to check out the kid's warehouse pad.

Luke was familiar with the location, a short cab ride away from the entertainment district. It was a hulking mass of three stories that rambled a city block from Queen Street all the way to the rail corridor. Built as a piano factory with grim, utilitarian lines, it had begun to fray and crumble. There were gaps where windows had been knocked out by weather or vandalism. Residents were a mix of artists, couriers, drug dealers, the unemployable, and hipsters with sleeve tattoos and rescue dogs on expensive leashes.

There was no formal entry, no directory, just a door to a tall metal staircase painted a grim shade of green. The door was missing a panel of safety glass. Just inside the door, the glass lay on the ground, a spray of cubed, rough-cut diamonds glittering on the dark concrete.

At the top of the stairs, the landing let onto an endless hallway clad with diagonally striped maple wood flooring. The massive space had been chopped up into unit after unit of housing reclaimed as live-work space. Eleven a.m. and the air was spiced with various strains of hash and weed. Dance music, bandsaws, reggae, and someone practising vocal scales bled out from the doorways.

The officer with Luke knocked and the two of them stood by. Chuck said that his roommate would still be home. Likely still in bed, sleeping off partying.

Through the door Pink Floyd played softly on a stereo. Luke rolled his eyes. It was always Floyd. After several louder knocks, there was finally a shuffling inside and the door cracked to reveal a sleep-stunned kid still in his tighty whities.

Inside, Christmas lights scribbled along exposed brick walls lit the ceiling beams of an old warehouse space. They had jerry-rigged a lopsided kitchen counter with a hotplate and a dish drainer. The sink drained into a plastic bucket. Battle-scarred pleather couches and man-sized speakers dominated the lounge area. Every surface was covered with empty beer cans and plastic cups. A leaking beer keg on its side. A toilet off to one side, festively hung with a flaccid Union Jack flag for privacy.

Luke wondered what well-heeled Jane must have thought coming to this shithole. It stank. Half the windows were foiled over, so eastern sun wouldn't disturb their beauty sleep.

While they glanced around, the roommate, Raj, sprawled on the couch, not bothering to pull on pants.

"We've chatted with your roommate, Mr. Patil. Mr. Stewart, Chuck, indicated that you were with him last night."

"Aw fuck. You guys are here because of that crazy bitch, aren't you?" he slurred.

Luke smiled mildly. "Raj Patil, it is my duty to inform you that you have the right to retain and instruct counsel in private, without delay." He spoke the words with careful inflection, but a mild tone.

The kid was heaved up from the couch and cuffed. It took two of them to lift him.

"Yeah. Well. She started it. She was the one who killed Rich, man. We were just defending ourselves. Bitch was fucking savage. She did that …" He gestured with his head at a sturdy maple coffee table that stood nearby, caved into a V shape.

Something glistening caught Luke's eye. He bent at the waist a little and it came into focus. A single, spherical black round button had come to rest in the hollowed-out knot of the wooden floorboards. He pointed it out to the SOCO who would bag it. Luke returned his gaze to the kid, who was still waking up. Luke smiled, a little jaunty.

"Well, we'll sort out who did what to whom with statements at the station."

Across the warehouse space an officer helped the kid pull on some jogging pants and shuffle to the doorway. He shook his head slowly at Luke but said nothing.

Chapter 24

LUKE

They worked the boys over in separate interviews. Meanwhile, the loft was meticulously taken apart by forensics. Cocky at first, the boys led with a story of a drunk, hot-to-trot Jane who came to their loft, attacked their friend, and that she and Rich left, together, alive. At first they feigned surprise that their friend had been found, a pathetic and transparent ruse. Luke worked them individually, allowing them to sit, to be bored and scared and alone with their thoughts. He'd go from one to the other. How had they met? How had they all come to be at the warehouse? How had they come to leave? How had Rich come to be alone with her?

In the first round, Jane left the club with Rich, and they never saw either of them again. But Chuck volunteered that they got into a cab together, while Raj suggested the roommates had returned home in one car, while Rich and Jane went to her place. Luke kept at them, asking them to repeat the steps from leaving the club, to waking up the next day. Over a long lunch, evidence of the four of them together in the back of a city cab, caught on camera, emerged.

After he'd had a leisurely bagel with a great Americano, Luke sat across from Raj, smoothing his tie. One of the few Beatrice had bought him. He didn't like it. It had a bad habit of kinking up along the seam. But he liked her knowing that he wore it. He found himself musing as he sat down to give them the final blow, that neither of these boys was likely going to know the pleasure of wearing a bad tie their wife had picked out for them for another twenty-five years. "You know, Raj, when we run the fingerprints of whoever dressed Jane and Rich, and when they turn out to be yours and Chuck's, it will make things easier for me. But harder for you. And harder for you to see your way through a plea. I'd appreciate it, and I think you will too, later, if you just make things nice and clear now."

It was Raj who back-pedaled first and offered the real sequence of events. Going back and forth between the two boys over the course of hours, the blow-by-blow emerged.

According to them, John Doe was an upper-middle-class kid, Rich Beauville, from an Anglo Montreal family, one of several brothers, and a party animal. This was his second post-secondary institution. He'd been kicked out of the first one for a laundry list of plagiarism, drugs in res, and an abysmal showing in class attendance, participation, and GPA. As far as his parents knew, he was minoring in business in a city college as a do-over. In reality he was majoring in clubbing. He was handsome kid, powerfully built, easily popular with women. Rich had certainly caught Jane's eye.

His wingmen, Raj and Chuck, were at university, enrolled in kinesiology. They were the heart of their rugby team. They'd found Rich through an internet roommate finder site. They had similar tastes in music and partying. Rich was good with what money he had. He was chill, liked to smoke up and hang.

They had Uber-ed to Nausea with Rich and were there by 10:00 p.m., when the cover charge went way up. The plan was: pound cheap bar shots before the women arrived and then try to pick up chicks. By 11:30 the dance floor was still sparse. They were separated temporarily, and by the time Raj and Chuck found Rich, he was standing behind a knockout in a tight black dress, grinding his pelvis against her ass in time to the music while she backed it up rhythmically.

They said Rich looked as surprised as anyone else to have that gorgeous cougar putting the moves on him. They gyrated through several extended mixes before she was all over him, making out hot and heavy, tongues and all, and grabbing at each other's junk right there on the dance floor. From the sidelines of the dance floor, they watched her drag him out by the shirt collar. They wanted to see where it was all going and decided to follow him out.

At the end of the alley, she hailed a street cab. She got in, then pulled Rich in after. Before they could speed off for their tryst, the roommates jumped in the back with them. They wanted to show her their loft. She wanted to go to her place. She was the one paying, so she got the veto.

She was loaded, they said. Fancy townhouse in midtown. Lots of good cocktails. Hash joints came out, then coke, and they all lounged on the couch in front of a big TV, while the drugs kicked in. Raj and Chuck were cramping Jane's style, so she sidelined Rich to her bedroom. They audibly made out there for a while as the roommates couched out, surfing on the TV, debating about going back to the club for a last chance to pick up girls. Before they could solidify plans, a disturbance brought them both running into the bedroom.

They found Rich in the bathroom, jeans half off, shirt gone, bleeding from his mouth. Chuck remembered seeing hectic spots dripping onto the front of his crisp, white boxers.

The guys wanted to split. But this was the point where Jane got pushy. She told them she wanted a four-way. This part was a stretch for Luke. She was an undeniably attractive woman. These guys were, aside from Rich, who was the handsome one, middling at best. Sure, they were built, and in their prime, but they were several rungs below what Jane could have pulled.

But Raj dug his heels in about staying. He didn't feel cool about the situation. He and Chuck fought about it briefly. Ultimately, they hatched a plan. Chuck approached Jane while she was all over Rich, who seemed out of it. While Chuck took over and started to make out with her, Raj called a cab and hustled Rich out. That was when Chuck said Jane bit him, hard, digging into his tongue. Sure enough, he still had marks on in it. Despite being the biggest of the three of them, Chuck had to really fight to wrestle Jane off to follow once the cab finally arrived. He kept trying to move out of her grasp, only to have her pull wrestling-worthy moves on him. She pinned him against the wall, he ducked. She stabbed her foot between his ankles, he fell. He arm-over-armed down the hall while she threw herself on his legs and tried to grab his hair. He was having trouble seeing because he was freaking out and crying. Raj came back only because he was wondering what the hell was taking so long. He kicked at Jane, hitting her in the forehead, dislodged her long enough for them both to sprint.

They raced out of Jane's. Rich was limp in the back seat of the Uber, with Jane running after them, shouting. She tried to stop the car. She put her hands on the hood, accused them of stealing from her, and when things got really crazy, screamed that she was going to charge all of them with assaulting her. This while their friend was bleeding from his mouth in the back of the nice Uber.

The driver gave them a hard time, letting them know that if it turned out they had attacked her, he would take her side. He turned around in his seat to look at them. He wasn't going to be a party to some frat-boy types fucking around with some poor woman. By this point Raj had tears in his eyes, Rich was almost comatose, and Chuck was freaked out.

Jane, in a wild-eyed fury, started bashing on the hood of his car, denting it with her fists and shrieking that she "would fucking kill" all of them.

The driver opened his window to yell at her to leave his cab alone. She drove a hand through the half-open window and grabbed a fistful of his face.

The driver gunned it backward. He drove the wrong way up a one-way while the GPS voice on his sound system commanded him to stop and perform a U-turn.

He drove them downtown and dropped them outside their warehouse pad, seething mad.

Chuck was helping Rich out and Raj was leaving five stars on the Uber driver's profile when another street cab charged them. Jane. She flew out of the cab, leaving the door hanging open with a look in her eye that they said could only be described as completely psycho.

They scrambled inside, one on top of the other. They fumbled with keys. But they were able to lock her out. They argued about whether they should call the cops, or an ambulance, or take Rich to a doctor. As they reached the top of the metal steps, the metal-reinforced safety glass on the front door shattered. Hinges shrieked. The metal door slammed against the bricks. Rapid fire: tap tap tap tap tap. That was Jane powering up the metal steps in her stilettos.

They sprinted to their apartment, where they deadbolted and barricaded their unit door with a hunk of plywood and a couch. They sat on the couch. Rich, red-eyed, sucked on a plastic bag full of frozen vegetables. They waited for the sound of footsteps and heard nothing. After half an hour, they got massively stoned. Chuck passed out on the couch, Raj in his room, Rich in his.

But that was not the end.

Raj and Chuck woke to find Rich stripped down, lying on his back on his futon, with Jane straddling him. It was Raj, generally the quicker one, who realized that nothing was right with Rich. He looked stiff, and Raj thought he might be in shock.

Jane came at them. Working together, with practised moves drilled on the rugby team, Raj faced her, and let her come at him while Chuck crept from behind. Raj was no small kid — as a hooker on the team, he was drilled in ways to haul other grown men packed with muscle off one of his teammates, and then incapacitate them with a vicious blow. Jane was no rugby player, but she was immovable as a wall. And then she was coming at him like a machine. He found himself clawing at her with both hands, while she repeatedly went for his neck with her hands. Frantic, he managed to immobilize her hands and Chuck, from behind, made use of a cinder block that held up part of their kitchen counter. The force of it brought down on her head, took her body down, and caved in the coffee table.

And after that her seemingly unstoppable force was finally, eerily still.

When they thought to check on Rich, he was still in his bed, right where he had been before Jane jumped them. On his back. Still and unbreathing, a smear of blood on his lips.

For the better part of an hour, they played speed metal to focus their thoughts. An irate neighbour banged on the drywall yelling for them to keep it down, and they tried to figure out what to do. They knew they were fucked — the story with the Uber driver could come out and no one was going to take the side of three college boys against one sharp, well-spoken, rich lady. No one would believe that three meaty boys were the prey of one woman. Surging hormones and fading alcohol and drugs and adrenalin added up to the half-assed solution they went for.

In the last shreds of night, they re-dressed Rich and the woman in the clothes they'd originally been in. They put on hoodies and caps and drove in Raj's beater car, figuring that they'd both been scared straight enough to drive by this point. They wove through alleys and one-way streets. Stragglers of drunk kids huddled in groups all over the club district, girls and boys fighting, last-minute makeout sessions. Most of them were too drunk to notice two guys dragging their drunk girl- and boyfriends along the alley, the rest too drunk to care. The woman and Rich just looked like they were two more drunken casualties. Chuck and Raj squeezed behind the dumpster and propped them against the wall.

"Sorry, Rich, man," Chuck had said. And he was choking back tears as he did.

It was Raj who'd propped Jane up and crossed her arms, feeling sick guilt at leaving her body there.

They scuttled out of the alley, mingling with the last of the sweaty, bug-eyed kids leaving the nightclub. They hoped the people who found them would just figure Rich and the woman had done each other in.

Chapter 25

RENARD

He became aware that he had been unaware.

Renard was on the move, but not under his own steam. Because of the dark, it was hard to tell at first, but it was the tilting of the sky back and forth that made him realize he was moving. When he thought he'd try to sit up to check out what was happening, he realized he could not. This terrified him.

Someone came into his vision, but he couldn't place their uniform. Croat? Bosnian? Brit? Pole?

Who could tell? Too dark. Whoever it was looked down on him, frowning. They spoke. The words were indistinct but tinged with clear contempt. The sky tilted itself back and forth a few more times, sharply, which was confusing, until an "aha moment" when Renard realized: they were kicking him. And he couldn't move a fucking muscle. *Tabernac.*

They swung their legs far back to get a good run at his ribs. The impact was enough to break them, but he couldn't feel those ribs, so it struck him as funny. He thought he felt a laugh bubble up from his throat, but he couldn't even do that. Just as well, it would only have enraged the kicker. So being immobile likely saved his life. For a moment someone else joined in the kicking, from the other side. The sky swayed back and forth. Then, quite suddenly, the assailants looked up, looked away, and moved on without a backward glance.

Morning, pre-dawn.

Flies arrived to eat him. And then, snuffling through the leaves, the dogs came.

It really was a shame about Josée, he found himself thinking. She'd had an actual head for business. And what an ass she had. And what a laugh. Now, if he could, he would have teared up.

Their plan had been to get married, then start working at the hotel with his mom and dad. Then gradually take over the operation and somehow convince the two old ones to get in their camper van and drive to Florida like they always talked about. Then Dad had the stroke. And Mom stayed put and hired some help. And without warning, Josée dumped him for that idiot, Patrice. Left to himself, he started drinking, for real, now that he didn't have regiment stuff to do. And then he may or may not have spent a bunch of money from the safe. Hard to remember what he'd done with it, but blackouts were a common feature of his mornings then, so he figured he'd been up to some shit. Mom had to fire the help. When she got into the three-way crash en route to visiting Dad in rehab — well. Some things are depressing. When the bank foreclosed on the *auberge*, it was a relief. So here he was. Minus girl, *auberge*, ring, or anything like a point.

And now some dogs were trying to eat him.

"This one is gone." Someone was crouched nearby, red cross on a helmet. The dogs ran when they heard the voices.

"Don't be an idiot, I'm not gone," Renard said to his rescuer, but he only said it in his head. He realized with a shimmery disappointment that he couldn't speak.

"Found a pulse. Get a stretcher!"

The sky passed by overhead and then he was slid under a tan-coloured, seamed ceiling. Windows sometimes tilted into view.

We're driving, he thought. *I need to keep thinking*, he realized with panic.

The tan tin ceiling. Sky, now with clouds. Overhead wires. More wires. Canvas. China hat lamps. Tubing. Curtains. Flashlights like needles in his eyes. He felt his pupils squeeze down against the invasion. *Stop it.*

Eventually, they did. For a while the canvas got dark, then light, then dark and light. And so on.

My name is Martin. My nom de guerre *is Renard. Probably I'm gonna die out here in a Red Cross or UN tent in Bosnia. I had a pretty good run.*

And then for a while he thought about Josée and the way her skin, by mid-summer, always turned the exact same colour as the way he liked his coffee. Dark coffee with just one spoon of Carnation Creamer. And when she laughed, she got that one dimple in her cheek, and her teeth were perfect except that front one in the corner that she'd chipped when they were kids.

I'm still thinking. I have to keep thinking. Or everything will stop.

Chapter 26

LUKE

Number 5 Playter Place, the address Luke had unearthed for the Jane Doe at the Medspa, sounded like a nice address. One that projected wealth and solid, detached brick homes. The moment his car planned the route to the deep northwest end, though, Luke knew it wasn't going to be nice. It was incongruous that Ms. Doe, with her taste in extremely high-end couture, was living in one of the last downtown collections of ungentrified shanties. Real estate agents loved the area, calling it the last place in the "core" to get "affordable" semi-detached homes, a step up from a condo for a growing family. Homes that were still south of a million dollars. Of course, any family that had a wife like his would require nearly a quarter of a million dollars in renovations to make those semis habitable.

Playter ran diagonal to most of the city grid, backing onto the train tracks. All the rowhouses had shallow, rickety porches.

Worker housing for a class of worker long gone extinct, each one with a little place to sit on a bench or a chair and stare at the neighbours on either side or across the way for a spell in the evening. Now the homes were being torn up and tarted into design-builds. A few rat traps remained.

The roof at Number 5 leaned so far to the right that it touched the next-door house. The pitch made it look like a wonky Doctor Seuss drawing. That reminded Luke: he had yet to order the full set of Dr. Seuss kids' books, as his wife had requested.

A woman with a takeout coffee and a fluffy cat sweater nodded warily at him as he mounted the stairs. The stairs sloped so steeply he felt a little drunk walking up. Nails stuck up out of the mushy wood boards. The porch floor unfurled like a roller coaster. The screen door was corroded and pitted with age and dirty enough to give him pause about actually touching it with his bare knuckles to knock.

"No point to that," the woman remarked from across the way. She sat on a padded kitchen chair with all its stuffing leaking out.

"Huh?"

"No one home."

"You know that for sure."

"I saw Helen dead myself and no one's been livin' in there since."

"How long ago was this?"

"Five years. I let the paramedics in 'cause I had a key. Landlord's a real asshole. Holding out to sell the place to one of these yuppies." She gestured across the way to where a semi was clad in pink insulation and a Bobcat was levelling the front yard.

"Helen. How old was she?"

"Sixty. Too young to go, but that's what two packs a smokes a day will do. Had the breast cancer. But I beat it. Cut out the smokes."

"Good plan. Did Helen have a roommate? A young woman?"

"Helen preferred her own company and didn't suffer fools. And pretty much everyone was a fool, the way Helen saw it."

"I don't suppose she looked anything like this?" He showed the photo of the woman as a formality at this point, since it didn't seem Jane and Helen could possibly overlap. The woman had to put down her coffee to cackle.

"You sure got a good sense of humour on you!" she bleated, with real delight. "Listen, Helen and me have the same dentist." She showed him a wide-open mouth of missing teeth.

"You ever seen this woman?"

"Sorry."

"Someone gave me this address; said she lived here."

"I guess you got sent on a fool's errand."

"I guess." Luke turned and gripped the handrail to leave.

"You got a couple bucks for a refill?" She jangled the empty coffee cup at him. He flipped her a toonie, and figured Cleo owed him a fancy espresso over this. Being mad at her was a balm. It smeared away the elevator memory.

He sat in his car and replayed the placenta argument with Beatrice in his mind. A wave of sick guilt hit him.

He was always away; she was home on her own with her fears and her doomscrolling. Her *What to Expect* pregnancy book trolled her with horror stories of fetuses strangled by their own umbilical cords. And he was looking for reasons not to be home. She was afraid of what she was growing inside.

They were both afraid they might not be up to the entire task. The whole notion of eating enough. Eating *right* enough for the baby. That wasn't the real issue. They were both scared shitless that they were going to cock up the entire thing. They were standing on a precipice, looking straight down into the maw of their own ignorance.

He dialed her cell. She answered, sleepy and surprised.

"Hey." He injected as much warmth as he could into it.

"Hey back." It was the closest to a purr that he'd heard in a long time.

"I got a dead end at work. And I was wondering …"

"Wondering?" A hint of wariness crept into her voice, as if she was afraid he was about to ask for a favour.

"Remember that place, near the ski hills? The Norwegian spa?" he asked.

"Nordic spa you mean?" She had perked up.

He was scrolling hotel aggregator sites as they spoke, realizing he may have spoken too soon.

"Yeah. I remember it," she said. "You said you hate those places."

Nordic Spa. The site said two bookings were still available. "Yeah, but you don't hate them." Shit. They were the two *most* expensive suites. He hit book. "You know how you want me to be all spontaneous sometimes?"

"Uh-huh." She laughed.

"Well pack an overnight, baby."

Chapter 27

LUKE

Luke avoided Highway 400 whenever he could. It wasn't a highway; it was a parking lot. But at least he was beginning to feel a sense of closure with the Jane Doe case. A slew of paperwork and forms and details to wade through, but a sense it was in the rearview. With the city slipping away behind them too, Luke felt his shoulders and neck unclamping.

It was capital-*R* romantic to be on a getaway with Beatrice, so he drove up the hilly, forested route along Airport Road instead. He was disappointed when dark gathered around them sooner than he'd bargained for. Beatrice sat in the passenger seat, her body tilted toward him for a change. In the theatrical light of the visor, carving her features out of the dark, her face beamed.

"Nordic Spa. This is so sweet of you." She ran her hand along his knee, building heat with the friction of her fingers. "This place is *very* expensive."

"I looked it up on Google all by myself."

"I told you about that place months ago. Good remembering." She stretched out — extending toes forward and hands up to brush the ceiling of the car. "Big marks for this."

"Any specific rewards on that front?" He exaggerated the innuendo.

"Keep it all up and maybe we'll see," she said. Her eyes were closed.

"Right, right. I'll stay in my lane. But I'll be hopeful."

"Perchance to dream," she purred. She was lit almost beatifically by that visor light.

It felt cozy in the car, a little speeding pod holding just the two of them. They hurtled not just through space but through time to great change. Soon enough there would be no such thing as cozy alone time, just the two of them in the car. It would be bottles, sippy cups, diapers, and tantrums and the Magical World of Disney on permanent repeat. It was good to mark a moment like this. And enjoy it.

It didn't last.

Beatrice threw her overnight on the bed without giving the room a glance, in a total snit.

"Won't let me have a massage. I shouldn't have even *told* them I was pregnant."

"You didn't know, babe," he soothed. For some weird reason, once a woman is carrying a child, she can no longer go in water any warmer than tepid or get a massage. No eating raw foods or drinking alcohol. The unfriendly woman at the hotel check-in had been very clear about services they would provide Beatrice.

"It's like you're not supposed to leave the house once you're pregnant or something. It makes me crazy!" She spat out through gritted teeth. "Sometimes it feels like the whole world wants to treat you like *you're* the baby, just because you're going to *have* a baby. My back is *killing* me. And the only spa treatment I'm allowed to get from Miss Mealy Mouth receptionist is a toxic mani-pedi or a dumb facial. Do I *look* like I need a facial?"

She did not. Her face was, and always had been, flawless. Dewy, pulled tight over graceful cheekbones. And right now, screwed up into a knot of fury.

Luke padded over to the bathroom, which thankfully had an extra big tub and jets. He started her a bath. By the time it was nearly full, he came out to find her a little calmer.

"At least they have no way of stopping you from taking a bath?" he said. She melted a little into his arms, and he thought there was a chance the evening could still be salvaged despite overly prescriptive spa managers-cum-autocrats.

He laid himself down on the bed, wishfully stripped down to boxers and wrapped in a huge white bathrobe while the bathtub worked its feeble magic. He intended to close his eyes and then give her the backrub she needed once she was out.

When he came to, the bathroom door was wide open, the light was off, and Beatrice's coat and Keds were gone.

Fuck.

Had he cocked it up enough that she'd walked out on him?

He bolted up, his heart pounding. A glance at the clock revealed the worst. He'd been asleep for over four hours. He was fully aware that a complete browbeating would follow the moment she came back. He dressed in a hurry and paced the room a little.

Twenty minutes passed and his pulse remained high, and he realized that he was actually a little scared of his wife. Not in a serious way, but it was exactly the same feeling he'd had as a kid when he'd gotten up to some shit and knew that he would catch it from his mom. And likely a volley of swats from the fly swatter over it. He tried a little box breathing to calm himself down and sat on the edge of the bed to check in with the concierge.

Just as he did, the door lock eased open mechanically at the swipe of Beatrice's card. The door opened, bringing in a gust of sharp freezing country air.

"Oh," she said, mildly. "You're awake."

"My god — I was out for hours."

"Mmm," she agreed. Impossible to tell how badly in trouble he was.

"Where were you? I'd been awake just long enough to get a little worried," he told her back as she stepped out of her running shoes and pulled her hair down from a ponytail.

"Just around a little bit. Walking. I probably left only about ten minutes before you woke up."

"Oh god, some romantic getaway. 'Man snores.'" He wrote the headline in the air with his hands.

"Newsflash. Love you anyway," she told him. She crawled into bed next to him and gave him a warm kiss on the forehead. Her lips and her cheek were frigid.

"Jesus. Get in here, Bea. You're freezing."

"Mmm. And so sleepy." That was partly code between them for: *Don't try anything.* He was just relieved she was back and not too mad. He wrapped his arms around her and felt her temperature start to warm up to his. Her breaths quickly evened out and deepened and she grew heavy.

He lay there willing and fighting with himself to settle back down into sleep. But years of split shifts and staggered wake-ups had long ago taken a toll. He'd slept. Now he was awake. And the choice was either to get up and do something or take a pill and be even more of a dolt in the morning.

He eased out of bed and into his puffer jacket, feeling a little bit of grief for the lost chance to really rekindle something. It was a cute room. Fireplace. He'd imagined canoodling in the sauna and making other guests uncomfortable. Still, he liked to think he'd earned some brownie points.

He slid out the door and walked along the outdoor second-floor walkway, testing the ground with his sneakers. If he was going to be awake, he might as well exorcise thoughts of Jane and the dead boys, and hopefully a few pounds around his middle, while he was at it. God only knew how often he'd be able to sneak out for a run once the baby came.

He jogged, light and creaky, the first one out in too long to remember. He did not remember his knee bones crunching down onto his shins quite so heavily, nor the feeling of the pavement jolting straight up his hip sockets and into his spine.

"Just a bullshit run," he told himself, as encouragement. "Take it easy." And he did, "running" for two blocks at most before subsiding into a brisk walk before trying another almost-tubby-man run. He was grateful it was frosty cold, as it kept him moving. Out here in the country, all the trees were already fully bare. He followed the winding road that had driven them up into the Collingwood ski hills where the spa looked out over the front door lights of scattered country homes.

He didn't expect to come across barricades and reflective tape blocking the road where they'd driven up. He was, frankly, winded and glad for an excuse to take a breather. A guy in a huge dark parka stood with his hands shoved into his pockets and his back to oncoming traffic. A tow truck driver.

"What's going on?"

"I got a call that maybe there's a car over the embankment. Turns out, no such luck."

What an asshole, Luke thought to himself. Only tow truck drivers thought of a car over an embankment as "luck."

"Someone's over the edge?"

"Scanner said something about a person. A hobo or something."

"You get a lot of homeless people out here?"

"Yeah, you know, the country has a few poor people too," the guy retorted. He must've read Luke for a city slicker in his J.Crew puffer jacket and technical jogging gear.

Luke swung his body between the work horses and headed toward where he could see amber and red lights swirling against the tree trunks.

"You can't go there," called the tow truck driver.

"Try to stop me," Luke called back, smug in the knowledge that he might be out of shape, but he was in a better place than Mr. Misanthropy.

An OPP cop did stop him, all thick in his vest and winter gear and attitude.

"It's okay. I'm a detective."

"That so. Where from?"

"City. What's going on?"

"Great, Detective of the City. Let me know where and I'll come and crash your site first chance I get."

"Come on," said Luke. "I've escaped the Nordic Spa and a mad wife. I'm out on good behaviour."

The cop rolled his eyes. "It's some kid. Likely transient. Not from around here. Probably on their way down to the big city from up north. Didn't make it there. Happy?" As Luke tried to make conversation with the cop, he swept practised eyes over what he could see of the scene through the trees. Only a few feet from the road's edge, a lot of footprints marred an early dusting of snow. The sneaker prints, one set big and deeper, possibly size twelves or more, another set small, less indented, indicating a person with a smaller frame, caught Luke's eye.

"Of course not. Someone lost their life, right? Who's happy about that?" Luke said it with levity, trying to ease the guy open.

"You know what I mean. Have a good night, sir." The cop said "sir," but he meant "asshole." Luke flipped a card to the guy.

"I just happen to be looking into multiple runaway boys who didn't make it. So, if your guys feel like chatting, let them know to feel free to spitball. Have a good night, officer."

The cop shot him a little side eye, but otherwise said nothing.

"Okay, try to have a good night," Luke said.

He turned and began the walk/run back up the hill, at once regretting that he had gone out at all. Up was torture compared to down. And the cold breaths of air he sucked in felt like icicles boring holes into his lungs.

Back in the room, he snuck back into bed, turtled in a blanket a few feet away from Beatrice, coveting her warmth, but fearful of waking her.

Chapter 28

LUKE

There was traffic on the way back into the city to drop Beatrice off and Luke cursed himself for not factoring that into a "fun" getaway. Beatrice rubbed her belly absently but stayed tight-lipped.

Underneath everything, Luke's brain gnawed at the fact of that boy in the woods. Jane was behind a string of deaths. He wanted that to be it. Hopefully he was overthinking it, connecting the unconnected, seeing faces in clouds.

"I'd like to formally return my husband points," he muttered as he unpacked their bags in the driveway.

"I appreciate you trying, sweetheart," she told him with a dry cheek kiss.

He swung the car back out into traffic heading downtown. "Heading" was an ambitious word for it. *Creeping* downtown. The rush-hour pace compounded Luke's bad mood.

He shared office space and a frosted window with two other detectives. Their melamine desks were messy, his was neat, but only because he swept a mass of papers into a drawer each night before leaving. He was also in the habit of leaving his last cup of coffee for the day on the desk, which meant the first thing he did every morning was ferry his old cup downstairs and scrub at the congealed ring of cream and coffee before starting the whole cycle over again.

Paperwork sprang up like a jack-in-the-box from his crammed drawer. Largely to be sorted, filled, and filed. Sometimes he imagined introducing himself as "Luke Stockton, filer" because it would more accurately describe his work life than Trainee Detective.

He found his notes from the useless trip to 5 Playter Place and groaned inwardly. But the Jane Doe file still had the other lead — the hastily scrawled handwritten taxi receipt.

The receipt had been filled out by hand by "Jimmy." Luke called the cellphone number written in ballpoint on the card and met up with the affable Jafar Baqri, who went by Jimmy for expediency.

Jafar was chatty. He wore a headset and fielded a dozen social calls from friends back in Lahore while he and Luke talked. He was organized. His vehicle was as neat as a pin and smelled of air freshener and Fantastik.

"Mint?" offered Jimmy. Luke declined. Jimmy had been a dentist back in Lahore. Luke felt that usual stab of guilt whenever he met newcomers with such a story. They came here, hustled their asses off, and had better work ethic than most people he knew. They left behind professional lives and clout to be demoted to taxi driving or hamburger franchise management, so their kids could get a chance. Jimmy's lot was to ferry drunken louts around the entertainment district so they could rock and roll all night and party every day. Luke knew what Jimmy probably did by now too — a new country with a strange name and a rigid accent rarely turned into a better life. For his kids, sure, but for Jimmy? Wiping vomit and beer off car seats to make ends meet.

Jimmy had a log of passengers, jotted down in a notebook. He easily found the night he'd ferried Jane to the nightclub. 9:15 p.m. pickup. Nausea at 9:50 p.m. The address on Russell Hill Road was a far more likely address for Jane than the derelict lump on Playter, and it was easily corroborated by cellphone tower pings and taxi dispatch logs. No more fool's errand.

Chapter 29

LUKE

Luke was professionally and personally curious about what Jane's apartment would reveal about her life. The image of her vaulting from her taxi to pursue those boys into their home like some kind of relentless valkyrie haunted him. He waited in his car, answering emails and getting distracted by iPhone games until the locksmith and the Paid Duty Officer arrived. In between wasting a bit of time on the games, he got a jump on filling out the forms. After today he would hopefully be able to start using a name on the forms for the deceased, and not just "Jane Doe."

While the PDO waited in a squad car, the locksmith had several locks and bolts to remove from the door. It wasn't high-tech security — but there were many of them. Nothing surprising for a woman living alone even if she was a Titan. The locksmith covered the holes he left with a steel plate and installed a single Home Depot lock and key set. Luke's Scene of Crime Officer would log and store that key. Before entering Luke switched his body cam on. As he slipped plastic booties over his boots, he spoke aloud his name, his rank, where he was, the date, the address, the time, and repressed the constant urge to add sarcastic details like his astrological sign and what he'd had for lunch. In the old days, when he'd started, it was all little black flip pads. Now it was all audio and video recordings. It had taken time to get used to the tinny, compressed sound of his own voice speaking out loud. Was it really that high? In his head it felt like it had a more convincing rumble. He'd had to learn to externalize his thoughts and actions in real time as he had them.

"Slight chemical smell on entering."

The smell was often the first thing he noticed anywhere, and years of investigations prepped him to expect the worst any time he entered a new scene. He breathed in, tentatively, through his nose. Under his mask Luke wrinkled his nose, bracing for what could be an assault of that rank cheese-like cadaver smell. Instead, he picked up a faint off-gassiness.

"Smells like brand new carpet in here." That could easily be a cover for something. Carpets held evidence like crazy. A brand new one could reveal a cover-up.

Deeper in the house, he sensed cleaning products infused with lavender. There was an undercurrent of mould from somewhere, likely a neglected garbage can.

A vestibule led up plushly carpeted stairs with metal banisters. At the top the landing led through double doors into a white-trimmed living room. The windows looked out through diamond panes to treetops outside. To the left, a heavy dining set, and beyond that a marble kitchen island and kitchen cupboards with big bones.

The cupboards and drawers moved on silent hinges. It was one of those show kitchens they venerated in design magazines, with a massive island big enough to serve as an altar for sacrificing entire cows. The chef-sized six-burner grill top, utter theatre: it was immaculate, with light wear on only one burner. No one in his experience ever used those things. Sure enough, off to the side of the kitchen in a pantry was a whole other work stove which showed more wear.

He found a sea of empty prosecco, champagne, and Italian wine bottles in the blue bin. Luke whistled looking at the labels. They would be "big deal night wines" for his wallet. She had folded her cardboard boxes down and filed them in a blue box. Where he also found several Medspa glossy baggies along with Medspa-branded aluminum canisters. He screwed the lid off one.

"Rinsed-out canisters from Medspa. Send to the lab for swabbing." He would definitely be talking more with Ms. Cleo.

The living room Berber carpet sucked his feet in. Perfectly white, and perfectly placed under a glass coffee table. The carpet was the source of the off-gassing. White on white on white — poufs and couches and chaises. Romantic gauze curtains. But no art. No photos. It felt like a hotel room. High-end but zero personality.

The coffee table told a story to match what the boys had said. A sea of dirty glasses littered the coffee table, along with tobacco shreds, dead joint roaches in a saucer, and lots of empties.

"Send smoking paraphernalia to the lab for DNA testing," Luke noted. He mentioned the schmutz on the coffee table that looked like it would test positive for coke residue. Quite the party. A flicker of a thought crossed his mind: the closest he got to a good time was investigating scenes like this.

In contrast to the party detritus in the living room, romantic touches waited deeper into the apartment. The principal bedroom was white on white with a tall and rumpled bed. Luke lifted a comforter with a pen tip.

"Scant blood spatter on master bedroom covers and sheets." It could have been nothing. Still, the tiny drips led away from the bed to an ensuite. They were spaced far enough apart to tell the story of someone rushing to the bathroom to staunch a wound. Sure enough, a cupboard hung open, and first aid gak was strewn around the otherwise empty and echoing marble-and-gold space.

"One pair men's athletic socks." He cocked his head at them. They were in a little bedraggled pile in a corner.

The walk-in closet had a dressing plinth, three racks of clothing with immaculate suits and robes and dresses and blouses on padded hangers, well-spaced from one another. Satins and silks and dramatic whites and darks. She had an entire cupboard dedicated to purses and still another to shoes. And here, front and centre, he found *the* shoes — those shoes with the curious cross shaped heel.

"Pair of black Givenchy boots. Size nine." Black and racy. Those he bagged right away and would transport himself to the lab where he fully expected they would find dirt matching the downtown alley the first victim was found in.

In the bedroom wastebasket, he found several condom wrappers, torn, as well as several single-use lube packs.

A small office adjoined the bedroom in a curtained alcove and in this, an elegant writing desk balanced on top of rose gold legs. There were keys and a wallet on top, a copper vase and dead flowers, sad heads sunk to their stalks. Here, at last, Luke finally found statutory proof of Jane's existence. A small leather folder contained her bank cards and driver's licence. Heloise Wu. Thirty-three years old.

He peered inside the drawers, his gloved fingers rifling through all the papers. More ID. Many more of them. A U.S. passport. A dual citizen, perhaps. A U.K. passport. Triple? A Swiss passport. Flipping through revealed various names: Helen Wai. Hour Chour. Hilary Wong. Maybe Luke was going to have to go back to calling her Jane Doe after all? The age on the Swiss passport put her at forty-seven, which seemed like a stretch. Pregnancy at forty-seven was remarkable.

The rest of the papers in the drawers disputed the driver's licence ID — insurance papers and bank accounts and household bills were addressed to Helen or Helene or Harriette with different combinations of Wai, Woo, Wu, and others. He recognized several Medspa receipts, a number of which were for the same $251.25 amount, spread out over the course of several weeks. A thick, cream envelope with ballpoint pen was labelled "Bank Box." Inside this he found a key. He held the driver's licence next to the open passport, side by side. The year placed the photos fifteen years apart. But they looked like they could have been taken the same day.

"I wonder how exactly you 'two' ladies know each other?" Luke said aloud.

Under the passports and various bills, he found stacks of folded stationary. Letters.

"Correspondence found in the bedroom writing desk. From … Turkey. Bosnia." Luke read fragments aloud.

> *New York, 1942, by Airmail*
> *My dear Heloise,*
> *I was told of your birth today by your mother. I write so that one day, you may know your history, and your place in this world. They said you latched well, ate greedily, and have bright, clear eyes. Adding a girl to our family is the greatest blessing I could ask for. Our girls are our future, a link between us and our children's children.*

Luke wondered if this was a letter to his Jane Doe's mother. Another letter was dated some twenty years later.

> *The locals here, who practise an interesting sect of Christianity, are saying "Hristos se rodi" or Christ is Born. At Easter Christians think about their Christ, and sacrifice. Give us this day our daily bread, the Christians always said. But what they really meant*

was flesh. We Sanguin are no stranger to sacrifice, are we? Left to their own devices, every animal would surely choose to life over death. But Christian guilt about all that so-called sacrifice was nothing new. It was an improvement on an ancient theological sleight of hand. When hunters whispered fervent thanks to the animal felled by their own hand, it made the sight of a sleek, lovely body reduced to hide and bones and meat and gore easier to take. It made the actions of the hunter seem less murderous. The act of killing to survive is elevated to an act of piety, godliness even. Men, play-acting at Gods, chose this one or that one to die and then thanked the hapless creatures. Little do they know it is they who are the flocks for the slaughter.

This grisly letter seemed to be from some auntie to her niece, or godmother maybe. Luke found himself sitting down on the chair, reading.

Did you know, Heloise, that humans have only been writing for approximately 5,500 years? Five thousand years is nothing compared to the vastness of time. In that little blip of time, man has counted his sheep, totted his grain, tallied his gold, waxed on about "darling buds of May," and grappled with his mortality. He created heroes and villains who ply the seas and fly too near the face of God. In the main he did this so he need not blame himself for the evil of the world. Now he snidely tears apart his peers in gossip and opinion columns in all the best papers and magazines, proud of his ability to slaughter with words when slaughtering with swords is frowned on. They quibble and parse words their ancestors wrote down in "Holy Books." They lay claim to who owns this or that and who may lie with whom and how persons are expected to pray, and how often. Sometimes I think they should get better material to quibble about.

The author seemed snobby to Luke. Pedantic letters from a professor to some long-dead relative?

Sapiens *love to talk about their revolutions — their great leaps forward. How they alone invented language. Art. Religion. Culture. Cultivation. Animal husbandry. Taxation.*

Sometime in the past, they edged out ahead of Neanderthals and other hominids who shared the nearly empty world with them. Humans were never as hardy as Neanderthals, with their skinny rib cages and their short noses. But they were wily. They figured out how efficiently nourishing bone marrow is. Their earliest ancestors learned how to crush the bones of their prey.

Time crept along. They fattened their grain, they fattened their herds, they fattened themselves. And they soothed themselves when they slaughtered lambs that this was just a different kind of reaping.

They fermented wines. They were docile. They gathered in snug little villages.

We watched. Always a few steps ahead.

The secret to our power was in our evolutionary edge. Homo sapiens *knew some of the things we did. But we learned faster. And we cultivated an easy and renewable resource. They were fat with marrow, in those early days, and warm with fire.*

We learned early that as long as they feel comfort and safety, those sapiens *will cow. I believe they desire to be subjugated.*

Whoever wrote it was some kind of insane. Luke made a note to hang on to the letters specifically, along with the Medspa canisters.

Silent on the thick broadloom, Luke exited the main bedroom and found a closed door. The cast iron handle turned effortlessly, and the door swung open on silent, perfectly balanced hinges. And for a change, Luke was surprised.

It was a nursery.

He felt an irrational pang of jealousy, imagining the financially secure life this kid would have had. It was followed by an internal flash of anger at himself: why let himself feel emasculated by a dead person's ability to provide for a deceased child? Was he that insecure about his means? Even so, the furniture was immaculate. Was there such a thing as California King cribs? Drawers and cupboards were stashed with baby gear, all ready to go. Heloise/Helen wasn't wasting time getting ready for this baby. Stacks of pristine flannel blankets. He always wondered what those flannel blankets were supposed to be for, anyway. How many damn blankets did a baby need?

But it was weird to him, looking around at the expense and precision and preparedness for this very much wanted and expected baby. Why be partying with college louts, doing drugs and drinking? Did Heloise/Helen — fuck it, he was just going to think of her as Jane — did Jane even know she was pregnant at the time of her death? Why the different personalities?

The scene was going to yield an avalanche of data. On a hunch he returned to the bedroom and rummaged through the bedside tables. Wrapped in a handkerchief, under a blank greeting card, he found a familiar sight. A purple-and-white pregnancy test with a faint positive on it. So, Jane had known her condition.

When he left, he sat for a time in his car, still wearing gloves, peering through the folded and worn letters.

> *We lived alongside them, in the shadows, for millennia.*
>
> *We have our own history. Greater, deeper, faster, more evolved. But* sapiens *won't find traces of their masters, the Sanguin. We have been canny since time immemorial. We have kept our secrets close, covered our tracks as we left. Humans have their fields, barns, and killing floors. And we have our own killing floors.*

Our own killing floors.

That made Luke shiver.

Who the hell was Jane? Who the hell was this relative?

He made a mental note to pick up more flannel blankies for the baby. Beatrice liked it when he brought baby stuff home. She liked when he got into nesting.

Chapter 30

LUKE

Being sent off to the wrong place made Luke feel suspicious and jerked around.

None of the pieces of information he'd found at Jane-slash-Helen's house verified the Playter Place address. Nor did any of them corroborate each other, either.

At the Medspa Genevieve was in full gatekeeper mode. Today her painted mouth was hot magenta.

"Unfortunately, Cleo isn't available to see you at the moment."

"Busy unavailable?" He perched on the edge of one of those leather chairs. "Because I can wait until she's free."

"Out of the country unavailable." This made a spring in Luke uncoil a little. He glanced up at the receptionist who held up a finger to say, hold please. While he held Luke noticed she had a different colour on each nail. He didn't get the way girls dressed anymore. "I have her on the line, Detective." She smiled winsomely. Sweetly. Helpfully.

"Mr. Stockton. I am so very sorry."

"Oh yeah? Sorry, about what, exactly?"

"I think there was a mix-up. I think you received the wrong address information."

"Huh. That so." Luke found the passive phrasing interesting. *Mistakes were made.* It was an increasingly common way to speak. But to a detective, such distancing between cause and effect could be telling.

"I looked into it after you'd left, and I've only just now gotten confirmation about the address. I'm not in the country you see, so communication is difficult. I hope you weren't inconvenienced?"

"No inconvenience. Just following up."

"There should be a package for you. I'd give it to you myself but I'm in Switzerland."

"What's taking you there, exactly?"

"The Swiss are always on the cutting edge of new treatments. It's a constant chase in this business to keep up with technology. Could we set up a time when I come back? Say two days' time?"

"Yeah, that'd be fine."

"That would be wonderful. And tell me, how is mother and baby doing?" She asked it smoothly. And it threw him a little.

"Still just a fetus at this point, so I imagine still having the time of its life. I'm the one who will have plenty to worry about later." He said it wearily.

She laughed a silky laugh that made him feel good about himself.

"You're wise beyond your years, Mr. Stockton. Most new parents are so focused on panicking about how the birth will go, they don't even think about the stress of the years to come. And there's always stress. I can see you Tuesday. May I call you to set it up?"

The detective in him took back over from the man getting his ego petted.

"No, Ms. Drover, I'll contact you. It's my job. Safe travels."

Chapter 31

CLEO

Cleo lay on a leather couch several thousand feet over the Alps, drinking Assam tea from a china cup so thin it was translucent. The Praetor jet she flew in held a dozen people luxuriously, but today she was the only passenger, tended to by an entire team of stewards.

"Thank you, Gaultier." She gazed at the finely boned young man over the rim of her gilded teacup. "You know, you have such lovely eyes."

He smiled and looked down.

"*Je vous en prie, Mademoiselle*," he said, soft and smooth. He knew she was no miss, and she knew he did. But she enjoyed the flirtatious lie.

She'd accepted the flight gracefully too, though she was perfectly capable of paying for it herself. It would have been churlish to do otherwise. Her Swiss colleagues deeply appreciated her patronage. She appreciated their product and their attention to many small details. Such as Gaultier. She did love those brown-haired boys with fine stubble on their jaws.

But Gaultier's charms were insufficient to soothe her today. The ache she'd had within for some time now seemed, if anything, sharper. Grief was strange like that. It ebbed and flowed, and sometimes surged back with a fierce intensity.

Foolish girl, Cleo thought to herself. *Stupid, foolish girl.*

She glanced down at the peaks and folds of the Swiss Alps scattered below, snow heaped on their limestone shoulders and mused about the many peoples who had crossed them or been barred by them. Although some found it stuffy, she'd always had an affinity for Switzerland. A castle of a country with mountain ramparts, walls, and moats. Here her business was safe, her secrets were carefully tended, and everything was taken care of with a cool, calm politeness. Of all humans, the Swiss with their careful alacrity seemed most like her tribe.

One thing that was less secure, though, was Cleo's own fate, in light of Heloise's death.

What a terrible end to come to, after so much promise. She'd been a comet shooting through their lives. Passionate. Irrepressible. Brilliant. But troubled. Full of appetites Cleo tried to curb. All that life and vibrancy, just to end uncouthly in an alley, lust and appetite on full display? To consort with beasts like that thick-necked boy? Worse still, to imperil everyone else she knew. Such recklessness.

Cleo sighed. She understood. She'd been that young once too. She'd felt the same rushing hormones and urges. But she had carefully constructed her life, built her empire to safeguard the rest of them from exactly these kinds of excesses. These kinds of tragedies.

The Playter address Cleo had made up for Luke was only ever going to be a brief smokescreen. One of several layers painted on her life to frustrate even the most dogged attempts to know Heloise, truly. Cleo moved with careful and long design. This life of theirs required an almost monastic sense of duty, role, hierarchy. If their castle walls were breached, it would trigger other events.

If Cleo wasn't careful, Heloise would become a symbol to the other women. It was critical now to manage what kind of symbol. To the youngest, she was dangerous. An uncontrolled blast of desire, teeth bared, a little feral. They all felt it. Internally, a life of carefulness chafed at their essential natures. Dogs are still wolves, deep in their souls after all, despite millennia of being kept by *Homo sapiens*. And *sapiens* were reliably *sapiens*, after all that time too. Lizard brains, basic urges, pedantic anxieties, sweet sheepishness, so easily led.

No, Cleo could not let Heloise become an icon for all things feral. She had to make her into a poster child for the true cost of waywardness. She was a tragic figure of a life gone terribly wrong. They could all prosper; they could all enjoy long fruitful lives if they only cleaved to the sober way of doing things. That was Cleo's legacy. Safeguarding their collective future.

In the old days, it was different. There were rigid guidelines. No one questioned the order of things. The head was the head, and the rest did as they were bid, swore their undying fealty, and were thankful for the gift of life. Now the younger generations were catching the same "me me me" that was sweeping the rest of the world. Me and my rights. Me and my identity. Tossing off the yoke of power. Claiming the reins for themselves. Oblivious to the costs of leadership, the travails of responsibility.

Cleo stepped off the plane and felt a rush of wind blast her skirt against her bare legs as she descended to the tarmac. Her Swiss colleagues were arrayed in a line — suited, sharp, full of smiles. They should be. They were going to be vastly enriched after meeting today.

As much as she relished conducting her business here, she felt a warm twinge when she thought about the curious detective, with his good genes. He had dark brown hair that curled fetchingly around his collar and a finely textured stubble, shot through with just a little silver. A silver fox in sheep's clothing. And the parts that remained feral deep within her DNA perked up at the thought of re-encountering him. She liked to shepherd.

On the tarmac Nicolas, her main contact, was virtually indistinguishable from his colleagues, all of them men with chalky white skin, immaculate suits, cropped silver hair, and bodies they kept chiselled with long-distance cycling or running. She was thankful he approached her first and kissed her three times, so she could keep up the ruse of remembering which one he was.

She was shown a fine time.

An excess of wines and international cuisine. There was a ski day planned for all of them, and contracts to be signed over champagne in a glass lounge perched in the Alps. One of the junior members of the team, Ulrich, visited her that night in her suite. He was so charming and passionate that she believed he might even have elected to come to her on his own, and not merely as part of the overall corporate hospitality.

The only sour note was right before signing. Nicolas was forced to stand and demand that another junior member of the team leave when he insisted on voicing some quibble with the details of the contract. It was some high-minded business. The junior executive was keen to impress on Cleo that though his compatriots might be fine with the age-old traditions of Swiss neutrality and diligent secrecy, he was not at all on board with everything, that the plan with storing comatose patients and shuffling them across borders was unconscionable and that it was high time that traditions that kept the money of the extraordinarily wealthy hidden or allowed for Nazis to hide treasures from the eyes of the world ended for once and for all.

There was shocked silence after the man was ejected.

"Perhaps we should make him a guinea pig on the new patient beds?"

Nicolas delivered the joke flatly, down the length of a table made up of still faces. But after a crackling moment, the whole room erupted into prolonged and relieved laughter. Cleo did not laugh. But she was pleased that Nicolas could joke about permanently silencing the junior executive. In short time, of course, she would see to it herself that the high-minded young man wouldn't be able to share anything with the world.

"So." Nicolas shook her hand when she set down the silver pen they'd provided. He closed the thick leather folder on the contract. "The first shipment will be in a few months, and from then on, you can expect perhaps every six to seven weeks. We are at the mercies of the various state departments, and each case will be … unique."

"Passports, transit nurses, ambulances …" murmured Cleo.

Nicolas waved her words away with a "tut tut." He handed her a very crisp glass of Bollinger and allowed his glacial expression to crease into a smile.

"No more business talk now. Ulrich, your glass is empty!"

Chapter 32

RENARD

He knew when they transferred him to an ambulance that the big move was coming. He could catch tantalizing snatches from his bed when they talked in low voices nearby. Sometimes some real go-getter even came up to him and said things directly to him, such as:

"Okay, buddy. Time to get cleaned up. Going to turn you over now."

Or, "Two more weeks and you move to the *Médecins Sans Frontières* and I go home for Christmas."

"Jesus, Handsome, what a mess. How the hell is anyone supposed to deal with this much mess?"

"Good luck in there. I'm leaving this place. Forever. You keep fighting."

He liked it when they urged him to keep fighting.

He knew he was still in Europe, and he guessed still in the Balkans. He knew they didn't know who he was. He'd been shelled and wounded, and he was in a coma. And he would have been more unhappy about it but there was a woolly kind of stuffing all around him that made thinking and feeling very porridgey.

He cycled up and down. Sometimes he wasn't really there. His consciousness was vaporous like a cloud. Other times he could feel a sense of self and knowing and awareness gather. Sometimes he would attempt to focus all the energy he could muster on trying to move just one finger, as though he was lying in bed, rigid with sleep paralysis, just trying to shake it off. More often than not, his attention would fade from the effort, and he would forget what he'd been trying to do. He didn't know if he was kidding himself about it, that there was no way to will himself out of this. But he didn't like to completely discount the idea. And on bad days, when he did discount absolutely everything, he was depressed. And he felt more bitter still to realize that all human feeling was denied to him except despair. But boredom habitually made him swim back to the notion that he might yet will himself out and he clung to that.

He got a lot of excitement out of the big move. Switzerland. He heard them say it: "Switzerland." He heard the word "clinic." Moving was at least a change and in a world where all change was denied to him, that was a very good thing. Clinics were good things. Clinics were more special than hospitals. Maybe they would be able to get to him. Wake up the body imprisoning him and get to his mind.

"If they think you're a candidate, you'll get some kind of special coma treatment." He recognized Melanie by her voice and the amount of jostling. He imagined she was strong. She had dark hair. Not as dark as Josée, and straighter. "If they don't … well, you'll just show them that you are, right, handsome?"

He wondered if he was handsome, or if she was just saying that. When she had given back the ring, Josée had said Patrice was a lot better-looking …

"And when you get better, you're going to look me up in Winnipeg and you're going to send me postcards, right?"

Inwardly, he chuckled. *Sure.* She had no idea how bad his handwriting was. He'd joined the army, *Calice*, not gone to college.

When they came, and the canvas ceiling gave way to bright blue sky and then a waffle pattern inside the chopper, and then more sky, dimmer, shot with red, he vowed he would not miss one moment of it all. But somewhere after being loaded on a plane, maybe it was the drone of engines and a self-satisfied feeling that *something* was happening, he went down.

When he came back up, there were new faces, a ring of them, peering down. A few men. A few women. Concerned. Kindly. One of the men had a wide-open face like summer fields. One of them was scrunched up, impatient. One of the women was alert, brisk, a human calculator. The other woman with blond hair looked like an angel sent from above. Glass-blue eyes. Almost white-blond hair. A pink flush to her fine-boned cheek.

After the others left, she remained for a moment and leaned down, very close.

"Very handsome. Good bones. Good eyes." She peered at him, pinched his flesh, stroked his arm, peered into his pupils with a bright light as she spoke. "I like you." She leaned in a little closer yet. "I'm going to call you Tomas."

He didn't like that. It wasn't his name.

His name was … it was … He flitted about the edges of all that he knew now. Why couldn't he think of anything but a furry red creature?

Chapter 33

LUKE

Jane's bank box was in a downtown office tower in a facility dedicated to high-net-worth individuals — in other words, people nothing like Luke. The atrium soared stories high and housed an airplane-sized hunk of stainless-steel modern art suspended over a shimmering pool of water. The silver and the water cast glinting light over the dark-red polished granite. A woman in a fur coat lounged on a leather bench and chatted with a man in a dandyish suit. Another man waited in a leather chair and stared off pensively like a dour cologne model. Luke was glad he'd taken the time to put on one of his better sports jackets and dress pants.

When the concierge was ready, Luke produced his badge, ID, papers, and Jane Doe's key.

"But where is Ms. Wu?" the concierge wanted to know with touching sincerity. Worry ruffled his Botoxed features.

"I'm on official business with an ongoing investigation. I'm afraid Ms. Wu is deceased."

"Dead? Oh my god, oh my god. This is awful. Will they catch the person? Do you know when? Or how? I'm sorry, you probably can't say that. Oh my god. She was always so nice to us here. She gave the most outrageous Christmas baskets to everyone here. Right down to the cleaning lady."

Luke mumbled out a "sorry for your loss, doing everything we can" type response. This guy wasn't privy to the things Jane had been up to, the mayhem and subterfuge. And he didn't look like he could have handled the cognitive dissonance of the truth, had he found out.

Once he'd looked through Luke's particulars, the concierge called someone else over to stand in for him.

"I'll take you down myself. I feel like it's a personal service. For Ms. Wu's sake." He pressed his hand to his chest.

They slid down into the bowels of the building in a black elevator clad in onyx and brushed chrome. It released them into a long corridor of polished concrete. Doors stepped away down the hall punctuating the dark concrete with bright yellow and bright red gloss-painted steel.

The concierge stepped along the hall with loud heels on the hard concrete, stiff and precise like a Prussian soldier. He stopped at a door and pointed to a lock. It was illuminated by a little kicker light. There was a little shelf nearby to put one's phone or bag down while looking for the key. The rich seemed to live lives where little details like this were always thought through.

"Allow me," the concierge urged, and took the key that Luke dropped out of its paper evidence bag. He was wearing black nitrile gloves already. The door slid sideways, which surprised Luke.

"More secure than a swing door," the concierge explained. "Can't be pried or rammed open. Thick steel embedded in thick concrete. Very, very safe. Which is why our clients love us. Discretion and safety."

"What's the weirdest thing you think is kept down here?"

"Well, I can't go into detail, obviously, but I believe we have some Roman artifacts. Intimate ones. And some highly sought-after baseball cards."

Luke nodded. Humans were weird. Baseball cards and ancient smut. Sort of seemed to sum people up.

The concierge produced a jet-black lock box on a silent cart. They had to place identical keys in the lock and turn them at the same time. Luke stifled the urge to make a joke about it looking like a nuclear strike key, since the concierge seemed so distraught.

While the concierge stood a few respectful feet away, with his arms laced around each other behind his back, Luke pored through the effects. It was almost entirely documents, a few pieces of unremarkable jewellery. The dates on the documents went back to the 1900s. Landing papers. Lithographs of beautiful women. One lithograph from 1904 said Shanghai on the back. A sleekly tailored western dress on an Asian woman. She resembled Ms. Wu. A grandmother? The photo was exquisite and well preserved in an onion-skin paper envelope.

While Luke picked through with his gloved hands, the concierge cleared his throat. Once. Twice. Enough to make Luke look up, expectantly.

"Ms. Wu once invited me to her place. At Christmas time."

"Is that so."

The concierge shuffled a little closer. "She'd had a Christmas Day levee. But the only people who came were the cleaning lady and me. And that was it, poor girl. I was a kind of an 'orphan' at the time myself — between boyfriends, no blood family. When no one else came to her levee, she and I got drunk on her couch watching trashy television. Drunk on champagne and cognac, eating truffles and Mimolette cheese."

Luke, unsure of the spelling, wrote "Mimmolet" as the concierge spoke.

"She confided to me that she had had no family — absolutely no one — no friends, nothing. Only work and racket sports and her on-again off-again boss-slash-lover. And he was never going to commit to her. She desperately wanted a child. More than anything she was ready for and wanted a child."

"Do you know where she was working?"

"Bosch Liebowitcz Burns. Some swish law firm in Chicago. I think she was in corporate law? She was always around the money, anyway." The concierge closed the gap between them. But his arms remained laced behind his back. "I told her," he said, lowering his voice irrationally since they were alone, "that I would offer her semen, myself. To just give it to her. But that I couldn't possibly do it via, you know, *sex*. But she told me, and I just find this so tragic, she wouldn't quote-unquote *do* in vitro. She said she was too old-fashioned for that. She wanted to do it the normal way — between a man and a woman who were attracted to each other. She said she believed in that energy. That something important, I think she said 'necessary' about that energy goes into the child, becomes part of the life force of the child. She said 'Mixing kids in a test tube? No thank you. And online dating, also no thank you.'"

"That was mostly my take too," Luke observed, wryly.

"Oh my *god*. Online dating is just the worst. The absolute worst. Bad for your soul. You just never *know who* you're going to meet up with on those things. Bring back arranged marriages, I say. Statistically, they say they're safer and people often really do learn to care for one another."

"I don't know about that. But I did find my wife in the end, on one of those sites," Luke chuckled.

"Well, there's always outliers. Congrats." He lapsed into silence for a while and the only sound for a few more minutes was the shuffling of papers, the click of Luke's phone camera, and the piped-in air, rumbling through overhead ducts.

There was a transcript from Harvard, which corroborated Jane's CV, but the dates were all wrong. The transcript was dated sometime in the '70s, and the CV he was looking at was from the 1980s. As were letters from several professors and heads of departments at Harvard enthusiastically recommending her for employment with a law firm. There were landing papers with her name on them. U.S. and Canadian dual citizen paperwork. A birth certificate from pre-communist China, another transcript from Cambridge. A marriage in Paris. Another in Turkey. Divorce decrees from Las Vegas, the Province of Ontario, and from the U.K. Passports from four continents, social insurance numbers, landed immigrant cards from countries that didn't exist anymore, tax returns from a United Nations of countries ... Jane's lockbox held a tranche of paperwork, none of which was real. There were at least six discrete women with lives supposedly going back nearly one hundred years. Which was ludicrous. And supposedly, all of which Jane had inherited. So, in addition to murder, he was looking at massive fraud; meticulous, decades-long, intergenerational fraud.

"I did offer to set Ms. Wu up on a date at one point."

"Really?" Luke flipped open a new page in his notebook, scribbling as the concierge talked.

"She scoffed, initially. She had gone on the date; the guy was totally handsome. They'd both started drawing up paperwork based on her having the child, having sole custody, never introducing the father, deleting any trail to his participation, signing off on him ever having to have any financial obligation. For his end he wanted children — but only to have them. Not to raise them. He'd apparently already inseminated other women, giving them the 'gift' they wanted — because something about their very existence made him feel virile, potent, important. But one of those women had, in the end, come back to him and started demanding money for the child. He was interested in more, but he had to be sure. Ms. Wu was as financially independent as they come and could have raised a dozen kids without any financial help. But something soured on the deal for him. He declined. She cried on my lap for a whole night while we watched romcoms and drank Cognac. She grew distant after that, and the Christmas baskets stopped coming. But I always saw her as a wonderful woman. A sad, lonely princess up in her townhouse."

"Here's my card. Can I get your number? I may need to follow up with more questions about Ms. Wu."

"Of course. Anything to help. Anything at all. Sometimes I think I would have done anything for that woman. Just to see her happy, you know."

Chapter 34

LUKE

Heloise's credit cards revealed travel plans, which connected her to an Iain Burns in the Chicago area, a hotshot lawyer at the same firm as Heloise: Bosch Liebowitcz Burns. His name showed up on a flight manifest. The romantic destination suggested he might be a boyfriend, or at least friend with benefits. Luke worked the data, calling up flight tickets, manifests, hotels. According to the front desk at the law firm, Burns was to travel on October 12, first class. Cross-referencing with one of several platinum credit cards, Helen Wu was his seatmate, meeting in Toronto, then changing flights in Doha, Beijing, Hanoi, and finally Ho Chi Minh City. But neither of them was on either flight. First-class seats, first-class passenger lounges, the sprawling beach suite overlooking the East Sea booked off for two entire months … none of them used. Burns had never left the country. But one of Jane's aliases had left Canada and crossed the border from Quebec into New York State in a rental vehicle on October 19.

Luke sat in his car, listening to clicks and burrs on his cell as it connected with the number of the law firm Bosch Liebowitcz Burns in Chicago.

Once he stated his business, he was transferred almost immediately to Mr. Liebowitcz via reception.

"I understand that Helen Wu was a junior partner with your firm, Bosch, Liebowitcz, Burns?"

"Was? Has something happened to Helen?"

"Unfortunately, Ms. Wu has met with foul play. And I'm following up on some leads. Is it safe to say that Ms. Wu reported to an Iain Burns?"

"She did. Mr. Burns is my partner. Senior and founding partner here. He was the one who originally brought Helen on."

"I understand that Mr. Burns is away."

"Yes, Vietnam. He goes every few years for a month. He's due back, well, any day now. Happy to help in the meantime."

"Seems that Ms. Wu came directly to your firm from Harvard, seemingly right out of school."

"She did. Whip-smart. I'm sorry, I'm finding it hard to conceive of her being gone."

"Is it safe to say she was made junior partner fairly quickly?"

"Oh, we fast-tracked her. This woman showed incredible determination and work ethic. One of the best assets at our firm. She would easily have made senior partner in short order. You know she boxed?"

"Boxed? As in the sport?"

"Yeah, with male sparring partners. She was vicious. Great hooks. She was in better shape than most of the guys here. I sparred with her a few times. Lost bad to her at a charity boxing event the firm held. Too rich for my blood. A real killer."

"Any relationships? Maybe with one of her boxing partners?"

"She lived like a monk. I'd say nun, but she was more monk-like than anything. I sometimes wonder if she even slept. I lost count of the times she was still here when I left and already here when I came back the next day. I never got the read off Helen that she was into relationships."

"So not married then, that you know of."

"Ha, family law takes up one entire floor here … and let me tell you — that woman was never going to make some man domestically happy. Stage a coup, maybe. Marriage? No."

"Hmm. And Mr. Burns … have you got an address?"

"Certainly. He has two. A *pied-à-terre* downtown when he's late at the office. But his real home is a beautiful place up in the Pistakee Highland, Spring Grove area, out in the forest. My wife and I summer with him every year. If you can hold on, I'll get the exact address from my file."

"I'll wait." And while Luke waited on hold, he started googling the nearest sheriff to Spring Grove, Illinois. And after that, he was going to have to get up and running with Interpol.

Chapter 35

LUKE

"En route to the crime scene, a line of vehicles made a convoy along a stretch of smooth, newly paved blacktop. In the front, the local sheriff from Pistakee Highlands and behind him, the country coroner. They drove silently down a forested, quiet county road with their cherries flashing. They are here today because behind the black fences and security gates, behind the sedate luxurious homes of this bucolic countryside, evil came to pay a visit."

Luke huddled next to Harry in a small, dark editing bay.

"Sorry about the stupid narration," Harry said. "It's the flavour of the show."

"When did you get to shoot all this?"

"A few weeks ago. I was in Chicago on something else, my producer caught wind of the case. It's a big one. I pulled some strings with guys I know on the force there. They let me in after they finished up."

"I'm surprised you got in so soon after."

"A few weeks ago, a buddy of mine on the Chicago force tipped me about the case. He let me in to the crime scene right after the CSI guys left."

Harry pointed out rows and rows of file folders.

"I've got thirty to forty possible shows on the go at any time. A lot of these never make it to air, but our whole thing is being on the bleeding edge of the media cycle. As long as the lawyers for the show approve it, in some cases we're out on the streamers before the accused even get their day in court."

This made Luke shake his head a little. But for today, he was thankful to be able to pick Harry's brain a bit. Even if it did involve looking at endless shots of Harry in his camel overcoat by a bush or Harry crouching in his camel coat by a stain, or Harry looking handsomely down the barrel of the camera.

"I know," said Harry. "But it sells shows. And people eat this stuff up; the grislier the better." He restarted the video onscreen.

"The Burns residence is situated in a graceful forest of cedars, pines, birch, and maple," narrated Harry's disembodied voice. "The air is sweet here, with sap, with flowers and bracken. It's a far cry from the loud, dirty streets of downtown Chicago, and that's exactly what drove corporate lawyer and Chicago luminary Mr. Burns to purchase this country home. That, and the safety of the quiet, affluent community. But as Mr. Burns was to discover, it was not a place he could be safe from murder."

"Laying it on thick," Luke smiled.

"Beats getting in a cruiser and crawling around in dirty alleys every day."

"Please. You miss crawling around in dirty alleys."

"In these suits? I don't think so."

"Have you and Beatrice been talking? She's been trying to get me to quit the force and become a TV type as well."

"Only if you think you've got the chops for it." Harry turned his head and showed off his long, ruler-straight jaw.

"Okay, Hollywood. Show me the rest of the house."

"Obviously, the rest isn't edited, and we have to take out certain things before it could air. Wheels of justice and all. But we try to be on the leading edge of ripped-from-the-pages crime. This one was a doozy. Lawyer bigwig. Brazen intruder, grisly murder."

"But not necessarily an intruder."

"It seems they used a key, which we found discarded. Knew how to disarm the alarm. So, someone who had been there before. We considered cleaning staff, other contractors."

"All ruled out."

"Correct."

Harry walked Luke through the video outtakes of a grey stone chateau, modern but modelled after the real deal in France, with tall, heavy, copper rooftops and a soaring front face. A sweep of stairs led up to a rounded stone portico with a swinging iron lantern. The place spilled out over a hilltop. There was a distant sight of Lake Michigan, luminescent blue when the trees waved their trunks.

"Just a massive place. The guy was loaded." Harry fast-forwarded through images of a huge, pillared mezzanine, salons and living rooms, panelled doorways, timbered ceilings. "The kitchen was down that way." The camera caught a glimpse of a lake of polished tile and soaring cabinets. Hallways that became bridges spanned galleries of art and sculpture.

The camera went down stairways bored down under the house, where more hallways tunnelled into bedrock. Discreet sconces hidden from view barely picked out the outlines of doorways. An unseen hand swung a matte-black glass door inward, revealing a regulation-sized squash court.

"I guess he was trying to save on having a gym membership."

"Pfft," Harry replied. "Where did I go wrong in life?"

"Well, you're still among the living, so I guess you're doing all right."

The squash court was an immaculate space with bare, sleek hardwood floors. Except for the ugly brown stain at the front left side of the court. A roughly man-sized brown stain.

"So, this is where he was found?"

"You should have seen it," Harry said. "He'd been here the whole time he was supposed to have been lying on a resort beach in Da Nang."

"Decomposing."

"Yeah."

"The place was a frickin' mess. Fluids seeped out and dried, in waves. Guys in there for two days sorting it all out. The body was sludge, really. Needed a shovel to get him in a body bag more than anything else. Criminologists from the city came to help the local guys. Sorry. Criminologist gals, I should say. They were all women. I'm trying to be more PC these days."

Luke smiled a tight smile at him. "So, what did they piece together?"

"So. This guy here, one of the head partners at the law firm in Chicago. Bosch Liebowitcz Burns. He's supposed to go on vacay. Comes home from work. Spends the night. Watched some Netflix, later watched some porn. Ate some takeout from a high-end Chicago deli. Boar tenderloin, Yukon Gold potatoes, and broccolini. No visitors, eats it alone. Plates are still by the leather couch in the study."

"Okay."

"He showers, sleeps, next morning he goes down to shoot some squash balls around his court. Security cameras show a vehicle come in at around nine a.m. Rental car. Silver Toyota. Which we still can't find. The visitor comes in here. Pretty much straight in here. Like they know where he was gonna be."

"Did you get a good look?"

"Nope. They had a key. So that narrows down our possibilities. Whoever it was had an idea of where all the security cameras were, so they managed to sneak around in here in a big grey trench coat and keep their head down, face turned away. Once they were in here, no good shots. Border guys gave me a match on the Toyota's plates — it's this Canadian gal who works with him at Bosch and whatever firm."

"So, they came in here and …?"

"They came in here and we figure they knew each other because they initially got a little busy. They found his clothes strewn all over, like there was a prolonged undressing. We found him naked, on his back. No struggle. At least, not like he was fighting anyone off."

"Semen?" asked Luke.

"Semen trace. And shortly after, hard to say how shortly of course, due to the advance decomp, death via exsanguination."

Luke nodded. "Can they tell how?"

"Best they could figure, COD was a major wound inflicted to the mouth — but when I say mouth, it was just a mess of decomp. A volume of blood missing, he bled out on the floor. The sheriff is getting ready to pry up the floorboards to see how much seeped between them."

"I guess no one at work missed the guy, huh?"

"The guy was separated," Harry said, "pretty much estranged from his kids. But the staff we talked to say he was seeing one of the partners from the firm on the side, low-key."

"Ms. Helen. Or Heloise, depending on who's asking, I guess," Luke said. "She was on vacation too. For the period while he was gone. The ticket she bought was what connected me to him. It was unused. The whole vacation seems like a nice and tidy way to buy time to carry all this out."

Luke handed over a photograph showing attractive Heloise with dark hair in a conservative suit. A single-strand pearl necklace, pop of white blouse under a tailored navy blazer. She peered out from the photograph with a look of sharp intelligence. Her mouth didn't smile, but there was a liveliness around the eyes.

“There she is,” Harry said, looking at the picture, impressed.

“The sheriff looked around for a bit to locate her,” Luke said, “but there was no indication of that Toyota crossing back over.”

“And she was chilling in a morgue in Canada,” said Harry. “My producer has a CSI contact who said Burns suffered exsanguination via a deep cut under the tongue. Almost deep enough to sever the tongue.”

Heloise had been busy. Luke’s own work had dredged up the rental car, the time it crossed the border, and the fact that it was one of her aliases who had booked it. Finding the car would be nice. But running the semen trace against Jane Doe’s body in Toronto was sure to start bringing some closure to things.

“You guys up for a dinner sometime? You won’t get the chance to much in the future.”

Luke raked his hand through his hair. “Maybe in a few weeks?” He didn’t want to seem desperate, but he also really wanted Harry’s steadying company.

“Sure. I got a window.” Harry gripped his hand, hard, like he always did. A few weeks felt like a long way off to Luke.

It was 2:00 a.m. when he got home, and the house was dark and silent.

He wandered the downstairs in silent bare feet, not wanting to wake Beatrice. He opened cupboards, as though looking for inspiration. He rubbed his belly while standing in front of the open refrigerator. It was pretty empty. A conspicuous package of Brie lay unopened. He hated the athletic sock stink of the stuff. As he glanced over the fridge contents, he was unaware he was looking for something more than inspiration or appetite. He listlessly lifted out something in a shallow bowl that had been left with a small plate on top. She’d been cooking. Beatrice preferred not to have Saran Wrap in the house in her futile attempt to save the planet.

He pulled it toward him and peeked under the plate.

The moment he did, the whole works fell to the floor and splintered loudly into wicked shards of glass and porcelain which skittered across the ceramic tiles. Stark against the white tiles, there it was: a thick, black, misshapen form and a burgundy smear of blood.

A whole leech.

What the fuck! What the fuck?

Black. Bloated. Tinges of red blood in the white bowl.

He could have sworn, but ultimately rejected admitting it himself, that just for a moment, he thought he saw the fucking thing move.

Chapter 36

LAUREN

"Hey, guys!"

Lauren pasted on her show face while she performed the material she'd practised in front of the mirror. Truth was, she felt like a hollow shell with dregs of disgusting shame pooled at the bottom. But she was driven to get her stuff out there. Just in case she could somehow pull things together to be proven right, one day. She sat in front of her pull-down backdrop, wore her lucky hat, and dug deep to beam a big smile at the red light on her camera.

"Lauren here, at *Missing Link Found*, where you can count on me to bring you the real, dirty truth behind archeology, to open up a world of secrets and lies, as well as the coolest and most up-to-date true archeological facts — all brought straight to you. I'm 'Professor' (wink wink) Lauren Esteban.

"I want to talk about murder today, my arch-y fans. Murder on a really big scale. So much murder, it counts as genocide. Or is that *hominid-ocide*? Think of today's YouTube cast as maybe the beginning of my own Ancient Murder Podcast. Red herrings! Dead ends! Dead species, what?! Don't forget to like and subscribe, all my little arch-y fans!

"Okay, guys. You don't need to have been a viewer for very long to know that I have an obsession: showing everyone in the world that there are more hominids on the planet than just humans. We know for a fact that other hominids walked the planet at the very same time as humans did. We all know the Neanderthals." She made an ugly face, jutting her bottom teeth out and growled, "Me cave man," for comic effect, followed by a self-indulgent laugh.

"Okay, that stuff is all pretty much garbage, and the Neanderthals were, in fact, very sensitive and intelligent hominids who lived in the same places as *Homo sapiens*, at pretty much the same time. And for some reason at some point around forty thousand years ago they disappeared. Really interesting timing given that's right when humans or *Homo sapiens* showed up.

"But did you know there were *other* hominid species around too? Yeah. Denisovans for one, from Asia. Indonesian *Homo erectus*, and *Homo rhodesiensis* from Central Africa. There's a fascinating group we charmingly dub 'Hobbits': small-stature hominids from Indonesia known as *Homo floresiensis*. Where did they go? Floods, food shortages? Climate?

"A lot of bets point to one big smoking gun. A flint-packing, murderous, fast-spreading killer I like to call *Homo sapiens*. I've covered this topic pretty thoroughly in episode seven hundred and forty-three, which you can look up in the archives. You get free access to if you become one of my subscribers!

"Today, I want to go off-book a little and talk about some what-ifs. Wild what-ifs. If you know me, you know I'm building up to a sweet big reveal at some point. What I'm about to say is something *you* won't want to miss."

Lauren knew the what-ifs, like "what if she was crazy?" or "what if that asshole professor *is* correct?" … even "what if she were wrong?" But she thought about that Jane Doe on the news. And she knew in her soul. She had to go on. She was on to something …

"Okay, here it is. We all know about food chains on planet earth, arch-y fans. Carrots grow, rabbits eat carrots, cougars eat rabbits, then wolves eat cougars. That sort of thing. We know *Homo sapiens* have been eating carrots *and* rabbits, and even wolves from time to time, although we were more likely to domesticate them because: Cute puppy eyes! But I digress." Here, Lauren planned to insert some stock images of lions and wolves into her recording.

"At the top of food chains are apex predators. Humans quickly became apex. So good at hunting that we hunted some species right into extinction. But I want you to imagine that maybe, just maybe, there's been a species that once hunted us. Not even because they had to. Or wanted to hunt us into extinction, but because they could." She paused, milking the drama a little.

"Some of the research I've done with bones led me to believe that not everything we dig up falls into neat timelines or categories. Hominid, human. Many bones have been dug up and really, just terribly miscategorized. I believe there's been a *huge* cover-up and that at some point on planet Earth there have been other creatures living among us who evolved to need and want to consume *Homo sapiens*, regularly. For the hell of it? Because they could? Because they had to? Who knows? Why did we evolve to be able to eat meat when we could have been perfectly fine with grubs and roots and berries? Once we did, one thing is for sure, we figured out that more iron in our diet made *Homo sapiens* smarter, grew cranial capacity, changed us into the creatures that crave more heme for our hemoglobin, more iron for our mothers, more iron for our babies, more iron for our nursing. My hypothesis is that this other species, who I like to call *Hemo sapiens*, took it a step further. Just take a look at this."

She showed an image of a skull and traced its jaw and teeth as she spoke.

"Imagine a jaw shaped like this to support a different kind of musculature. You don't need a big crushing jaw if you're getting your protein from blood and not crunching hard grains or tearing raw meat off bones. Imagine how the tongue would change to support that? Think about what the teeth would look like. Wouldn't molars become obsolete? Crazy, right? These are just ideas of course, but it makes you think, doesn't it?"

She spent two hours dropping text and images onto the recording. And sent it, a little paper boat of hope, out into cyberspace. She was building her pathway into history and infamy.

Chapter 37

LUKE

Luke stood outside his car in a light misty rain. He was an hour's drive north of Steeles, out where relentlessly creeping subdivisions met with fields and forests. Sprawling houses hid from straight country roads behind gracious fences and trees. It reminded him of the Chicago lawyer's spread. It reminded him that he sure hadn't accumulated all that much wealth in life.

Cleo's address led him to a place on the car's Global Positioning System where roads were too new to register. The map showed his car flipping as if confused in a field of neutral grey pixels, lost. Uselessly, the GPS kept messaging him to "return to the road."

A steel mechanical gate that led down a winding black tarmac drive would not open when he buzzed the intercom. He sat in his car, with the heater blasting at his face and feet against the damp in the air, legs and ass aching after hours sitting in traffic just trying to get out of the city.

Squeezed through the small speaker of an intercom, Cleo's voice told him to hang on. She had to manually open the gate to let him in.

A handsome man approached, coming up the steep incline, his long legs eating up the distance. He was an L.L.Bean type — rugged, with a light-brown beard, trim enough to look downy. He wore a doeskin jacket, army-green T-shirt, and regulation Ken doll jeans. The jeans hung on him too well to be Walmart or Gap. That was something Beatrice had pointed out to him in exasperation at some department store: seventy-dollar jeans looked like shit; four hundred dollar jeans looked like what this guy wore. Draped, hung, and clinging to his long shanks just so.

"Hey man," L.L.Bean said brightly as Luke eased out of the car, feeling like he must look like a used takeout napkin. "We'll get you going here in just a sec." The man beeped a few buttons and then put both hands on the gate. He braced against the bricks and heaved with his body weight. The gate complained with a metallic *eek* and then gave, popping and shuddering. "It gets caught on the bricks here. Foundation's going. See you down there." The man gestured for Luke to go ahead. In the rear-view, Luke watched him close the gate. Luke made a note to himself of the entry code: 12-24-5. Said it repeatedly to himself until it was a kind of beat. A mnemonic that sometimes worked to keep things in his head short term.

The road wound down, black tarmac vibrant against the dull greens, into a vale of slender pine trees. Young ones, spaced far apart, with a second growth of deciduous, brambles and Virginia creeper underneath. The mist gathered silver on dark-green pine needles, congealing into ice. The house appeared at the base of this vale, all glass, looking like a massive ice cube. A few hints of light flickered within. The effect was of a snow globe hiding a secret world.

Cleo appeared at the door, holding it open to the damp frigid air. She was barefoot in a long t-shirt. She braced the door open with a slender, naked foot and cradled a mug that steamed in the cold air. Luke got the distinct impression he had interrupted a woodland tryst between her and Mr. L.L.Bean. If she was annoyed, she covered. She gave him that bright, hot, white smile that curved her mouth but not her eyes. And she looked through him with that pinning gaze.

"Thank you for coming all this way."

"No trouble. It's my job, Ms. Drover." He kept it on the clippy side today. He was still pissed about the misdirect and he allowed the energy of that to keep him in drill-sergeant mode. She stood back to let him pass and closed the door. Her home was an expanse of blond wood and white textiles, floor-to-ceiling windows open to forest and sky on four sides. Luke indicated them with a glance.

"Not a very private place you got here."

"The woods are the only curtains you need here. If someone's really going to bother to scale the chain-link and hike in here, I guess I don't mind if they see me in my underthings." She lingered near Luke.

He was still standing there, rooted. This was calculated on his part. He wanted to build hesitation into this interview. He had and was going to keep the upper hand. He was going to stay focused. Not focused on the length of the hem of her T-shirt and her polished toenails. No. He was going to stay off that.

"Do you want to sit?" She kept her own cool and offered a long dining table.

"Kitchen counter suits me fine." He strode that way after her, his boots heavy on the blond floors. "Company?"

A man wearing a tea towel tucked into the top of his sweatpants swivelled around to face him. His arms were soapy up to the elbow. He offered a thick elbow to bump. He was a solidly built fellow who hadn't yet bothered to put on a shirt or shave. Scruffy with light-brown hair and an easy, open expression. He looked like he didn't have a lot of stress in his life.

"Oh, Sergei's not company. He lives here," Cleo noted.

Luke enjoyed the little electric jump that went through Sergei's expression when he introduced himself and his homicide investigation.

"I'm gonna go throw on a shirt." Sergei brushed his hand from the small of Cleo's back to the top of her flank as he passed by. She gave him a warm look as he did. Luke had definitely interrupted a romantic weekend moment. Maybe Mr. L.L.Bean was just the caretaker. Luke already had his little black book out, old school style. All business.

"What's Sergei's last name?"

"Oh, uh, Roberts."

He clocked her hesitation. "Sure about that?"

She laughed. "Sorry. One of those, what do you call them. Petits mals? Coffee hasn't kicked in. Yes. His last name is Roberts." She swivelled onto one of the Plexiglas stools that were pulled up to the creamy travertine island counter. Luke didn't sit. He stood to his full height, spine straight, shoulders back, writing.

"And how long has he lived here?"

"Three years."

"And you?"

"Five years."

"Is it your home? Are you both owners?"

"It is our home. I'm the sole owner. Do you want me to pull out my mortgage papers?"

"Not necessary."

There was a noise at the front door. It was Mr. L.L.Bean coming in. He knocked his boots together and then took them off, neatly by the front door.

"Cleo, we gotta get that gate reshored. Hey! Dean." He introduced himself with an outstretched hand. He crossed the distance with a few strides of those long legs. "Everything okay, sweetheart?"

Sweetheart? Was he her … brother? Cousin?

When he gripped Luke's hand it was with enough of a squeeze to seem meaningful without crossing the line into aggression. He helped himself to coffee. And then kissed Cleo's neck.

Okay. So, not her relative.

For some reason, Luke felt a tingle. A feeling of elation and disappointment all at once.

Cleo threw Dean a warm look. Turning back to Luke, she got back to business.

"This is Detective Stockton. He's here about the woman I told you about."

"Does Dean also … reside here?" Luke's voice caught on the question a little when Dean slipped a well-manicured hand across her slim shoulder and let the fingers trace up under the curtain of her pale, smooth hair.

She didn't answer. Luke's pen stood poised over the blue lines. He put all his attention on that for the moment. When he looked up, she was smiling wickedly.

"He does. And it's Queinnec. Q-u-e, i two n's e-c." She nearly winked. "Coffee has kicked in. I'm so sorry. May I offer you one? We can make you a pour-over. Or a tea. Or espresso …"

Luke paused and looked at her levelly. "I can't. As you know I can't accept anything …"

"Right, right, yes. Sterling. Policy. I remember. Sorry, it's hard not to jump into hostess mode. Water, at least? Detectives can't get dehydrated, can they?"

"Not at the moment, thanks. Dean here is your …"

"Boyfriend." Dean called the word over his shoulder as he mounted an open stringer of metal stairs, which ascended perilously without a banister or risers. Luke looked at Cleo, eyebrows questioning.

"Yes. Dean is my boyfriend. He's lived here for three years also."

Luke couldn't help a little involuntary "huh!" of his eyebrows but said nothing.

"Elias," she called out, quite loud, without breaking her gaze at Luke.

Luke expected now that he would hear small feet. A child. Or a dog. He pictured one of those weird stringy-haired dogs with a mop of fur.

"Yo!" called another voice. A human male. A grown-up one.

A dark tousled head poked up from a staircase on the other side of the house that led down.

"Say hello to Detective Stockton."

Elias jogged over. He at least was fully dressed. He flashed a nice, warm smile at Luke. Shook his hand. He said his last name, which sounded like Mewler and wrote it down for Luke, complete with umlaut over the *u*.

"No one gets it. It's Swiss German," he explained. He stood behind Cleo. "You got everything you need?" He spoke it close to her ear, and ran his hands down her waist, and rubbed along both flanks. She stretched, leaning back against him, unfurling her spine, and laced hands up his chest. She linked them around the back of his neck for a peck of their lips. Elias stayed there a moment, his face leaning against her crown, while Cleo looked at Luke down the length of her nose, a little curl at the edge of her lip.

She laughed and tilted some coffee into her mouth. "Um. Cold."

"Oh, I'll top you up." Elias took her cup. "You need me to stay?" he asked Luke who shook his head no politely.

Internally, Luke was really shaking his head thinking *what the fuck?* but maintaining a blank face.

"You can put down that Elias is also my boyfriend, Detective. But I'm sure I can assume you didn't drive out all this way just to investigate my love life." She leaned close. "Or did you? That would be enticing."

"I don't make judgments, Ms. Drover," he lied. "I'm just here to clarify some things. I have a homicide case, an intricate one. I'd like to make sure I have as much clarity as I can."

"All right, then I suppose I have a confession to make."

This caught Luke off guard a little, but he kept his voice level. "Do you?"

"First of all, I am mortified about the business with the invoice. That was a mistake. An honest-to-goodness one. A filing thing. Someone doing data entry got something mixed up. I received this from my assistant after I landed." She pulled out a blank envelope. A folded piece of paper with a printout of an email detailed Jane's proper address as well as one of the names that agreed with some of her pieces of ID: Heloise. And it matched the physical location Luke had been to. "A mistake," Cleo reiterated. "But that's not my confession."

Luke adjusted his posture, slightly.

"I had met her before. And I omitted telling you that."

Now this was something.

"I know that to some people it would be considered sordid. But I, for one, am not mortified about it in the least. We had sex."

"Mm-hmm." He made his tone as bland as was humanly possible, flipped pages in his little black book. "Can you elaborate?"

"Certainly. Two separate occasions. In the city. At a club. On Mercer Street."

"Uh-huh."

"You're probably familiar with it, in a professional capacity of course."

"Want to just give me the address?"

"Number 5 Mercer," she drawled.

Of course he knew it. A four-story brick Victorian tucked away in between the financial district and a crappy part of town. Every day of the year with half a day off for Christmas, decent folks could go pay a cover and have sex with other consenting people. It was a regular stopover for vice. Even so, everything was perfectly legal about the place, and they were assiduous about keeping prostitution out. Just a nice, clean, pleather-clad dark lounge where strangers could go fuck. It was popular with plenty of racy first responder types who relished the abandon of kink and intrigue as a life-affirming antidote to grim death and its bleak attendants of sorrow, trauma, and fear. Not him, of course. He was way too chickenshit. And lately, way too married.

"And the second occasion?"

"That was here. With us. Hello, again," she said to Dean who was back. He sat nearby with a concerned look at her, which she waved away.

"A-ha. A-all of you?"

She laughed. "Elias and Dean. Sergei wasn't with us."

Dean smirked a little. "We had a pretty crazy summer," Dean said, lacing hands behind his head and tilting his rib cage out in a stretch. "Man. So much drinking."

Luke allowed himself to scrub his forehead slightly. "I'm going to have to take statements from everyone."

"Sergei too?"

"Everyone."

"I imagine this must all seem a little wild to someone in a conventional relationship, like you."

"Takes all kinds. I told you I don't judge. But I do appreciate getting all the facts. And the fact that you were involved with Ms. Wu, now deceased, warrants investigation. As does the fact that you concealed that information. But the more forthcoming you can be, I'm sure we'll be able to clear everything up."

"I'm not going to be in trouble, am I?"

"Let's not worry about that. Let's just get everything down, nice and clear. It's in everyone's interest to be clear as possible. People remember things at different times. So now that you've remembered, let's get into it."

"In my defence I compartmentalize a lot. Work is work. Play is play. Love is love."

Luke bit the inside of his cheek a little. He was compartmentalizing at work like fuck.

"We met at Mercer Street. In the upstairs lounge. Elias pointed her out to me."

"Was she alone?"

"I'd say she was on the prowl. Dramatic makeup. Dramatic lingerie. Dressed to be noticed. Most people walk around that place with lumpy towels wrapped around their lumpy bodies. I mean, try to make some effort."

"And she had?"

"I approved, so I sent her a drink. She came over to talk to us, seemed to like my boyfriends. She had some ground rules. Prophylactics, for one. No drinks for her. Nothing too crazy. No binding. And for her no PIV."

Luke glanced up, puzzled.

"Penis in vagina."

He looked right back down. She looked at him over the rim of her mug. "After we played we had a cooldown. She talked about a partner. Long-distance relationship. Very sad."

"Sad, why?"

"She was lonely. Unfulfilled. A woman like her, in her absolute prime, physically, mentally. No PIV was because she was desperate for a child. She wanted a child with a long-distance boyfriend. At the time she was ovulating, so she had to be extra careful. But in their relationship, he was holding out. This made her feel like a prisoner, watching her best years tick by, both of them knowing what a power he held over her. Her little jaunt to Mercer Street was a way to take her power back."

"Did she come to your Medspa before or after this encounter?"

"Her Medspa visits were completely unconnected. She happened to be a client of the city's best Medical Spa, of which I happen to be the owner."

"Coincidence."

"I'm sure you could draw socioeconomic lines if you really want to. Women of a certain class and age, they just know about my business. And I make it my business *to be* known to women of a certain socioeconomic standing."

"So back to the club on Mercer."

"We all swam a little …" She paused when he looked a little confused. "They have a fully heated swimming pool. Up on the top. Didn't you know?"

"Yeah, I've … yes, that's my understanding. I have never frequented the place, if that's what you're trying to get at, Ms. Drover."

She laughed.

"Of course. Mr. Conventional Relationship, I remember. The rest of us had more drinks … then we took over one of the playrooms until a little past dawn. My car service dropped her off at home that night. And then took all of us back home after."

"And this would have been?"

"July. Mid-July. I can look up the date in my invoices with the car service."

"And the next time?"

"The next time, I suppose I was on the prowl."

"Uh-huh?"

"I took all three boys with me. We were looking for her. Hoped to see her. And as luck would have it, she was there."

"And this second time was …?"

"A month later."

Luke caught the sly smile Cleo gave.

"When she was ovulating again."

The smile twisted a little more. "She was hungry. So was I. And when you're on the prowl, it is wise to pay attention to things like that. Lions stake out watering holes. I knew she'd be back. And I knew she would be ravenous. And grateful." Cleo stretched. "We convinced her to leave Mercer and drive out here. I had a second car put on the service, to wait outside at her convenience. She was game. Very adventurous. We all had a very, very nice time. Remind me to show you the hot tub here. Sunk in the back deck. Incredible view."

"Of the outside?"

"With so much glass, the view is great no matter where you look."

Luke interviewed the three men separately at the same seat at the kitchen counter. Mr. L.L.Bean was last. Luke rubbed his forehead wearily.

"So. You're one of three boyfriends." He chuckled. "Are you guys … with each … I mean, are you bi?"

"Nope we're all straight. Except Cleo. She's bi."

"So, is everyone, uh, satisfied with the, um, arrangement?" He was trying hard to sound utterly uninterested, bored even. And hip to all the different forms of … whatever this was.

"Do we all get laid enough, is that what you want to know?"

Luke made some word-like noises. He wanted to know. He also didn't want to know.

"You're married, yeah?" Dean pointed out Luke's wedding band.

"Uh-huh."

"You get laid much?"

Touché, thought Luke.

"There's a lot of communication." Dean launched into an explanation that sounded rehearsed to Luke. "Like, an unbelievable amount of communication. And you and I both know, that isn't most guys' strong suit. Two of us, me and Elias, we had folks who split when we were really young. Shuffled us back and forth between two or more sets of parents, splintering custody time, the whole divorced-kid thing. Deals, working things out. Becomes a habit. As is not expecting someone is going to be your Only, and your Forever. No one owns anyone, you know? Every line between every person is a thread you spin together. You connect. Things get frayed, you work to repair the connection."

"Jealousies?"

"Sure. I mean, look at you, for example. Good-looking guy. Cop, to boot. And she's sitting there at the counter in nothing but a T-shirt? Shit. But hell, I can feel jealous of the wet guy in a soap commercial. Wish I had better lats, wish her eye landed on my abs that way."

"Yeah, I don't know if you have much to worry about."

Dean poured out two glasses of water. "You're so her type."

This caught Luke off guard.

"Oh yeah, light-brown hair, touch of salt and pepper, bit of stubble. You got naturally broad shoulders." Dean drank his glass fast in a few swallows. "You know, you start doing regular reps, you'd be ripped in no time. But truthfully, it isn't ripped she likes. It's the rugged understated shapeliness she likes. Potential energy."

As Luke finished up with Dean, Cleo stood on the staircase, leaning over it. One bare foot propped against the other.

"If we're all done, Detective, I'd like to go have a long hot shower."

"We're done." Luke ground his molars together. Absently, he took another swallow of the water Dean had poured.

"Thank you for your time. I expect I'll need to do follow-up, so please keep me apprised of any travel or major plans."

"Of course. Drive safely."

It was dusk when Luke stepped outside. The mist had hung around and the cold was already seeping into his bones. His stomach growled.

"Jesus fuck."

The front driver's side tire was completely flat. The car sat heavy on the metal rim, showing through the flaccid rubber of the tire. It made the car look exhausted. "Here the donkey lay down and died." He laughed at the expression some guy at work used to say to him. Translated from Calabrian or Sicilian or something. The part where everything goes to shit.

Cleo and the others offered him a room to stay, which he declined. They offered to set him up at a neighbour's, drive him to town. All firmly turned down. He accepted a glass of water from

Dean while he waited for the local tow truck to come. He drank the water slowly, watching the last of the pale-yellow light bleeding from the sky and the first sight of Venus, twinkling through the pine boughs.

The car was going to a mechanic. A leak that bad meant the whole rim would have to be looked at, probably replaced. He got a room in town at a little motel with eight rooms. A police-account tow truck would take the vehicle first thing, and him with it.

The tow truck driver was aggressively chatty. Luke felt like an asshole, but just couldn't make simple small talk while the kilometres rolled away. When Luke asked for quiet, the driver sniffed, pushing the air out of both nostrils to register his contempt for Luke's unfriendliness.

The hum of the road nearly lulled him to sleep. He leaned his forehead against the cold glass and let the asphalt drift into a blur. It was a strange feeling to be a passenger, to feel himself being driven instead of driving himself. And it allowed his mind to wander. He found himself fixated on the image of Cleo standing on the staircase, one bare foot tracing the top of the other one and stroking up along her shin, rhythmically. He pulled his thoughts away to the details the boyfriends had given — for they *were* mere boys. The oldest one was at least fifteen years younger than Cleo. Old enough to consent, obviously, but there was a distastefulness to it all. What could she see in them? Besides the bluntly obvious? Sure, they might be good lays, but what do you talk about with a twenty-year-old? Maybe that's why she had three of them, for Chrissakes. So they could entertain each other when they weren't entertaining her.

And then somehow, the blur of the road drifted into slate tiles and the patter of tires became the patter of water falling on slate and the beads of water were glistening along the length of a hamstring and strung up along the slight s-curve of a taut, twisted back, glittering against tawny-coloured skin, faintly flushed with pink in the heat of the spray. The drops clung and clung until they fattened and merged and trembled and yielded to gravity, melding one into the other, coursing down the inside of an elbow shimmering at the edge of a kneecap, gathering like tears on wet clumps of darkened eyelashes. And Luke realized, with a shock, that the door to the shower was open, the door to the bathroom was open and she stood in the light, and turned to him, turned knowing to him, both arms up behind her neck, gathering up her hair, rib cage sucked in, streaming with water, and smiling at him.

He shook himself. The hum of the road meshed with the gaggle of voices on the radio and the driver made another annoyed snort to suggest he was unimpressed with Luke.

By the time he talked to the mechanics, dropped off the car, and checked in, he was weirdly wiped. The interview, and probably the drive and the grilled cheese with bacon he'd had on the way up were conspiring against him.

He called Beatrice at home. But she didn't answer. It was weird that she didn't answer. But his head was swimming too much to puzzle about it. Instead, he lay down on the brown plaid blanket and felt the bed bow under him. It was so lax he had a head-swimming moment that made him feel like he was in deep water.

He woke sometime later with a start. In the bathroom he looked grey and sweaty. He looked at his own shoulders in the mirror, which he admitted fuzzily were okay. But it was a half-thought thought. His head felt like cotton. He wondered if he'd caught a bug. Hungry? The grilled cheese was a long time ago. He considered sleeping until morning. He considered dragging himself to the motel bar. In the end he construed a flip in his stomach as hunger and staggered out. If he was sick, he was sick. If he went to bed hungry and wasn't sick, he'd be useless the next day.

He walked out of his room. He noticed that the key in the lock felt odd. So, too, the indoor-outdoor turf carpet on the walls scudding under his heels. He felt disconnected from his feet as he walked. He felt taller. The crunch of pea gravel outside seemed a long way down.

He woke with a start on a couch.

He knew for certain his room did not have a couch.

He was wrapped in a blanket. And otherwise naked. *That* was fucked up.

And he was in Cleo's home.

His head hurt. It pounded. And when he stood, he had the impression of the floor being farther away than normal. Just looking down at his feet gave him a feeling of vertigo. And swinging his gaze back up made his brain feel like it had gone for a swim inside his skull.

He had a sudden intrusive flash of Cleo, of her face, too close to his, her mouth, smiling, her eyes serious. Her teeth. She seemed to have so many of them, straight and flashing white.

He was clammy, dry mouthed. His face was greasy.

"You're up!" Dean sauntered in. He tossed something Luke's way. Luke reached to grab but fumbled. His car keys. "We picked it up for you, first thing. Figured you would want to be on your way."

"What the hell is going on?" Luke demanded, making his voice big. Partly to cover his nakedness.

Cleo entered behind Dean. Jeans. Turtleneck. Looking like some kind of regular next-door neighbour.

"You would *not* wake up," she said with a smile.

"How? What am I doing here? I left here."

"Oh. You don't … remember?"

Luke sat, heavily, on the couch, perched on the edge. She sat near, but not too near. Thankfully.

"The bar. You called me. You were eating. I joined you. You still wouldn't let me buy you a drink. So, you bought yours and I bought mine."

He had a flash of his room. He had a flash of his dark room. He couldn't see it, but he could feel the cheap, fake, pressed wood panelling nearby. He could smell the mustiness of the brown plaid blanket. He could hear a drip of a tap.

A burst of amber light shattered the darkness and fell, making a skewed trapezoid on the bed. And splayed in this cell of light, her body. Her skin glowed the colour of tungsten, hot against his retinas — the pupils still clamped down in protest against the burst of light out of dark.

He approached, cloaked in darkness, outside that oblong of light. He clung to the edge of plausible deniability. He wanted to break against her sharp edges. She lay on her belly, at once offering and mocking, lips curled. Urging. Daring.

Had that been real? Had he? His head pounded.

"Oh please, don't worry, Mr. Sterling."

He looked up at her.

"Absolutely nothing untoward happened."

He let out some air. Just a bit. He was still clenching the rest of it, anxiously.

"Oh no," she said. Sitting back in her chair, smiling with her mouth and unkind with her eyes. "You were very clear. That's not the kind of guy you are." She passed her tongue along her top lip. And for the first time, Luke noticed her tongue was pierced through the centre with a long, flashing silver piece of jewellery. "You felt terrible at the bar. I took you to your room. You made it very clear to me that you're still very, very, very married. And then you were sick. And then you told me you were okay with me bringing you here, in case you got worse. You really don't remember any of that?"

Her face swam before him. Sitting on her couch with a blanket wrapped around his waist, Luke felt creeping panic, sickly. Some of it felt mechanical. Something was wrong with him. But a lot of the sick was a heart-faltering feeling of disappointment in himself.

How could he have let himself? How had this happened? He would have to quit the case. He would have to hand it all over. It was too messy. Too weird. He felt waves of shame. Had he done anything? Accepted advances? What had he done? Had he dreamed the room? Her on the bed? Just like the shower?

Dean dropped a pile of his folded clothes next to him.

"I threw your stuff in the dryer, man. You'd spilled a couple of drinks on yourself at the bar." Luke nodded, dimly. Was it possible he'd felt sick, and a few drinks had made him black out?

"I'm sorry but I have to run out and attend to a few things," Cleo told him. "Will we be able to talk to you if we want to hear how the case is going?" She looked so wholesome and concerned.

"Yeah," Luke mumbled. "I'll keep you posted."

Chapter 38

LAUREN

Lauren sat in a maroon Dodge Caravan in a parking lot, kitty corner from Ontario Forensic Pathology Service. It had occurred to her to call and get someone on the phone. She could have told them she was still doing her grad studies. She could have asked to come in, so she could observe. But she knew that doing so would involve a series of bureaucratic steps including background checks, letters, references. Which would result in denial. And even if she could have passed muster, it wouldn't have gotten her what she really needed. And none of it on the timeline she needed it to happen by. They would fob her off. They would dismiss her. She would miss her window.

Time was wasting. That Jane Doe they showed on the news would be bagged up in the morgue. They still had the appeal for any leads or next of kin on the police website. She was still tantalizingly fresh. Full of data and details. Lauren *knew* she was the missing piece — her own private Mina, her own anthropological missing link — and her way back into good graces and studies and professorship, privileges and grants, tenure, and, when she permitted herself to indulge in the biggest picture, worldwide fame.

She considered walking straight into the morgue, unannounced, to simply smile and brightly charm her way in. Lauren bit at a crust of cuticle where she'd managed to get a deep cut right through it. They were always dry, and she was always picking at them with her fingers, or teeth. She sat behind the wheel of her minivan, watching the coroner's, nibbling on that exquisitely sensitive triangle of flesh.

Periodically, black vans drove around the side, along a boxwood hedge and down a cement ramp to an automatic door. There was a surface parking lot with a loading bay, a set of double doors. Lauren watched the place over the course of several days. She packed lunches. She brought a thermos. She used a bathroom in a local doughnut shop. She bought doughnuts to justify using the bathroom and discarded them on the way out of the store, so she wouldn't be tempted to eat them. In the car she packed all her wrappers and containers with her, lest her trash lead anyone back to her.

She noted that the cleaners, a third-party service provider, came every single day. While she ate her sandwich, she watched as they manoeuvred big plastic grey bins filled with oversized yellow hazardous waste bags and others with large regular black plastic bags of waste through a set of doors onto the loading ramp. The crew was two slight ladies, and one large guy, all of whom wore hazmat suits cinched around their faces, with goggles, masks, and gloves. They chattered between themselves whenever they appeared outside. They handled the large bags as a team, holding either side, swinging them to build momentum to push them up and over the lip of the bin.

In addition to the cleaners, a wide array of men and women came through the main doors. Many gained entry using a fob.

Others paused and identified themselves over a speaker and then the doors swung open to admit them. Sometimes they arrived in bunches. In those cases the first one to arrive there went through the rigamarole of identifying themselves and being allowed to enter. The person who sauntered up right after them just breezed on through, on the coattails of the first person. *Some not-so-ironclad security right there*, Lauren thought.

Over the course of days, Lauren watched who came through while she googled the day-to-day inside a city morgue. There were detectives, coroners and assistants, crime scene investigators, police officers, admin staff, HVAC people, morgue technicians, morgue beauticians, funeral service managers and staff, the bereaved relatives, and more. It was a far busier place than she'd ever thought.

While she ate her sandwiches of egg or tuna, leaving the crusts for last, she formulated a plan. She'd once read an article about a man who had fibbed his way to within a few feet of the sideline of the Superbowl simply by carrying a cellphone, a clipboard, a headset, and a brisk attitude of authority. *Surprise*, she thought as she washed down a crust with some cool tea and honey. Surprise and brisk, pleasant authority. That was the way in. The way out? That would be more of a trick. She noticed her thumb was bleeding again, from the crack in her cuticle. She must have caught it on a thread of her sweater. Again.

She kept a printout of the Jane Doe image folded up in her pocketbook. She had a kind of tingle inside her stomach when she looked at it. She knew deep within, with every fibre, that this woman, this incredible specimen, was the one thing that could change everything for her. She could finish her studies. She could pay off her student loans. She could quit the soul-crushing job at the dry cleaners that she hated with every ounce of her being. She smiled to herself.

She returned the next day and left her car in the loading bay. She'd noted this spot was never taken by anyone else. She backed in carefully and had to reposition a few times to make sure her bumper was snug against the black rubber lip at the edge. She took a deep breath and felt remarkably calm. She'd lain in bed at night rehearsing her steps from the car to the front door while reminding herself to stay loose in case things changed.

She'd repurposed a university ID card and stuck it on a lanyard. She'd decided to pose as a mortuary aesthetician, but a confused one, on her very first day at a new funeral home. People like to help people, generally. As soon as she cautiously approached the speaker, someone else bustled in front of her. A guy wearing a brown uniform and moving in a hurry passed her on the sidewalk. He barked his name into the speaker and the door clicked and swung open. And just like that, breezing behind him, she was in.

She walked purposefully along the terrazzo floors, her rubber heels making a kissing sound as she went. She scanned for wayfinding signs but found none. When the hallway ended at a dead end, she turned on her heel and walked back. A guy in scrubs nodded at her. Did he know? Could he tell she was faking?

When she didn't instantly reply, he cocked his head at her. Now her heart was starting to feel like it was working its way up her throat.

Chapter 39

LAUREN

"Are you lost?"

The lady in scrubs was looking at Lauren intently, with a birdlike expression, head to the side, eyes so piercing they were almost beady. Lauren felt trapped.

"Uh, bathroom?" she ventured and tried to look desperate. She laughed, good-naturedly.

"Yeah, this place is a total rabbit warren. You're new?"

Lauren summoned a laugh back at her and followed through two sets of double doors. The lady in scrubs used her key card. She showed her the door and gave her a little semi-comic bow, after rendering her service. Lauren tittered and fled inside the bathroom. She counted silently to fifty before exiting and doubling back one set of double doors to where she saw the wall of cold storage bays.

She hadn't counted on there being so many. So many silver doors. Nor had she counted on them being identified the way they were. Of course, there was more than one Jane Doe housed in the morgue. And coming up close to them, she realized the doors were sealed with a piece of laminated paper that screamed "Evidence" and "Chain of Custody." Lauren sighed. This was where she would have to put on her methodical brain.

"Separate the data, Lauren," she told herself.

A scan of the doors showed her dates. There were forty bays. She scanned over them, ruling out anything more recent than the Missing Persons plea on the news. She ruled out the unidentified males and focused on the Jane Does. She also ruled out anything that was two weeks prior to that. She was left with three doors.

"Door number one, door number two, door number three?" she whispered to herself. At that moment the double doors crashed open, and a technician entered, wheeling a gurney in.

"Can I help you with something?" he asked in a surly tone that suggested he'd prefer not to help her with anything. "I'm almost on break, so nothing too big."

"The uh, Jane Doe, police uh, they put out that media appeal."

"Yeah, A-23. You have to wait. They need to send a SOCO over to witness the seal."

"*Soh-coh*?" she asked. She hoped her helplessness was charming.

He manoeuvred the gurney to the wall and transferred the bag into one of the refrigeration units.

"Scene of Crimes Officer? Oh god, you're new, right? Look, can you please just go wait up near the front with the others? The SOCO will get here when they get here. When they are good and goddamned ready. Welcome to my life." He slammed the door shut using his hip, getting a sound out of it despite the cushion of air. "It's *all* hurry up and wait."

He shoved the empty gurney against the wall and stalked out, presumably to find a coffee and hopefully a more positive outlook on life.

Lauren hunkered down to put her purse on the floor. She pulled out a pair of rubber boots and a hazmat suit, a hardware store one, but still. She shucked off her sweater and heels, shoved them into an open garbage bin and slid into the hazmat suit. Now her heart was surely racing.

She put both hands on the handle of A-23. The evidence tape sealed the opening and would leave a telltale mark once she opened it.

She took a breath, put both hands shakily around the handle and heaved with both hands. The tape made a squeak as it pulled and snapped. When the door opened, she tugged on the slider and the black-bagged form slid out toward her with a cough of frigid air. Even through the surgical mask she'd donned, Lauren suppressed an irrational urge to not breathe in the air that had just recently enveloped all the cadavers within the unit. She closed the door and smoothed the tape back down so it wouldn't immediately draw attention to itself.

To her, the bagged body had an electrical buzz to it. Hope was here. Her specimen was here. Future was here. She was on her way.

The gurney would have been useful. But she opted instead for a wide, long grey garbage bin. She tugged on the body, needing all her strength to budge it and felt sick when it landed with an unhealthy thump in the bottom of the garbage. She pulled the half-full garbage bag out of its stand and threw it over top.

She hurried the cart to the doors where she had to shimmy back and forth between them to get them both open, using the bin to brace first one and then the other. Outside, she had two more false starts going down the wrong hallways. But she kept her cool pulling garbage bags from receptacles and heaping them over the body.

At last she found the double doors that led to the loading bay. And here she was stuck. The doors wouldn't open. The crash handles did nothing. She allowed herself to pace a little, thinking.

"All right, all right," came an echoing voice down the hallway.

It was an HVAC guy.

"I know. They should be open this time of day. Here." He waved his key card over it and slid a garbage can over to brace the door open. "Just remember to close it. You'll let all the heat in." He tapped his HVAC flash as though to indicate he was the temperature police. "Take it easy." He went out via the loading door, hopping down from the ledge easily.

Lauren was thinking all this time if she'd wanted to meet guys, she could have just walked around the provincial morgue, looking helpless.

Outside, the top of her minivan door was too low to let her easily move the body out. There was nothing for it now, and she regretted the damage to the specimen it would cause, but she would have to tip the bin. She had to hang off the edge of the thing with all her weight before she could lever it over. When it went, it scraped her viciously through her pants and the hazmat suit. But she bit the inside of her cheek against the pain on her thigh as she worked to haul the body out. She threw all the bags of garbage in after it and slammed the minivan door shut. Once she was behind the wheel, she was shaking.

At first she threw the car into reverse and gunned it and the car slammed against the loading bay bumper. A slight bump, a change of gears, and she peeled out. One block away, shimmying in the driver's seat, she tore off the hazmat suit and mask. She shoved her hair up under a baseball cap and joined traffic headed for the east end. She had rented a storage container near the lakeshore that waited to receive her precious specimen.

By the time she backed up to the lip of her storage unit, some of the adrenalin had begun to wear off. Her back was killing her. Likely she'd pulled something while lugging stuff around. And now her whole neck and spine slick with sweat under her top, and her muscles crying out for a hot shower, she knew she had to source a big dolly to make the final metres to her space with her cargo.

She cheered herself up thinking about how she could spin this. The video entries for her YouTube channel. The glowing recognition from the university. The disgruntled looks from Professor Broady when she passed him in the hallways. The day she could take the goddamn quotation marks off the "Professor" in her name.

She moved the body first. The room contained several mobile air conditioners. While it wasn't as cold as it should be, it was at least chilly. She had sourced ice and a large chest-type freezer. She would perform a full dissection. After a lot of documenting, specimen jars, photos, cells, everything she could, she planned to have the full, de-fleshed skeleton. Then she could compare that one goddamn bone she knew was proof of the missing link.

She stuffed the rest of the garbage she'd collected into open-mouthed bins in the hallway. She felt a little twinge of guilt over sending the biohazard yellow bags off to regular landfill. But in the big picture, was that really going to cause much of a problem for anyone? There was a garbage transfer station not far away. She doubted there were many human interactions between here and there.

Before getting to work, though, she had one last thing to do.

She had to get rid of the van.

Commissioners Street was a wide, sere wasteland on the edge of the city. It greedily hogged the shoreline, littered with derricks and industrial slips. There were several wide canals, big enough to accommodate massive tankers that now lay disused. Some still had the rusted metal moorings jutting out of the old concrete along the long slips where massive hulls had once rested. The land nearby was fallow. Abandoned warehouses were the last testament to what had been a working city port.

She'd read about a crime once that had involved a man driving his car into a canal. He'd left the car running, got out, reached in through the open window, and switched the gear shift over to drive. They'd found it later because the damn canal wasn't deep enough. The tail lights had been visible from the surface. Shoddy work on his part. Lauren liked to think she was pretty thorough. She'd even looked into city planning documents that made mention of the canal depths. There was no issue with depth here.

Rather than drive, she selected neutral. She wasn't keen on getting dragged with the damn thing over the edge and down into the fetid, dark water below. No, she was taking the hard way. She put it in neutral, and, knowing her back would complain later, she pushed.

For a moment after the vehicle's front wheels bumped over the lip and the whole thing jolted and tilted and shoved its rear end up and toward her chin, knocking her jaw, she was worried that it would stay stuck on the edge. She thought about the intricacy of reaching inside to grab the tire jack to help it along. But a sick grating of metal against concrete soon rattled her tooth fillings. And a moment later, with a heave of rude bubbles, the thing slipped below the surface.

Lauren waited for a bit. For what, she didn't know. In case it honked? Or, laughing at herself for the thought, leapt back out?

From there she began the long, hot walk back to the storage facility.

She'd done it.

Chapter 40

LUKE

He came home in the evening and found himself in an empty, dark house.

"Relax, calm down," Harry was saying to him on the phone. But his voice was vacant and absent. He was on set and Luke could tell he was annoyed but covering. "I'm sure there's a reasonable explanation. Plus, you gotta go get a blood test or something. I think you got roofied."

"I *did not* get roofied," Luke shot back. But he wondered if he had been too. He had six days. He could go get a test. Did he want to know?

"Well, whatever else is going on you need to communicate with Beatrice. You guys need to get it together. Be a united front, you know?"

Luke wanted to scream. That was all he'd ever wanted.

The front door slammed. Luke felt guilty, instantly. For talking to Harry. About everything that did or did not happen. And how much it made him ache to think about it.

"Beatrice!"

She gave him a nice smile, dropped her bag, and slipped into the hallway powder room, like nothing at all was going on.

Luke hammered the bathroom door with his fist.

"Beatrice! What the actual fuck?"

"Wait." Her voice on the other side of the door was ice. He counted breaths. He calmed himself the fuck down and heard the toilet flush and the faucet run.

The door revealed a much less serene face when she opened it.

"What," she said, flat.

"What?" He could not make the word sound any nicer or calmer. "I call you at eleven p.m. and you don't pick up the phone? I find goddamn leeches — live *leeches* in my fridge — after thinking that maybe for once my wife made me leftovers — "

"Oh. So, I'm supposed to be here all the time being wifey-poo to you and have no life of my own?"

"That's not what I'm saying."

"Maybe I was sleeping." Her hands were on her hips now.

"You didn't seem too fucking concerned about me coming back, maybe you don't even really care."

"And *maybe* I don't have to report everything to you."

She slammed the door again and Luke heard the faucet turn on with a fierce wrench.

"I don't know what's going on with you. With the doctor. With the baby. With us," Luke told the door, his lips almost touching the fake wood panel.

There was a pause before she spoke. He thought he could feel his heart breaking and sinking inside his chest. But he made himself wait.

"I don't have to tell you everything. We're married. Not each other's jailer."

Was it her who was sinking? Or him?

He wanted a kind word. Just one. He wanted a rope tossed his way.

But it was not going to be tonight.

"I love you," he told the door.

The door did not answer.

Chapter 41

LAUREN

The body lay on a fold-out table flanked by eight air conditioning units, still partly in the black body bag. Lauren learned the hard way that the body was still actively decaying when she unzipped the bag and fluids gushed onto the floor. Lauren had worked with cadavers before, but only in a well-controlled environment with staff to take care of the unexpected. And drains in the floor. The sudden spill gave her the urge to retch. But Lauren swung into action, knowing this necessitated a quick trip to the nearest hardware supply store she could find for bleach, mops, a bucket, antiseptic.

Once things were cleaned up, with tarps and bins placed under the table, Lauren took stock.

The body had been damaged in transit. A hank of skin flapped bloodlessly open over the right kneecap. There were other dents here and there. As though the body was more plasticine than human. No point being too upset about it though. She was going to have to cause a lot more damage to the specimen in order to get to the evidence she really needed. She had to deflesh the entire cadaver to get to the all-important skeletal structure, because that was where she was really going to show the science, the proof of her work. Of course, she planned to take lots of tissue and DNA samples, carefully labelled.

Just looking at the jawbone, and the pelvis, while fully fleshed, Lauren could tell this specimen proved absolutely everything. She could picture the skeleton, on display, articulated. That jaw, that narrow jaw, with its unusual shape. Definitely not classically human. There was an elegance to the shape of the skull — refinements no *Homo sapiens* had. And the powerful bones that structured the dense muscles of those legs. This was a predator. And a cunning thinker. With organs missing, and no doubt stored separately, there was a lot of guesswork she was going to have to do. A cursory look in the cavity suggested certain internal organs were enlarged. But she was gorgeous. A gorgeous, splendid, glorious piece of evidence that would change everything. Lauren brimmed with hope and a thrilling sense of discovery.

"Mina, my darling. Hello. We are going to do so much together."

For the moment, though, she had a timetable. Her podcast was a hungry beast that required regular feeding, lest she lose her sponsors. And her head was swimming with ideas, phrases, snippets that she knew she just had to get down, had to record. She wanted to capture the immediacy of the moment — she would hint by degrees what she was working toward in a careful campaign, but she needed to get something down now. Big reveal later.

Ahead of securing Mina, she'd made a workstation here in her makeshift field lab. Two folding plastic tables held her papers and various monitors. She'd lashed her pulldown screen to the ceiling and even thought to bring along her bush hat.

"Hi, guys!" she didn't have to work to inject warmth into her voice today or dig down to manufacture enthusiasm. "Lauren here, at *Missing Link Found*, where we always bring the real truth behind archeology conspiracies and lies, opening up a world of secrets, to bring the coolest and up-to-date and absolutely true archeological facts straight to you. I'm 'Professor' (wink wink) Lauren Esteban. And today, gosh, I am just so incredibly proud to announce my first day of some *very* important fieldwork from my new! Field lab! And to let you know that something big is coming. Something world-changingly big." She allowed her eyes to wander from the camera and to stare up into the future. "It's really starting today. Don't forget to like and subscribe, arch-y fans! So, I made an absolutely paradigm-shifting discovery years ago, which you can hear all about in *Missing Link Found*, episode three, parts one and two. That day set me on a journey that has led me to right here, right now. In a few minutes, I'm going to get to work on an actual specimen that I will prove is connected to that first discovery and that I promise *will blow* the *lid* off the entire archeology and anthropology worlds and rewrite all the textbooks written by fossilized professors out there on *Homo sapiens* and non-*Homo sapiens* beings on this planet. Stay tuned!"

She paused for a second, and slightly under her breath added …

"Cut. And save this next dialogue bit for the big reveal." She took a breath. Sat up. And stared down the barrel of the lens.

"*Homo sapiens* are not alone on earth. There is another humanoid species. Walking among us. Like us. But so very different. And I, Lauren Esteban, former Ph.D. candidate, was the one to recognize the first clue in a bone forgotten on an archeology shelf, and I am the first one to identify and acquire an actual specimen, recently deceased, and boy was that hard to do. And with no exaggeration I can safely say, this will change everything. What's more, I plan to prove through autopsy and analysis that this … creature — I call her Mina — is the product of millions of years of evolution geared with a lust to survive that outpaces *Homo sapiens*. In fact, it feeds on *Homo sapiens*."

She pulled up a newspaper that bore a headline from months back, featuring the boy in the alley.

"Police have been totally stumped by this crazy case. This hyper strong woman has killed at least three boys, practically men — that we know of. And the police are just bumbling along, totally inept, no clue what is going on. I'm going to prove that it was this specimen here, Mina, who is responsible. And that she isn't really guilty, in the truest sense — she did it because she needed their blood. Not like some woo-woo vampire out of the movies, but out of a biological process that makes her need heme in blood to live and procreate the way people need oxygen to live. Mina, like you and I, just wanted to live."

Here she paused to place her hand on her heart, as if to honour Mina. "Years ago, I had the intuition that we were not alone. And not one of my colleagues would give me the time of day. I got kicked out of my program, my school, from the only life that mattered to me. I've worked dead-end jobs for years. Dry cleaners. Cleaning houses." Her voice broke for a moment. "It's been … hard. You guys, my dear fans, you know all this. But I never, never gave up."

She hit pause on the camera. She noticed she was trembling slightly and could feel her entire back was sticky. It was enough for now. She would have to play it back and finesse it. Likely re-record the whole thing. This was posterity she was working toward.

She set up for her first lab shot. This would be rehash stuff, teasing at new information — but showing close-up details of the hip bone, the famous hip bone from the Spadina facility. She always kept off the bone itself and used drawings or photos instead, lest the wrong person identify it. She had a plaster cast of it she liked to handle while on camera.

For now the body was kept hidden. She had all that defleshing work to do on it. And she was going to have to keep mum about where she'd acquired the body exactly. And would stay off anything too identifying. For now. Once she had lined up all her evidence, she was going to have to figure out how she would get it in front of the public.

She set up an overhead camera, above the table, to cover the entire operation, so she could document everything she found. She pressed record, checked that the data was getting laid down, let the thing run, did her "Hi, guys!" intro looking up into the camera and then got to work.

Samples, containers, verbal and written notes. It felt so good to be back in the field, doing the work she knew she was meant to do, was destined to do, and better than all the other hacks.

While she was bustling around, happy as could be, she heard a sharp rap at the metal door.

Which she knew was odd. No one expected to find anyone *in* the storage units. Had she been too loud while recording? Was there a rule against being inside your unit for too long?

She was still wearing her bush hat when she reached for the doorknob but swept it self-consciously off her head before opening the door.

Outside was a woman, flanked by two men. A fancy lady woman all done up, pale and wealthy-looking.

"I'm looking for a dear friend of mine," said the woman.

"Sorry. I haven't seen anyone." Lauren shrugged, and she pushed the door closed. But it wouldn't budge. One of the men had put his foot in the way of its passage.

"Oh, I'm quite certain you know her." The woman smiled.

"Let us into the unit now, or I'll just call the police," one of the men added.

Lauren's body convulsed with a sudden sick feeling.

Chapter 42

LUKE

Luke spent two days with his head down, churning through memories of the surreal visit to Cleo. He was still pissed as hell about the redirect. And now Cleo had crossed a line from witness to suspect in his mind. In his experience anyone with money like she had was usually circumspect, but she was next level. Shadiness didn't translate directly to motive and means but they could be cozy neighbours. Worse, he was swimming in guilt that he'd come close to fucking around on his wife, and his wife wasn't talking to him, and he almost wished he had fucked around on his wife, just to see if it even mattered to her anymore what he did … Of course, more guilt surged in for even considering that. It was not the way he was wired. He'd made vows. He kept them.

"Don't speculate," Harry was fond of reminding him. "Work the details. See where they go."

Shaking off a greasy skin of guilt, he'd had to go down to Mercer Street to see if there was any corroboration for Cleo's sex party story. He didn't exactly relish the task of making a daytime appointment in order to meet the manager. He'd met with her in the past while chasing info on various cases. The sex club management kept their noses clean. They also held him and his entire ilk in sheer contempt. The manager had made a point of wearing a "Defund the Police" sweatshirt and bikini bottoms the last time they talked.

In the old days, such a place would have been regularly raided for illegal activity. Activity like sex with people of the same gender. And though the club was operated strictly on a basis of consenting adults meeting with other consenting adults, it appeared to the narrow-minded and more puritanical of society much too much like a bawdy house.

A reedy creature wearing a bikini bottom and a T-shirt showed Luke to the manager's office. Her office was in the hallway that led to the swimming pool, where the air was thick with chlorine.

The bright, chirpy club manager, crouched up on her chair, hugged one knee. Her brass nameplate said, "Ambassador of Good Feels."

"Afternoon, Ms. Feld," Luke told her. Her aggressively asymmetrical haircut made him feel a little seasick.

"Well, been a while since I had a visit from the po-po. Did they offer you a coffee? Doughnut?"

He smiled. She was just being sassy. "I'm trying to keep it tight for the wife." He patted his belly.

"That's so heteronormative of you."

"Yep, boringly born this way." He shrugged. "I'm here to request some security camera footage and guest logs. Ask about a few patrons ..."

"You'd better not be trying to pull some morality crap."

"A murder investigation. Would not dream of interfering otherwise. So, I'd appreciate any light you have to shed."

"Oooh. Tell me more." She sat up, balancing in the wooden swivel chair on both feet.

"I'm looking for footage and logs from these nights." He slid his notebook over with dates Cleo had given him. She jotted the dates into her phone, typing with both thumbs.

"And any thoughts on these two."

"Oh yeahhh. Oh my god, between us, that woman is so incredibly hot. It's always a good night when she's here."

"This one — the blond."

"Mm-hmm."

"Regular?"

"Ish. I think she's super loaded. Always tips well. Super polite. A little distant."

"What about her?" Luke indicated Jane. "I was led to believe they met up here. Got … uh, involved."

"Sorry. Never seen her. You know how much of a personal touch I am. If she's been here, I've never had the pleasure of seeing her. And trust me, word gets around here. If those two came in to play, together, *every*one would be talking about it forever. Best way to know would be to comb through the security cams. We've got a lot of them."

It wasn't a dead end yet, because there was a chance someone else had worked the door the night Jane came in.

"You know we have a really well-attended service night here. First Wednesday of every month. You might even see some people you know. We have an in-joke about it — It's *like*, Fire. Except it is fire, and EMS, and —"

"I get it," Luke said putting up a hand. "I wouldn't want to pour water on anyone's fun by showing up and recognizing them. Especially not with my soon-to-be dad bod. Can you provide me with upload links from your security cams for me by tomorrow?"

"Sure can. Thanks. It's been kinda nice to see you, for a change."

In real life Luke would have made a sarcastic joke. He was nice. Especially when others were nice and helpful. Instead, he said, "Thanks for your time."

But helpfulness and niceness were not to pay off. The bricks and mortar and vinyl and alcohol-based hand sanitizers of the club were the weak link.

Overnight, before he was supposed to receive links to the security footage, an eight-block section of the downtown around Yonge and Adelaide was sectioned off to make way for a multi-alarm fire and all the attendant services. They brought in transit vehicles for all the displaced people to stay warm while crews sprayed everything down, putting a damper on the activity at Mercer.

Seven trucks and their crews had to work through the night to contain the blaze. The club was part of a row house with connected attics and a long-forgotten underground coal-delivery system. Fire had raced along both conduits and tore through fifteen row houses, gutting them entirely.

It depressed Luke, knowing that as time ticked by after Jane's death, the traces of her on this earth became ever more finite and were at the whims of weather, catastrophe, and the greatest leveller of all: time. A lifetime of walking the earth only ever left a passing trace.

Returning home at the end of a frustrating day, Luke heard the kitchen wall phone ringing when his key was just sliding into the keyway. He had to use the bathroom, but he sprinted for the phone. How many times in his life had he sprinted for a phone only to get a gutter cleaner service?

"Is this Mr. Stockton?"

The woman's voice was just stroppy enough to irk him, so he deployed his rank.

"Detective Stockton, yeah," he replied, inflecting the "tec" just enough to convey annoyance, but otherwise neutral.

"Oh, good. Sorry to bother you on your home line, Detective, but we couldn't get through to your wife on her cell. I'm calling from Dr. Ko's clinic. The ob-gyn? You're Beatrice's emergency contact."

"What's this about? Is everything okay?" He let his case slide down to the floor, hands fumbling to get at the writing pad and pencil he kept nearby. The ones that Beatrice called old school, along with the land line.

"It's about her blood work."

"Oh Christ, is something wrong? She's been really worried about the tests."

"No, and really, I'm afraid I can't go giving out results of blood tests over the phone, but it's the blood tests themselves."

"Uh-huh," he said, hand poised over the paper to capture whatever was coming next.

"The blood tests are all missing. We've been trying to get through to Beatrice on her phone, and this is, I'd say, my fifth call. I've left messages. I sent an email. I'd appreciate hearing back."

"No kidding?"

"No kidding. Look, she really needs to get down to the office and get some of this redone. From my records she's moving along in the pregnancy, and she's considered geriatric pregnancy at her age. We really need to get data happening so we can make sure that she and the baby are both fine. There was also the issue of the DNC she had booked. Can you tell me when she had her last ultrasound?"

"Last? Try first," Luke joked. He didn't expect a strained silence. "And I'm sorry, did you say DNC? As in an ab—"

"Mr. Stockton, look, there appears to be some miscommunication and it's important that we speak to Beatrice herself. Please have her call us and get in for an appointment right away. Her ob-gyn is willing to stay late if he needs to accommodate her, just this time, because we really need to start getting some data to replace what we're missing."

"Sure. As soon as she comes in."

"I'll be here, at the clinic — you have the number?"

"Okay. It's just … my wife changed health care providers — did she not tell you?"

"Beatrice is still rostered with us as a patient."

"What the hell is the Medspa place then?"

"I'm sorry, sir, I don't know anything about that."

When she hung up, he stood there pondering this, feeling a rush of emotions as he did. DNC. Dilation and curettage. She was planning to abort their child?

At that second the phone rang again. He snatched it out of the cradle and barked.

"What?"

"Jeez," said Tymika with a detectable pout in her voice. "Don't you check your texts lately?"

"Tymika. Yeah. I'm kinda in the middle of something. Sorry."

"Yeah, well I just thought that maybe you'd like to know that our primary piece of evidence has gone missing."

Luke rubbed his face, hard. Anytime paperwork or items or photos went missing it was a big drag. It was a big blot. It was a missing link in a chain of evidence carefully forged so that it could practically stand up on its own in court, incriminating a suspect through sheer force of rational, chronological, objective, plain cause-and-effect steps. Missing links, especially if they went missing after being carefully catalogued, spoke to sloppiness, botched efforts. Even if it was through no one fault of any person, the severed links left questions, possibilities. Doubts. Case-killing doubts. God knows he was starting to have many of his own.

"All right. What's the problem?"

"Our Jane Doe."

"Yeah. Someone steal her brain or something?" It was a morbid joke, but he felt a bit of panic. The case could move forward without her clothes, sure. Or even some of the weird specimens they retrieved from her.

"Yeah: or something. Jane Doe is missing."

"I'm sorry, I don't think I understa—"

"The evidence has gone missing from the morgue."

"What evidence?"

"The entire cadaver. There was a break-in of some sort. Seal had been broken on the drawer. But no one seems to be able to gather when."

"Jesus. I mean … what? What th— How the hell does a body, a piece of a critical chain of evidence, just walk like that?"

"I know."

"Okay. Great. I'm heading down there. Jesus."

Luke hung up and sank down to the floor with his back against the wall. He felt the baseboard scrape along his tailbone as he hit the bottom.

He was heading down all right.

Chapter 43

LUKE

Luke took comfort in walking the long, narrow corridors of his division. In the bland industrial grey carpet and the beige walls, trimmed in blue. There was a comfort to being in a place where he felt competent and needed. And where he could concentrate on working instead of being a failed husband.

He smelled the toner and the brand-new paper reams in the photocopy room. Passing by the coffee station, burned coffee drops lingering on an element coloured the air. The powder puff sugar scent of Coffee-mate hung there too. No one drank station coffee. Someone always made a run to Timmies. At the end of the day, someone eased the dense black dregs down a drain. This morning, someone had made a run to Timmies but the idea of drinking one didn't sit well. In his mind's eye, Luke still saw that bloody leech splattered all over the white kitchen tiles. All the more disturbing when he'd been holding out for maybe paprika-fried pork chops. He was going to have to get to the bottom of whatever science experiment Bea had going on in the fridge.

His desk was a weirdly welcome sight. And the prospect of a few hours filling out various pieces of paperwork was soothing, like filling out an easy sudoku. Badge number, name, rank, date. Badge number, name, rank, date.

He had phone calls to catch up on as well.

Gertie had many connective pieces for him. A blood match on the park kid linked him to Jane Doe. The kid had never awakened, but at least there was some closure on who his killer was, though strained and fantastical. Likewise, tests came back linking the unborn child genetically to both Jane Doe, obviously, and the lawyer who'd met his end in the squash court. Gertie was also able to tell him that the conception lined up with the night of his death.

"Some weird family," muttered Luke. "Some date night."

"Oh, you've have had some doozies yourself. Remember the one who got so wasted you had to call an ambulance, and then she tried to rob the till at the bar?"

"She thought the cuffs were some kind of flirting," he replied, wiping strain from between his brows.

"Sounds exciting. Most nights I just have a shower and watch *Seinfeld* on endless reruns."

"So. No more Jane?"

"Oh yeah. You heard about our own personal Walking Dead."

"I guess it's asking too much that she just stay put?"

"She's been our most exciting customer in some time, I'll admit. A real superstar around here."

"With some super fans elsewhere, I suppose. I understand there's some surveillance available."

"Yep. Please bring real coffee when you come."

"There's some fresh Timmies across the hall."

"You heard me say *real* coffee."

So, the coroner's office now had to do double duty as a crime scene. A SOCO he hadn't worked with was busy, photographing the broken seal on the drawer. They'd narrowed it down to the day, though not the hour, by interviewing several of the workers around the facility.

"Still waiting to hear back from an HVAC guy who was here that day, but his company says he's up north at some fishing camp."

Muddy surveillance cameras gave them a look at the flow of people through the place on the day. The investigation would prompt the coroners to get better cameras, but the truth was no one really expected the bad guys to come right inside the sanctum. It took them a while to sort out who Lauren was, and a longer while to sort that the hazmat-suited person later on who was moving garbage bins around was also her.

Gertie groaned. "I saw her myself. Walked right by her. I just thought she was some new kid. Stupid. Stupid."

"You weren't looking for it, Gertie. And you had a full-time job to do. What about the HVAC guy? He just let her walk right out."

"I guess he was in a hurry to go fishing."

"You know what I miss? I miss the post–nine-eleven days when suddenly getting inside *any* public building was like getting into Fort Knox. People are just getting lazy about things like buzzing in. What's the point of fobs, security, surveillance, locks if no one uses them?"

"People can't stay on total alert forever. Most people just assume nothing weird is ever going on around them."

Partway through logging the data and timestamps as they watched security footage, Luke volunteered to grab lunches for them. A perk of seniority. He'd used to hate being the junior guy getting sent out. Now he relished the chance to move, clear his head, see a few glimpses of the sun on a nice day.

He drove up University Avenue, glad that the day meant the streets were full of people in T-shirts and jogging gear, enjoying a freakish late fall blast of warm weather. Girls in dresses peppered the streets around Queens Park. Along Bloor Street pedestrians slowed the traffic more than normal. The sun through the windshield was warm and golden.

He was preparing to park near Charles and Bay. A café in a three-story Victorian there served tuna melts twenty-four hours a day. While reversing into a spot, he automatically clocked yet another summery-dressed girl. And then realized with a start that he was looking at Beatrice.

It was a strange sensation seeing her out in the world, out and about on her day, lost in her own life. Her own person, as though she was a stranger to him. It was like looking at a stranger and having a celebrity sighting all rolled into one.

She shifted her bag, and he allowed himself a moment to just appreciate that his attractive wife still commanded his view, from across a sidewalk. She walked with purpose and a swaying skirt toward a set of glass double doors and went in. He pocketed his car key and jogged, jaywalking across the wide expanse of Bay Street.

On the other side, though, he stopped short. He turned and looked back, across the street. He was parked outside the Medspa clinic. And this was where Beatrice was headed with such particular focus.

It was at this point that Luke found himself propelled forward. He felt a rush of energy within that he knew, somewhere in his head, was the heat of months if not years of unexpressed anger. Its explosiveness propelled him back across the street, and pounding hard on his heels down the sidewalk so that the force of each footstep jammed his bones against each other. He was moving too quickly for the glass door to swish open fully, so he pushed at the side of it, and he felt the satisfying give of its mechanics groan against the force of his hand.

He was going to walk straight in and straighten some things out, this very moment.

"Hello Detective Stockton." Genevieve behind the desk seemed almost happy to see him. "Can I help you?"

"I'm here to meet my wife," he told her through gritted molars.

"Oh, and she is ...?"

"Beatrice Stockton." He laid into the last name. There was no way the redhead could have missed checking Beatrice in mere seconds ago.

"I don't seem to see anyone here with that —"

"I'll just go up and find her."

"I'm so sorry, we can't just have people walking around — a lot of private procedures happen here and —"

"My concern is that my wife is about to have some private procedures involving my baby here, and I'd kind of like to know what's going on. Take me to wherever you guys do your treatment stuff. Please." The please was not a "please." It was a "now."

She moved quickly and brought him into a sleek elevator — a different passageway into the Medspa inner sanctum than before. He was through the door as soon as the doors opened a crack, and could hear her heels skittering like a tap dance along the floor behind him trying to keep up.

As he stalked down the hall, scanning left and right, he could see patients in various procedure rooms, most of them half concealed by frosted glass. But at least one room gave him the sight of a woman wincing and turned his way. Her face was covered with a mess of gore. He started back for a second and then realized he was looking at one of those vampire facials Cleo had mentioned before. The woman was wincing because she was being injected.

"Beatrice!"

"Oh!" Genevieve stopped short behind him, almost colliding. "You found her."

"Thanks. I got this."

Beatrice looked warily up at Luke from a low reclining chair in a procedure room.

"You want to maybe tell me what's going on here?"

"Don't you think you're a little too worked up?"

"I have a lot of questions, Beatrice."

"So have we reached the 'stalking each other while we get facials' stage of our relationship, then?" Beatrice was quiet, and her voice was level. But frigid.

"A facial? Is that what this is?" He could do cold right back at her. He also couldn't help but notice that the room had an ultrasound machine set up and a bed with a paper gown laid out.

"We can resume this later if this is a bad time," suggested the nurse practitioner in the room. Luke watched her lean into Beatrice, and he knew what she was asking was if his wife felt safe right now.

"Please don't worry. I'm fine. I think my husband and I just need a chat."

The nurse left the room and closed the door, but not before casting a lingering, accusing glance Luke's way. Beatrice indicated an empty chair with her eyes.

"Out. Side," responded Luke. "I'll wait downstairs."

Beatrice held his look for a moment, and he could see that there was a well of rage inside her too. On some level all this was good. They never really fought. They just retreated to different parts of the house and allowed things to simmer. Maybe what they needed was to just let a bunch of shit out.

She sighed. "I'll need to change."

"Fine." He stalked out and made his way back to the elevator. The door to the vampire facial room was closed now, and he heard laughter behind it.

In another room a row of women sat in luxurious reclining leather chairs, their arms hooked up to thick IV lines, apparently getting blood infusions. Several of them were heavily pregnant. Some of them had red goo smeared all over their faces. He caught a glimpse just as an angry-looking nurse swung a door shut. The vampire facials were, indeed, a big business here. It struck him as odd — a woman could have some bizarre blood facial but wasn't allowed to eat raw cheese while expecting?

Waiting outside on the street, he paced, still propelled by his anger. Irrationally, he started to wonder if she'd bolted and left the building by another route. His mind whirled with a toxic mess of questions, accusations, tallied and nurtured hurts over the last few months, and not a little bit of unregistered guilt and shame over the way Cleo's very presence had made his blood race.

At last the glass doors swished open, and Beatrice appeared, in her coat. Shoulders hunched, clutching her bag. Seeing her outside, the knot of frenzy and anxiety inside him loosened. He wanted to grab her, hug her, rewind, just slip back to an easy existence.

"Beatrice, why are you here?"

"Why are you, Luke?"

"Beatrice, I'm working. My work involves murders, so you'll have to forgive me if randomly seeing you out at a place I'm investigating makes my mind go into overdrive."

"Okay."

"Okay? *Okay*?" He rammed the urge to yell right back down his own throat and breathed a deep breath instead. "Beatrice. I got a call from the ob-gyn's office. What's going on?"

"What do you mean what's going on? I'm having a baby. I decided to see a different doctor. It is *not* like I need to ask your permission."

"Of course you don't. But I think I have a right to know if you're considering things like a DNC."

This brought her up, sharp. "How do you know about that?"

"I'd like to think that you'd at least keep me in the loop about something that big happening to us. To …" He gestured with both hands at their unborn child still inside her and her autonomy. "You are freezing me out."

Her arms were crossed. "I wanted to have a midwife. I wanted a completely natural birth. And I knew you'd say no."

"DNC? What gives?"

"Again, how did you know?"

"The clinic called. So?"

"It was a just-in-case scenario. One of the tests had come back indicating that the genetics could be … bad. Additional chromosomes. Or something else. It was totally just in case something was seriously wrong."

"Is there a trisomy? Have you had genetic testing?"

"Luke, calm down."

"Were you planning on telling me about all the bad genetics? About your choices? What if I didn't agree? I want to know why, damn it, Beatrice."

"Luke, it doesn't matter what I say to you. There is no way you could ever understand my reasons."

"Okay. I mean it's not okay, but moving on for now, your ob-gyn called and said your blood work was missing. All of it. All the tests."

"Those people at the ob-gyn's are idiots."

"What happened to the tests?"

"I don't know, Luke! I changed doctors. Maybe they lost them? I'm here instead. I'm going to come here and I'm going to have a doula and music I like and I'm going to have a water birth. I'm going to have as much natural help as I can and I'm not going to have a drugged-up birth run by a bunch of bureaucrats and I'm going to start getting the nutrition this baby needs and these people are the absolute best there are in the entire world to help me do that."

"What if I told you I think the woman who runs this place is dangerous and I don't want you coming here?"

"I'd say you were controlling and paranoid. I joined a moms' group and they all raved about this place. It's what. I. Need."

"Well, I don't want it."

"Well, that's just too bad. Because it's what's happening. And maybe I need to have a long think about how much you're going to be in this baby's life at all."

"What the hell is *that* supposed to mean?"

"Stalking me downtown while I'm just trying to live my life. I'm not one of your cases. And this is not about *you*."

She turned on her heel. He tried to follow and grabbed her elbow. She wheeled around and put her hand on his, gripping. It was a vice like nothing he had ever felt from her before. For a moment he had the impression she could pick him up and toss him. He shrank back.

"Walk away, Luke. Now. Or I'll call the police and you'll have to explain to some of your colleagues why your wife was scared enough to call them in for a domestic disturbance. I don't think you want to have to deal with that."

He dropped his hands and watched his wife walk away down Bay Street with a stiff, straight back.

Chapter 44

LAUREN

Lauren stepped back from the two men who were jamming the storage room door open, one with a foot he'd shoved into the storage space. They both towered over her. Both handsome, all teeth and tans and beard stubble and soft, warm cologne. Under the handsome smiles, they had such a hard look in their eyes that Lauren fawned, stepping meekly backward. Inwardly, Lauren knew that they knew what she had done. She'd been caught. This was bad.

They were both wearing medic outfits, but without any kind of hospital lanyard or city hospital badges. No-name paramedics. They each held a medical cooler in either hand.

As soon as Lauren stepped backward, they calmly entered the space and set the coolers down on the floor.

The woman entered last.

Unlike the men, she was fashionably dressed. To Lauren, she looked like a real estate agent or a weather woman from a national newscast.

The woman walked right around the screen that Lauren had set up, her heels ticking lightly across the concrete floor. Until they stopped dead, and she sucked in a sharp breath.

One of the two men crossed the floor to her in a few long strides to be at her side. One arm went around the woman's shoulders. She clutched at his other hand with both of hers. Lauren got the impression she might fall over.

"Heloise …" managed the woman. For a moment she was overcome and held a clenched hand to her mouth. Then she let out a softer breath and her shoulders sagged. "How is it that she's still so beautiful?" she said as one of the men caught her in his arms.

"I know," the man murmured into her hair.

"Look, I'm in the middle of important fieldwork here," Lauren blustered. The woman turned to her, standing back up at her full height. There was sadness in her eyes, but her tone was fierce.

"Important fieldwork? This woman is my kin."

"Oh," said Lauren in a tiny voice.

"You've broken any number of laws and standards and ethics and morals. What kind of monster are you?" She spat the words and they lashed out at Lauren like whips. Those were details Lauren had carefully protected herself from admitting to herself. She was doing great work. She was making steps for science and self-improvement.

"Dean?"

On her word the other man stepped forward and calmly walked over to Lauren. "Relax," he said to Lauren, both hands out, palms facing out, unthreatening. "It's okay. Don't worry. Relax."

Lauren drew in a shaky breath. And in a few steps, he was upon her, one big hand clamped around each of her elbows. He manoeuvred her backward until her legs bumped into a fold-out chair.

"Let's sit."

She nodded a little. At the moment she felt drained of all power in her legs, especially her knees.

While she sat the woman walked over to the specimen on the table. She reached a trembling hand out and let it touch the dead woman's shoulder. The trip from the morgue had compromised the body more than Lauren had wanted, and time out of the refrigeration had hastened the relentless march of decomposition. Otherwise, Lauren was certain the woman would have kissed her cheek.

"My poor, poor girl," whispered the woman, and she smoothed the glossy black hair that cascaded over the edge of the table. "You were too wild for all of us." She wiped at thick tears that fell, one after the other, but could not stem their flow.

The man stood over Lauren, faintly smiling at her. Lauren had to crane a little to see what the woman was doing. But the woman's back was turned.

"Care for the dead, that ironic tenderness for the empty body, the empty vessel — it's something that *Homo sapiens* pride themselves on. It's one of the ways we distinguish ourselves from the rank animals of the field. We care for our dead. We cradle them after they've had grievous harm done to them by injury, by weakness, by the ravages of time. Strange, isn't it, that increasingly humans don't bother with priests or ceremonies. The only way anyone knows they have gone is a note on some computer application. Death has gone digital. Not you, my love. We will send you off properly. We will honour you."

While she spoke she circled the body and Lauren stared raptly at her. She didn't notice Dean approaching with the medic coolers. She did notice when he opened one and marked that it was filled to the brim with fresh ice.

Dean laid out some equipment on one of Lauren's folding tables.

The man in front of her said kindly, "Would you give me your arm?"

She hesitated a little but raised it. The other man quickly cinched it with a tourniquet and before Lauren could start struggling, they had her held down and a thick, angled cannula brusquely pierced through a vein in her inner arm.

"Ow!" managed Lauren. "What are you? Agh! Jesus."

"Just relax." The man encouraged her, and he connected plastic tubing to the other end. A sprig of red blood raced along the length of it and gushed into a plastic collection bag. Still holding her down, they zipped a second cannula into her other arm and Lauren had the impression that the bore of the needle and the plastic tube were thicker than they normally were.

"Hey, uh, that's a lot, like too much, don't you think?"

"It's all right, relax. Just relax," he said again.

"Stop telling me that," Lauren said. "I don't consent to this. I want you to stop."

"Pity for Heloise that no one was there to stop you from taking her. I wonder, if you were caught, what were you going to tell the police?"

Lauren looked up at the woman and it seemed to her that her eyesight had become a little dim. "It's for science. There is something very different about that woman. Something very special. I think she's proof that *Homo sapiens* aren't the only hominids to live on earth."

"Now this is one thing that you and I are actually in agreement on." The woman came close and bent a little at the waist. Dean was swapping out the first bag and replacing it with a second one, which started to fill. He handled it carefully, cradling it with both hands, and laid it inside the cooler, covering it with ice.

"That's too much blood. You're only supposed to take a pint. That's already at least fifteen hundred millilitres."

The woman was level with Lauren's face, her glare stern, punitive. "Heloise was my goddaughter. And she is something other than normal. Not *Homo sapiens* at all. Your precious missing link, as you are so fond of saying in your long-winded, self-important YouTube screeds."

"You've watched them?"

"I like to keep my eye on all sorts of things, 'Professor.'" The woman smiled, making air quotes around the title. "You were not mistaken about that jawbone. A shame you couldn't have managed yourself better. You could have made a decent academic if you weren't such an intolerable narcissist." She drew her fingers along her own trim jaw. "High heme, high protein, low carb, and meat diet. *Homo sapiens* jaws are also shrinking with time. But our jaws developed differently much earlier. Much, much earlier. Our greatest minds think, perhaps as many as a hundred thousand years earlier."

"One hundred. That's … I don't think that's possible." Lauren was finding it hard to get the words out, like she was wading through mud. The woman looked sideways at her but added nothing.

Lauren writhed in her chair. They were swapping out another plastic bag. She was feeling sharp pains in her midsection. "People should know. The world should know. I want them to meet Mina …" She couldn't lift her arm to gesture, but she nodded with her head toward her precious specimen.

"No, my dear. People must never know. We have taken great pains to make sure that they don't. And on my watch, that won't change. You must be feeling quite faint by now?"

Lauren was drooping in her chair. One of the men was holding her shoulders back against the chair back.

"Almost there."

Lauren buckled over. She felt a sharp stomach pain. She tried to pull her arms away from the two men so she could hug it and curl over. Lauren looked up at the woman with wide eyes.

"It's normal to feel some anxiety at this point. You've lost well over fifteen percent of your blood."

"You need to stop," Lauren said, between sips of air. She had begun to pant and swallow frequently. "Why are you here? I don't have time to give blood today. I have work." Even as the words came out, she knew they were irrational.

One of the men was holding her wrist.

"Pulse thinning out fast."

"Am I going to be okay?" Lauren asked him. He smiled down at her. He was handsome and looked friendly. Lauren looked down at her arms and saw that her fingernails were turning blue. Turning them over, curious, she saw her palms were quite pale. "Would it be okay if I lie down?" she asked the woman, with a small distant voice. And as she did, she slid completely off the chair, pooling onto the floor.

"It's fine," one of the men said. The other man was swapping the full bag with a new, empty one.

"What will happen to the specimen, to my Mina?"

"Heloise. We will take very good care of her."

"What about me? Are the police coming for me now? Are you almost done with this?" She raised her weak arms, hampered by the tubing.

"What about you? I imagine that eventually they'll find you. Right near the van you dumped in the canal." The woman leaned closer and hissed into her ear. "But I want you to know this … You are nothing more than an *animal.* She was a specimen to you. To me, you're less than a lab rat. A sheep for slaughter. And now you're just refuse." The word sliced through the fog seeping into Lauren's brain, and she groaned weakly at the castigation.

Lauren blinked at the fluorescents overhead. They were dim, as though someone was pulling on a dimmer switch. The ceiling looked almost black.

"Okay," she said faintly. And she allowed her eyelids to slide closed.

Chapter 45

LUKE

By the time he made it home, Beatrice had been and gone. Were he not actually trained to detect things, he might not have noticed she'd been there: she packed like a guy. Her one bag was gone. Her Keds. Her toothbrush was still there, but damp. No note. She was ghosting him. She knew exactly how much he needed to hear from her, so this was her punishment. Looking back, he realized this was always her way. Retreat when he advanced. Shut him out when he asked for a word. Turn her back when he needed her face. What a fucked-up way to get through life. To constantly push away the one person willing to accept anything. Be anything. Just in exchange for a little warmth.

The sight of her walking away down the street haunted him. It looked like an end-of-the-movie scene.

He tried unsuccessfully to nap on the couch, after clearing space among the baby magazines. He put off eating until the shadows stretched along the kitchen tiles and he was feeling a little light-headed. He ate small, reasoning that she would yet come in and they could begin their usual dance of reconciliation.

He flicked through mindless television. Allowed himself a light beer. Watched trashy reality shows about dysfunctional people and gave up when he realized he was as dysfunctional as any of them.

The problem with me and Beatrice is that we have problems we never discuss … He imagined explaining to a critical reality show interviewer under the glare of a TV camera.

His phone display hit 1:00 a.m. and he felt sick to his stomach. At 2:00 a.m. he rationalized that she was somewhere, likely blissfully asleep, likely not even thinking about him, completely unconcerned by his concern. At 3:00 a.m. he started watching *Vertigo* on an old movie channel but couldn't focus on Jimmy Stewart and his wobbly post-traumatic stress issues.

Bleary-eyed, and desperate to focus on anything but himself, he pulled the copies of files and letters from the Jane Doe safety box. "My Dear Heloise." "My Dear Goddaughter." It made no goddamn sense. Some of the letters were dated back to the 1940s. So maybe her mother was a Heloise too? Had she assumed her name?

One of the letters talked about a miscarriage. It took him a while to read through the lines of the fine handwriting. "A terrible loss … I can only imagine the pain of what you are feeling …" A lot of it was indirect; the writer was trying to be discreet. "I know you are angry with me because I insisted you come here and let yourself be taken care of in our old family ways."

Reams of letters, with dense but disconnected information. He found himself drifting mentally, which was when he was most at risk of intrusive thoughts. The drained, pale face and the smeared mouth of the boy in the alley, for example. His face could pop into Luke's mind as vivid as a photo at any moment. The sunken eyes of the boy in the park. The improbably athletic jogger they'd found … The pathetic cloth-and-velcro wallet of the boy behind the alley, and his still, handsome face. The stain on the floor of that squash court.

Instead of parrying the images of them away, he let them wash over and then soak into him. It was his fault the victims weren't better served. What the hell had Jane been up to? Were there more victims? How could she have been stopped? Why the hell was her cadaver missing? Something even larger than several dead runaways was at work. He felt like he was sinking in the murk of it all. He was trying to get somewhere, just trying to take one step forward. But now the office was out of coffee, and he was wandering the hallways with an empty cup trying to figure out where he could get some.

And then he had to make all these weird detours that drove him farther and farther away from the office, out onto the street it was on, out of the city itself. He was driving up the 400, which was a bad idea. He was looking for coffee but for some reason he was running slowly and out of breath up endless forested hills and a cop was trying to stop him from looking at some bloodied kid. Beatrice was there for some reason, standing nearby in her jacket. And he was laughing, pointing out that the footprints everywhere looked exactly like her Keds. She was angry. To try to placate her, he offered to get her coffee too, which she seemed unimpressed by.

He woke sometime later, shaking off the dream, to find himself near the end of *Vertigo*. A crazed Jimmy Stewart was urging a pliant but reluctant Kim Novak to change her hair. And then she emerged, reborn as the woman Stewart was crazy about. He was an idiot, of course, because he could have had that nice gal with the glasses who would've done anything for him. Instead, he was wrapped up in the mysterious blond woman.

The blond walked toward Stewart, stilted, ghostly and garish in the reflected green light of her cheap hotel room, transformed into some twisted thing of his making …

She looked … Luke sat up, squinting, and spilled what was left of a beer. She looked eerily like Cleo — that same platinum-blond, the cool construction of her face, and her carefully wrought expression. But, no. Just a trick of his addled mind. A 4:30 a.m. mind. He felt a lurch because he realized the house was still empty but for him.

Jimmy Stewart in one of his many grey suits bungled around the screen. Somehow, he managed to look elegant, no matter how distressed he was. His well-cut suits made him think of Harry. The consummate dresser. Ever handsome. The kind of man Beatrice wished Luke would be. Maybe she would have been happier in life with someone like him?

He pulled out his phone and tried to compose an email to Harry. He wasn't sure if he was confessing something or trying to ask something … But every time he started writing, it spun out of control and became a senseless rant.

Need to talk.

It was terse but it was the best his addled brain could come up with. He lay back on the couch and didn't wake again until sometime Saturday afternoon.

Chapter 46

CLEO

Dean and Elias zipped Heloise and Lauren into heavy black body bags, which they covered with blankets. They used a gurney to wheel Heloise outside to the unmarked ambulance parked outside. Dean carried Lauren. Once Heloise was rolled inside, they slung Lauren on the floor. An employee working for the storage facility, a young kid with cotton candy facial fuzz came out, looking concerned.

He caught them heaving the second body bag into the back of the vehicle. Something about that didn't look right to him, even with the official-looking uniforms. He approached the ambulance timidly while Dean got in the driver's side. He rolled down the window and gave the kid a friendly smile.

"Visitors to the facility are all supposed to check in with the front office."

"Not to worry," Dean told him in a soothing voice.

"What's going on?" the kid wanted to know, craning around. "Was there an accident?" He was trying to look past Dean into the ambulance while Dean used his bulk to block him.

"Nothing at all to worry about. We got a call. Some lady had a dizzy spell. We're taking her in to get her looked after. It's all good."

"What else did you put in? I thought that was a body bag, or something."

"It's all good. That was just some stuff we were loading in."

The kid scratched his head under his ball cap. "What about you, lady? Do you need something?"

Cleo shook her head slightly and pivoted on a high heel to get behind the wheel of her own car.

The slightly bewildered kid watched them go, sighed, and wandered back to his dull job where nothing ever happened.

As dusk fell, they stopped briefly a few blocks away, within sight of the city's downtown which caught the setting sun in jewelled tones on the facets of tower windows. Wearing hats and aviators and using gloves, Dean and Elias hauled Lauren out of her body bag and straight into the canal. She slipped into the water feet first, hands over her head, with a high-pitched musical plop as the water closed over her head, and was lost to sight. The intention was that Lauren would soon resurface as decomposition caused gases in her body to make her float.

When night fell first Cleo and then the unmarked ambulance drove down the nearly empty streets of the downtown core. A mechanical door on the side of the Medspa building raised to admit them. They descended to the sub-basements deep below the building.

Dean and Elias wheeled the gurney into the elevator. At the lowest level, the doors whisked open silently. Dean held the door open with a button. Elias passed the gurney through the doors to the waiting hands of attendants but didn't leave the elevator.

Cleo walked stiffly behind Heloise's body. She felt heavy and sluggish.

One of the attendants cast a glance back toward her. "At least she's back home with us now."

Cleo managed a nod.

Female attendants took the gurney through a set of automatic doors, and she passed through, the wheels silent on the thick carpets. Here it was Cleo's turn to watch the doors close, and stay on the other side. Here their paths diverged.

She walked back down the hall and let herself into an office, plainly panelled with dark red wood, with a large desk and islands of modern furniture. She stepped out of her heels and shed her jacket. She unzipped her sheath dress and let it slide down her body. She knelt to take it up in her hand and cast it to the leather ottoman against the wall. She hugged the wall, leaning on one smooth hand and found her way to the bathroom where she stepped numbly into a shower.

The steaming water hit her skin. She welcomed the hot needles, conscious that Heloise was also being meticulously cleaned, and that Heloise would never know or sense anything again. She let the hugeness of that thought, the massive, completeness of death sit in her heart and spread through her entire body. She did not fight it. She did not plead with it. She did not even weep at it. She took it in, completely.

While she shampooed and rinsed, she had the impression it was her hands squeezing the water and foam out of Heloise's hair. As Cleo combed out her wet hair, Heloise, too, had tangles and knots brushed out. Cleo put concealer on under her eyes where the last few weeks had left a trace of wan care. On Heloise they applied dense concealers to cover scratches and discolourations. When they were dry, they both slipped into long dresses of plain, heavy woven material, raw hemmed and without seams. Cleo was wooden. She felt like she was becoming stone. Heloise had petrified into her final form.

Cleo sat for a while at the large desk and pulled a letter out from under the blotter. The envelope was unmarked and unsealed. Inside, a folded paper, many times refolded, so that the puckered seams were supple and fragile.

Dear Heloise, it said. And Cleo found it was hard to make out her own words through a blur of tears.

She didn't need to read them to know every contour of that unsent letter. Heloise had run away many times over the years. She'd run from Cleo and her rules. She'd run into the wild, wanting what she thought of as "organic" food, over Cleo's processed, careful diets, sanitized with secrecy. And over the years, Cleo had begged her to come back to the fold. Letters like this one were proof of her futile efforts.

> *I know you hate me now. I know you blame me. I don't blame you. We've had our debates. I know your heart is wilder than mine. You are a forager. A hunter. And I am a conservator. A shepherd. You want to take what you need, and feel it hot and immediate. I want to cultivate. We all know wild strawberries explode on the tongue with sweetness and that cultivated ones are just a pathetic imitation.*
>
> *You believe with your soul that staying with me during your pregnancy is a death sentence for your unborn child. I know you believe that she would grow emaciated and anemic on a strict, planned medical diet. You want her to feed from the source. It is true. Sometimes the child is lost. Despite the very best efforts.*
>
> *Out in the wild, the child might have thrived at some point, but her birth could have killed you and I would have lost both of you. Here, I could save you*

from that future. Your cravings, and those of the child could be met — and surpassed! Because I have worked my whole life, and tailored the old ways to make sure that the source of life for us is secure so we can continue and thrive, unseen, but safe!

We have always lived in uneasy balance with our needs and the footprint of our need on this planet. We are part of a system. We are the greatest predators in that system. Even the most savage, ruthless predators don't hunt their prey out of existence. Homo sapiens *do. We are not them. Let us not make the same fatal errors. Do you really think it a mistake that they allow themselves to be yoked? They are venal and lawless and base. We are their natural masters. They are our crop, our blood, our birthright.*

Dear child, come back to the fires I built where we can all be warm, and safe.

Cleo refolded the letter and slid it in the envelope.

There was a gentle knock at the door. She admitted Dean, who came into her office and folded her into his long arms. For a moment she allowed herself to be weak, and to lean on him for all the strength in his body. But she left him there to see to the end on her own.

A passageway led directly from Cleo's office to a long, low stone space with sere stone benches. She approached Heloise on noiseless bare feet. The attendants, four of them, stood against two walls, with gazes fixed on the floor.

Cleo breathed around a lump in her throat. It was impossible to process the many thoughts, regrets, dashed hopes she felt standing here. She had vowed to never have her own child. She herself had never crossed to the other side, drunk from the full cup of life, though she could have. No, Heloise had been her assigned successor. The replacement for children she would not have. And now all of that was gone.

Cleo slipped the letter into a fold of the pale wrap Heloise wore. Standing over the body, Cleo held out her arm, open palm upward.

"We are of one blood. Your struggle is done. Go in peace, child. Sister. Mother."

With an acute flick, her other hand moved and the dim overhead lights caught a brief shimmer of light. The drops ran from the wound, in a tiny river, warm against her skin, and instantly cooling. She arced her arm, and a trail of thick, heavy drops followed and drew a pattern, landing on the white cloth, sinking into the dense fibres, staining them with a reckless Jackson Pollock pattern.

An attendant handed Cleo a cloth to bind the small wound, which smarted. She stepped back when the four of them approached the wheeled table.

With a rumble, a heavy door split open and Heloise was birthed into a fire. The flames glared, orange and stinging on the smooth planes of Cleo's face as she watched them surge.

Chapter 47

LUKE

Early in the morning, as cars and trucks hammered along the lakeshore highway nearby, a man and a woman visiting Toronto were exploring the Port Lands by canoe. Residents of Hanover, Germany, they were well acquainted with canals around Hamburg. They'd sailed on the Alster Lake many times, embarking from the Bobby Reich dock near the Krugkoppelbrücke bridge to explore the lakes and canals that made Hamburg sparkle. Bad enough they found Toronto to be a land choked with strip malls and their flavourless cousins, glass condos. They were unimpressed with the lack of city art, public restrooms, or nice places to eat outside.

They were further disappointed to learn that the Keating Channel did not allow them access to the Don River. Instead, as they canoed through the abandoned, sludgy water space, they were forced to agree the area had nothing to recommend it save an interesting view of the corporate downtown and a few torpid ducks, overfed with bread crusts. They clucked their tongues, deeply unimpressed. In Germany they could easily make all kinds of sport throughout the city. Such was the European way.

It was nevertheless a good moment for the pair of them. Their relationship had been on the rocks the last few years, and this vacation was meant to bring them closer together. What Toronto lacked in terms of architecture and culture it made up for in making them feel a tighter bond with each other.

Sniffing with disdain, they agreed to put their tanned, muscular rowing arms to good work and make a circle canoeing around Toronto Island. As fitness nuts, they wanted to be properly tired out ahead of their long flight back overseas. Unfortunately, as they exited the Keating channel, they were alarmed by a slight thump against the hull of their rental canoe.

For at that moment, Lauren's body hit just the right composition of gases to surface and bump up against the hull as they glided by.

She floated up, face down, hair billowing around her head. For a wild moment, they considered paddling on ahead. Someone else could make the report. But they were forced by a rigid moral compass to do the right thing and call their discovery in to the police. It took some frantic internet investigating to find words they never expected to use on vacation: Corpse. Bloated. Marina … no, harbour. Their next hurdle was to figure out how one called the police in this country. The internet came to the rescue again: a 911 call instead of the familiar 110. Only then, there was the question of, was it an emergency, since this person was clearly long past helping, or was it a different number they needed to call?

The upshot was that fire trucks and ambulance and police arrived in a hurry, none of them fully certain what the nationality of the person in the water was. And it took some sorting and a half-German SOCO to figure out that the death was nothing to do with boating, canoes, or travelling Germans.

A dive team quickly sorted out that there was a vehicle nearby, settled in the sediment, nose down in the water. For a while there was a grim worry that someone had perished after accidentally driving into the canal. And for a while there was confusion as to whether perhaps it was a German tourist in a rental vehicle. Once the plate was run, all speculation was put to rest. The car was Lauren's and the body was Lauren's and the Germans were merely bystanders, which put an end to their role in the bizarre story.

Luke spent time on the shore, resting a foot on a rusted-out bollard while divers continued to poke around below the surface of the canal. They sought Jane Doe. They knew their search was further complicated by the fact that they were looking for a body that was past the point of creating gases the way Lauren's had. There were earnest questions as to whether she would rise to the surface or stay below.

But after an exhaustive search of the Keating Waterway, Jane Doe was not to be found.

At the coroner's Gertie stopped what she was doing to come greet Lauren's body.

Partly emerged from the body bag, which lay open like some great damp clamshell, Lauren was unusually pale and waterlogged.

"My god. I talked to her that day," Gertie said with a head shake. She stood with her arms tightly crossed over her body. "She walked right up to me and asked me where the bathroom was, like she belonged here. Jeez. We'll know for sure once we get her examined … but I'd say that looks like a person who has been completely drained of their blood. By amateurs, at that." Both Lauren's arms had massive bruising due to blown veins on the inside of the elbows. Nothing was wrong with the tongue. But then, they knew it couldn't be Jane with her macabre modus operandi who was responsible. Death made for a solid alibi.

Luke reminded Gertie to be kind to herself. No one thinks to question if a random stranger asking for the bathroom is on the cusp of committing an intricate crime like body theft.

“Thanks. I appreciate it. I’m still going to feel guilty as hell about it though. And we’ve got to do something about that entryway. No more people coming in when someone else shows their badge or whatever.”

“You just learn to live with the constant guilt. The shouldas. The couldas.”

“Yeah. Is that your story? Cumulative guilt, honey?” She was organizing sterilized instruments on her tray but squinted up at him with her sharp, birdlike eyes.

Luke thought for a moment about telling her. He toyed with the idea of telling her all about Beatrice, the craziness, the fight, the move. Her apparently having moved out. Not sleeping. The words made their way to the tip of his tongue but not through his lips.

Chapter 48

LUKE

He was sitting in his car, on a side street near his division. At first he was answering emails on his phone while steady rain pattered the car roof. He soon found himself going down the rabbit hole of Lauren's loopy world of YouTube posts. He'd have to watch them and take detailed notes, but for now he scrubbed through her inane banter. She was always hinting that she was about to reveal something, only to yammer on about herself, sponsors, fans, liking, subscribing. And *Hemo sapiens*? He was no history buff, but he was sure the stuff she was spouting was pure crazy. As crazy as Bible-thumpers who claimed dinosaurs and cavemen lived at the same time. Or people who believed aliens "seeded" the planet with intelligent life.

The world outside his car was reduced to an impressionistic green through sheets of rain coating the windshield. He was avoiding the clarity of the office.

His eyes were rimmed and bagged. His shoulders slumped. He had a dozen unanswered phone calls and texts out to Bea. And only one answer, by text:

Don't want to talk.

He was sure that as soon as he walked into work, someone, well-meaning but annoying, would take one look at him and then command him to get on the phone with e-counselling. He knew where that would lead. Some really nice chap would kindly say things like: "And how does this make you feel, to think that your wife has left you? Perhaps permanently? Please realize that the feelings you are having are perfectly normal under the circumstances. The important thing is what self-soothing would get you through the next few minutes? If you can get through the next few minutes, you can surely get through an hour, a day, a week. In this way you can find yourself coping, Mr. Stockton."

Luke knew how to get through minutes, hours, days.

Work.

He was delighted to get through a surprising amount of report filings and correspondence, sitting there in the peace of his front seat. He'd spread out items on the passenger side. A pile to be filed, a pile to be filled out. He was cherry-picking the easy ones with mindless data and details to scribble in. He had worked his way up to finalizing the Keating Channel crime scene report, including splicing in details from the manufacturer about the red Dodge. That was when someone rapped their knuckles on the outside of the passenger window.

He waved them off, deeply annoyed. He'd just gotten into a decent flow. But the rap came again, sharper. He looked up to see Cleo. She was wearing a pale pink trench coat and was stooped slightly to see him. Something about that pale pink bothered him. It was far too girly and innocent a shade for her. It was the colour of infants and nurseries and daycares and toy bunny rabbits.

For no reason that crystallized in his brain, he hesitated before he hit the unlock button. It wasn't fear or annoyance or distrust.

It was an amber caution light that glowed for a brief moment deep inside his brain, just barely on the edge of his consciousness.

She swung in as he was clearing the passenger seat and for a flicker, his hand inadvertently grazed the pink coat hugging her flank. He pulled his hand away as though burned. She noticed the gesture. And laughed, lightly.

"Oh, don't worry, I won't sue."

"This is disturbing, Ms. Drover. I look people up at their home or work. I don't like it going the other way."

"You gave me your card. I happened to see you parked near the" — she glanced at his card, pulled out from a pocket — "Fourteen Division. Right here."

Luke sat back in his seat, leaning against the driver side door. Which was as much space as he was able to create between them in the car. Her scent filled the vehicle, subtle cardamom, and orange.

"What can I do for you since you've come all this way? Anything I can put in my report?"

"I can't believe someone took her. It's utterly barbaric." She turned, as though acting on a sudden thought. "Can you … drive us? Away from here."

Again, Luke hesitated. Some competing force in his brain compelled him to press his foot on the brake and punched the ignition on. He slipped past 14 Division as she settled into his passenger seat, head leaning back, chin up. Eyes closed. Okay then.

"You want me to look for an abandoned car park?"

She turned to look at him blankly.

"Like in the movies. Cloak-and-dagger stuff. That's what this feels like." He turned away and gripped the wheel. "Never mind."

"I suppose a car park would do."

He nodded. The air in the car felt like syrup. She was completely relaxed in his passenger seat, and leaned her head back again, eyes closed. Hands limp and easy, one on each knee that peeked out from the opening of her pink trench. She could have been sleeping. But he could sense her energy coiled up inside her.

The car plied the side streets of the west-end neighbourhood around 14 Division until they emerged on Croatia. The vehicle slipped behind a shopping mall where loading bays and chewed-up asphalt met a wild overgrowth of poplars and grass. Cabbies came here to get forty winks. It was busy most evenings with drug dealers on BMX bikes.

"How's this?"

She opened her eyes dreamily. One eyebrow made the slightest lift. Any higher he might have read it as judgment, but he couldn't parse this.

"Fine."

Strange, empty moments passed, crackling with potential energy, unspoken words. Despite years of training, learning to patiently wait for perpetrators in cinder-block rooms to break under his charm and affability, it was Luke who broke the silence that surged into the car first.

"What's this about, Cleo?"

"You," she said, simply. She leaned against her door. Not to be distant, but to take him in fully with her gaze. She added a warm smile. And the silence surged back again, while he processed the shock. It was the elevator all over again. He swore his arm hairs were all standing up.

He laughed a little. "Okay. I …"

Before he could speak, she put her hand on his kneecap, at which point for Luke all the air went out of the car.

She was leaning in toward him. He wasn't leaning into her, but neither was he pulling away.

"I …" she said as though she was starting to say something. But she stopped, and it hung there as an imperfect sentence. She reached her right hand across him, letting it brush his shirt, and laid it along the side of his neck, just under the jawbone where his blood pulsed under his skin. She ran her hand over the sand of his stubble, the faint creases in his flesh, the throb of his heart.

She swung over. Somehow, she was still elegant in that compressed space. With the inside of her knee laid on his thigh, she put her mouth on his. He was aware of her warm, spiced scent, and the line along his inner lip where it changed from dry to wet. Her lips were strong, her lips plush. He pushed into the kiss, felt the lightning bolt shock of her tongue that flickered through him from mouth past navel to groin. It was *her* tongue of all things, a wicked, unsanctioned knowing hot dart of energy. This was when she swung over fully, losing one shoe, to sit astride him. Locks of his hair and his skull in her two hands, she commanded full commitment to this kiss.

He arched against her. That was his action. That was his choice. He had a pent-up hunger of need and abandonment and hunger for touch and warmth. And the atavist surge of desire in tandem with it. No wonder they called it getting some action. There wasn't a molecule of him that wasn't firing.

But he ripped his lips, his jaw, his head, his whole self away. He tore free like a surfacing swimmer looking for air.

Cleo leaned her head back, looking down at him from a tilted face. She fell back into the passenger seat, withdrawing and folding back first one leg and then the other.

She heaved a sigh.

"It's a mistake, of course," she admitted, and the tone of her voice, the frankness made everything so much more awful and naked and knowing.

"Yeah. I'll say." His voice cracked like an angsty teen.

"I couldn't not, though." There was that chuckle again. It felt mocking.

"Hmm." Silence. "I'm married. I'm working a case. That I've questioned you on. This is … no. This is a no."

Silence again.

She laughed soft, and slightly cynical. “Oh, but you’re the big game. You’re the prize.”

“Come on. I am a regular person. And this isn’t a safari.” That felt idiotic as soon as it came out. “I have a life. My wife has a life with me. I can’t do this. I *don’t* do this.” He thought he should shut up more. He was certain she would read that he was telling himself more than her. That he was weak and would crumble to dust at a mere touch, only to re-liquify if pressed further.

“You’re a regular, committed person. A good man. A decent man. You’re big game to someone like me, because in the trenches of polyamory and fluid commitment, turning you would be a … feat. I think there’s a fantasy to someone like you. Can the domesticated be turned back to the wild …” She’d been staring forward out the window. But she turned to him. “You’ve been so very good. You’ve done what you’ve promised. We’re not so different on that account. Do you ever wonder, even a little, if you picked the wrong thing to apply yourself to?”

“Yeah, no. I’m firmly in the barn. In the stable. In the pen, whatever. Leashed.”

“Stop it,” she said. “You’re not helping.”

“Ugh, yeah, I didn’t mean it that way. I’m happily tied down — oh, forget it. I’m not available.”

“It’s nice I hope, to feel … wanted?”

Now he was the one to lay his head back. He had a lump in his throat he was not going to tell her anything about. He had an ache in several parts of his body; chiefly, a Beatrice-sized one in his heart. His eyes were prickling at the edges. He just wished Beatrice had come to him. Just once in a while.

“Look, I’m sorry. I don’t want to be hurtful by rebuffing you,” he stammered. He wanted to take care of her feelings, even though he was aware that she had come on to him without a shred of empathy for his. “We’re all animals. We’re all barely civilized. Feelings. Urges. Fuck.”

"Fuck, indeed." She laid into the first syllable with a particular heat, sounding the *K* unnecessarily loud. Like someone biting into something.

He adjusted himself in the seat. Made himself think about filing taxes. Watched his finger as it pressed the ignition.

"I'll drive you back."

But her hand was on the door handle and then she was out of the car. "I'll order myself an Uber. Please don't worry about getting me back." She held a hand up against his weak protests. "I've taken enough of your time." She started walking. She didn't look hurt or wounded. In fact, when he pulled up next to her, powering along in her ever-present heels, she almost had, he thought, a smirk?

"You going to be okay?" he asked through the window.

She was still walking. After a beat she turned to him with a placid expression, and then threw in a cool smile.

"Oh. Absolutely."

Chapter 49

LUKE

Luke sat on one of the twirly stools at the Olympic Diner. One of the bad ones, wobbling with a seasick to and fro. It was probably an easy fix. An extra couple of ball bearings and maybe a spritz of WD-40. He kept feeling his sacrum tilt when he shifted, or glanced one way or even breathed, for Chrissakes. The wobble made his stomach list and dance.

He'd rebuffed the waitress four times now. He could tell she was annoyed with him for taking up a seat at the busy time without ordering. He thought several times about ordering Harry's regular, so there would be a hamburger and a coffee waiting, ready to go. He wanted to blast through the pleasantries like "pass the ketchup" or "hi, how are you" and plunge straight into "What the fuck am I going to do with my life?"

But Harry was late.

Luke ordered one of their Greek plates, which always seemed to make them happy. It gave him about eight different perfectly executed items to shove listlessly with his fork.

Can't make it. Gotta reschedule.

When Harry's text came in, Luke swore out loud. He threw two twenties down on the counter and fled for the exit, dialing Harry on the run.

"Hey." By the sound of his voice, Harry was annoyed. That was fine. So was Luke.

"I'm sorry, man."

"Uh-huh." Harry was really annoyed. "I told you I needed to reschedule because I didn't have time, Luke. I'm snowed under here. I thought you'd respect that."

"I need help, Harry. I made contact with a witness, maybe a suspect."

"Okay." Luke could tell Harry was distracted, shuffling papers.

"Intimate contact."

The shuffling stopped.

"Luke, what the fuck."

"She found me. Came onto me. And Beatrice left me."

"Luke!" There was a pause. "Did you fuck her?"

"No, I did not fuck one of the chief witnesses, maybe a suspect in a murder investigation. Give me some credit. But I'm neck-deep in a whack of cases it means I have to just walk away from."

"So, you walk. Done. You could also lose your marriage."

"Yeah, that too."

"One, you need to do some slow box breathing, my friend. Two, you need to get off the phone from me and talk to someone who can really listen. Call the mental health hotline."

Ouch. Friend and not friend in one breath. "Yeah. You're one hundred percent right. Glad I called."

"And you need to take yourself off the case."

Luke knew that. And it was the last thing he wanted to hear. So instead of answering, all he did was breathe into the receiver.

"Hey buddy, I'm about to go on camera, call me whe—"

Luke pressed the red button. He didn't need to hear the rest: *I'm busy. Tell your problems to someone who cares. You're on your own. Yada yada.*

He power walked around the block, running things through his head, and the power walking drove more breaths into his lungs, which was a bonus.

There was no way Cleo was mooning over him, of all people. She had three guys on tap, completely under her thumb, and she needed to travel across town just to hit on him? At best if she was interested, it was as a tourist. She was curious if she had enough power, enough draw to make him cheat on his wife. He was big game. Well, maybe more like small game. More like a mouse she wanted to bat around.

One small glimmer he held on to was that, despite all his fucked-up feelings and needs and wants, he had not given in. He was still a good guy. He could look at himself in the mirror in the morning and know he was a fuck-up, yes, but not a low-life cheater.

He had still done the right thing, even if Beatrice had completely left him. He was clean. And he did not appreciate Cleo coming into his life and fucking with his head.

No. Cleo had not come to seduce him. She was up to something else.

And then he had a sick thought: Harry, Beatrice. Could that explain her strange behaviour? Or Harry drop-kicking him? That thought was as far as his own brain would allow him to go. Because it was too much to bear.

Chapter 50

LUKE

He pulled into the double car driveway, a little off the asphalt because the neighbour was too close to his side, again. The lights were off. The door was firmly locked. No signs of Beatrice.

He almost missed the package in the mailbox. And as soon as he saw it, his heart sank. Divorce papers. He knew it. She didn't want to talk. She just wanted to race straight to a separate life. He seized it in an angry fist and whipped it onto the couch.

He fixed himself a slow, leisurely meal. He sliced garlic and onions into painstakingly small pieces. He gently sautéed, he carefully browned. He seared a lamb chop and let it sit and mellow while he made a thick, luscious sauce. He made rice and wilted spinach. He sat down, and forced himself to eat, slowly, cutting off reasonable bites and chewing with a measured pace. He forced himself to fucking savour it. He paced himself through one glass of red wine and didn't finish the last swallow until the meal was done too. He walked to the sink. He rinsed oh-so-carefully.

Only then did he walk to the couch and pick up that goddamned manila envelope from where it lay face down and crumpled on the couch.

His name was on the cover, typed. On a label. No mention of a law firm on the outside, so just how many thousands of dollars this would cost him was still a mystery.

His heart seized for a second in a peristalsis of grief.

How *could* she? After everything they'd been through. Why? *Why* would she? Everything they'd worked for together was just being casually thrown away.

He swallowed the panic and denial down. And tore open the envelope.

Inside, no legal papers.

Instead, he found a photo of himself, which he had to stare at for a few moments, stupidly, in order to comprehend. Tilting his head, he saw his body was completely wrapped by Cleo. And their mouths were clamped on each other. His head thrown back in what could only be considered by a casual observer to be ecstasy.

Never mind the whole thing had lasted maybe three minutes and was punctuated by a clear and firm "no thanks" and buckets of guilt and shame and upset and absolutely no ecstasy. These photos of lips, mouths, hands, eyes, legs expertly captured by an adept, long lens were not going to editorialize about consent. They were a clickbait headline meant to drive the viewer to immediate condemnation and a conclusion: Luke Stockton didn't deserve his wife, or to stay on the case he was on. Or to carry a badge at all.

When the photos were spread out across his coffee table, he realized he was looking at the deconstruction of a career, spelled out over twenty-five glossy black-and-white eight-by-tens. Delivered straight to his doorstep. Which meant she knew where he lived. And as long as she was still his wife, where Beatrice lived.

He paced through the house, lapping his kitchen island, thinking. He mentally rehearsed going straight to his commanding officer: "So, I got caught up in this thing ..." No. He thought about putting something through the plate glass windows of her house. Like his boot. Or his whole fucking car. No. Of course not. He could try coming straight out — media? Whistle blow. "I was set up, this wasn't consensual ..." That was going to be an uphill battle. The photos did not make it look like he was fighting her off.

It was time for Luke to colour outside the lines he'd spent a lifetime abiding by.

He pulled out his phone and sent one text to Harry.

Thanks for the advice. Will take it. Might make front page of *Toronto Sun*, or fill a body bag in 3 days, in which case, pls call 14 Division. Also, made you executor for my will. Meant to tell you. Sorry. I trust no one else.

Chapter 51

LUKE

Luke needed something he could drive, but not be recognized by.

Several vehicles were at his disposal in the division's garage, usually through strict channels of requisition for undercover guys. He pasted on a menschy face to shortcut some red tape with the guy who signed them out.

He selected a set of wheels: an ugly little minivan. Tinted windows at the back, tinted windows for the driver and passenger seats. A plain white panel van. It could park anywhere and disappear into traffic.

Hunched down in the driver's seat, Luke waited outside the Medspa, parked on Bay. He watched her arrive in her silver Maserati and nose down into the private garage entrance. He was prepared for a long stakeout with beverages and food. But he ate nothing and nursed an ache in his belly instead, which felt like staying keen.

Around lunchtime, as rain clouds threatened, he almost missed her peeling out of the garage and into dense traffic. He cranked the van on and shot out in front of another driver going well over the speed limit. He bore the angry woman's honking and middle finger and tailgating for blocks while he weaved through traffic behind Cleo's car. He kept two vehicles between the van and the Maserati to stay out of sight. Cleo had a habit of running yellows that turned red halfway through the intersection and Luke was forced to drive right when they'd gone red or risk losing her. Which meant even more paperwork at some grim point in the future.

She drove herself to a members-only club, where Luke was forced to drive around a boxwood roundabout several times before parking in a loading zone. From there he saw her emerge on the heated, glassed-in patio with several men in grey suits. When she arrived, all three men stood and kissed her on the cheek not once but three times. While he chewed on cheese sandwiches, they collectively put away three bottles of wine, and Cleo drank her fair share. There were many toasts. Luke would have given a lot to know what the celebration was about. He also noticed, while appearing engrossed in his iPhone screen, that the man on Cleo's side kept sliding his hand along her knee, just under the hem of her skirt.

When they finished the meal, a valet brought Cleo her vehicle. She slipped behind the wheel, looking loose and cocky. The hand-to-knee man got in the passenger side of her car. A valet brought a conservative BMW around and the other two men got in that. He could have simply pulled her over then and there for blood alcohol level but his stakeout would have ended then too, with nothing to show for it.

They inched through grim traffic made worse by a now-steady downpour. He almost lost her toward Downsview but caught up thanks to a road crew blocking a lane. She was followed aggressively by the BMW. Moments later they were all westbound on the 401, cutting through a fine spray off the asphalt. At the turnoff to the airport, Luke felt a squeeze of concern. If she was leaving the country, he was fucked.

He tried to stay calm and reasoned that there were many reasons to exit near the airport. The fear edged back in as they took the airport exit. But they didn't go to any of the terminals.

They bypassed the nest of twining Arrivals and Departures roads. Instead, Cleo took a side road. The rarified world of private jets. So … not out of the woods. Cleo and the BMW slid past security at the compound with plastic fobs. Luke pulled his badge out of a pocket as he watched them enter.

He felt a prickle of anxiety. Things could go a few ways with the security guy. As a semi-public space, even a security guard couldn't really bar a member of the force from conducting police business without looking sketchy. If Cleo was up to something nefarious, the guy could well be on the take.

"Hey," said the guard through the window on his booth. He looked dead-eyed tired.

"Good afternoon. I'm conducting some police business here today. Need to access the terminal." He passed his badge over for the kid to look at. If the guard wanted, he could kick up a fuss. Ask for a warrant. Fifty-fifty chance he might, and Cleo could escape.

A hint of light came into the security guy's eyes.

"You down at Fourteen Division?" he asked.

"Yeah," said Luke. It said so right on the ID.

"You undercover?"

"In my civvies," said Luke with a cheerful lilt. They *were* his clothes, so it wasn't a lie.

"Huh." The interest in the guy's eyes dissipated, and he looked away, but waved Luke through the gate with a limp hand.

Chapter 52

CLEO

At YYZ a private jet with a Swiss registration number was cleared for landing only ten minutes late, and this was only because of the usual congestion at Toronto International airport, and nothing to do with the Swiss pilots who'd circled, waiting for a strip for almost half an hour.

Cleo waited in a chilly arrival lounge, legs casually crossed, unhurried, unconcerned. The warmth of several glasses of Pommery still coursed through her veins and synapses. She knew the Swiss arrivals would clear customs quickly. The paperwork was impeccable. Her shipment was routine.

Thanks to her friends in Switzerland, Cleo had frequently arrived to accept medical passengers transferred to her clinic's care. Their needs ranged from the dull to the pathetic. Some were cosmetic clients, sent by the sister clinic in Geneva. These were purely for show, for the Medspa's public face. Increasingly, the focus was experimental treatment of various consciousness disorders. There were those with profound catatonia who had lain in hospital beds for years. Cleo's colleagues recruited these clients. Many of them had parents with some means who had not run out of hope. Cleo's Medspa offered full coverage, daring treatments, and 24/7 dedicated care to grateful relatives ready to try anything. Some were the unresponsive wakeful — those once unkindly called "vegetative." Others were trauma-induced coma victims. And in one case, Tomas they called him, an unknown soldier of misfortune, plucked from a Bosnian battlefield. His body was in perfect condition, but his mind was held captive. He'd never been claimed by any country.

The treatments were real, and progress had been made. Cleo thought of their work as mental physiotherapy for the unconscious. They walked unresponsive patients through talk exercises that bade them to imagine preparing their favourite meal and then sitting down to eat it with a loved one for example. Or they might picture helping a young child tie their shoes or untangle a kite, or picture getting out of bed on a hot day to take a refreshing shower. Remarkably, nearly half their patients registered brain wave activity as they were talked through these steps.

The researcher's voices descended into the depths of the sleeper's deep solitary confinement, bringing new notes, new ideas, new stimulus to their long-forgotten souls. Cleo's team was able to prove unequivocally that the patients had wilfully formed thoughts in response, despite the severity of their persistent states of outward unconsciousness.

The clinic's poster child was one young man who had sat up in his bed one morning by himself. With a creaky, chalky voice, he'd asked a nearby nurse for a drink of water. He'd been unconscious since he was a child, and now, almost twenty years later, had rejoined the living. He'd undergone an aggressive approach of mental imagery, powerful repetitive transcranial magnetic stimulation, transcranial direct current stimulation, vagus nerve stimulation, sensory stimulation, and manual physiotherapy to encourage physical arousal and aid and encourage postural control, some of which aimed to "trick" the patient's body into connecting with the mind, which had brought him back to the surface.

Despite the jubilation of the patient, his family, the team, and the media, it was all a ruse. None of these pilot patients was the point of the exercise. The medical gains were beside the point. The money coming into the clinic from international families was beside the point. The international teams formed and research papers written: beside the point.

Most of the patients arriving today were themselves the entire point.

They were lost souls. They were those who had given up, spirit and body. They were Medical Assistance in Dying candidates who had consigned themselves to calm, graceful, thoughtful, and thorough care of the Swiss clinic they'd entered. They never expected to leave. They'd paid quite handsomely to have their lives medically cleaved from their bodies. The clinic was very good at what it did, which was to give clients what they wanted: death.

For the most part.

There were certain cases though, carefully sifted out from the others, generally in the best health as far as that was possible, and those with the slimmest ties to the material world. The childless orphans. The young widowed. The coma victims who'd had paperwork carefully wrought absolutely not to resuscitate. For an enormous fee, and under cover of criminal secrecy, they'd been earmarked and rendered not dead, but commercial.

To all outward appearances, there was a thorough and meticulous paperwork trail. It included exquisitely forged birth certificates and passports. They arrived at the clinic in Switzerland as would-be medically assisted death clients. They arrived in Canada as repatriated persistent vegetative citizens. The smooth paper trail lied about patients who'd sought their deaths and received it. And the paper trail, with perfect penmanship, did a sleight of hand: the dead lived on, renamed. Silent sleepers, they were reborn. They were submitted to changes of identity and citizenship. They took late-night ambulance rides and transatlantic flights. They arrived in Canada as lovely, warm bodies in need of Cleo's particular care.

It was victimless. It was beautifully constructed. It simplified a supply chain issue. All good corporate management sought to vertically integrate wherever it was possible. Close the loops between product and consumer to shorten the chains. Cleo had a hungry clientele with an unending need. And a need to sanitize her supply.

A Swiss doctor deplaned at the same time as Cleo's cargo, walking just behind them. They made quite a parade: four patients rolled through the doorway, each one with several wheeled IVs and orderlies to pass them through. The cost was astronomical, and entirely worth it. Through glass partitions, Cleo watched the handover observed by border guards.

They met in a glass room where they could be seen by guards and customs on all sides. It was a tiny international zone. The Swiss doctor came in one side, she came in from the other. As soon as the paperwork was complete, and the vitals were checked, Cleo took charge of her patients. Patients who were never to wake again, nor know that they had journeyed onward from Switzerland. They had given themselves over to eternal embrace. Little did they know there was so much more in store for them.

"Who have we got here?" asked Cleo as she leaned over one of the patients. "Why, Tomas. Hello." She placed a hand on his cheek.

"You know him?"

"Oh yes." She stroked his hair. "We've been acquainted for a while, through Switzerland. Incredible case. Such progress. I'm excited for what is ahead for us."

She walked out with them to the tarmac to see the gurneys loaded into three helicopters. Each one carried a patient, a doctor, and two orderlies. The airport wind whipped Cleo's hair and jacket against her, but she stood still as a picture, unbothered, eyes sharp on the transfer.

Chapter 53

LUKE

Outside the arrivals door at the executive terminal at the private airfield, Luke hung near his vehicle, wearing a grey windbreaker and a hipster toque. He pretended to check things off an empty clipboard. He was relieved to see Cleo re-enter her car, meaning she hadn't disappeared into the air on a private flight.

As soon as she exited the private terminal building, he tossed the clipboard in the back and got behind the wheel, ready for wherever she went next. Luke followed Cleo back downtown to Bay Street and arrived in time to see the distinctive red cross on the belly of the last of the helicopters circling the rooftop. Cleo slipped down the parking ramp.

Luke pulled a duffle bag from behind the passenger seat and unzipped it. He was ready to change into a contractor cover — collar shirt and hard hat, City of Toronto Engineering ID, silver clipboard, laser measuring device. That and a bunch of bluff would get him only so far. It was that or attempt to convince Genevieve the receptionist that he was here on urgent police business. Which would be strictly untrue. And crossing that boundary meant crossing into an unlit room full of pitfalls. Not that falsifying identity would be any better. But he knew that Cleo was after him, willing to go to his home, willing to put him in a compromising position, willing to blackmail him … for what? For what bigger purpose?

His phone buzzed with a text.

His heart leapt. Beatrice, finally. His brain was tripping over itself with things he wanted to say. But no.

Harry.

WTF? Will? *Sun* front page? Did you call the mental health hotline yet or not?

It was rare for Harry to seem so histrionic.

Luke texted back: Sure. Called. Took a Chill Pill.

It still stung to see Harry's earlier text "talk to someone who can really listen" sitting right there in the back-and-forth window. He stared out the window, thinking about how terrible the calculus of all this was. His phone pinged again, and he thought, *Thanks for nothing, Harry.*

Instead, this time, Beatrice.

I'm sorry I have been out of touch. Things are weird.

The elation at seeing her words there was surreal.

Weird is right.

The pusling dots told him she was responding as he continued typing.

I'm at the Medspa now.

He'd hoped she was at the Medspa too. Then they could meet. But then her response disappeared. And no text came from her.

Please trust me when I say I think the place is dangerous, he added. He typed it fast. Hoping some combination of words would make her see he was on her side, always. Only. Her response leapt up again. Disappeared. Reappeared. Went quiet.

A ping.

I do give a shit about you.

Another flood of feelings. Relief. A lump in his throat. And then he saw … Harry?

He'd thought it was Beatrice telling him that. Instead, it had been Harry. Which was confusing.

Don't do anything I wouldn't. Where are you now? wrote Harry.

Medspa. Luke punched the text in and sent, with heat. And then regretted it.

Stay put, wrote Harry.

Then Beatrice: Let's please talk in a couple of days. I'm at the house. Picking up some things.

Luke's blood ran cold. She would see the photos. They were out. On the coffee table, intermixed with her baby magazines. Nice picture that would make.

Beatrice. I –

He didn't get a chance to finish. There was a sharp knock on the driver side window.

Luke rolled the window down at the sight of old Mr. L.L.Bean himself, standing right there on Bay Street. Smoking a cigarette.

"Dean?"

Chapter 54

CLEO

Inside the building a dedicated elevator waited to take patients from the helicopters down to the sub-basement. Tenderly, they were ferried like precious works of art. They were transported through hushed, seamless halls. Support workers moving through the hallways came to a halt and bowed their heads as the patients passed by.

The patients were not destined for hospital rooms. Cleo fell into step behind the last of them and traced a path to a set of double doors that opened on a massive space. Far from looking like a patient ward, it had the aggressive architecture of a public building, an opera house or a court. It was hushed and serene, lofty and light. The ceilings of the sub-basement were high. In this space they were gilded and vaulted.

The new patients were wheeled in through the massive double doors that opened on silent hinges. The staff lined up to greet them in long queues, with solemn deference, as though they were some kind of dignitary. They were wheeled toward the centre where interlocking cubicles fanned out, part of a massive grid. Two hundred spaces arrayed in strict geometry, each one of them fed by IVs and tended to, as honeycombs are, by diligent workers. Nurses paid constant, careful attention.

Cleo walked among the aisles. She trailed her hand along the partitions separating the sleepers.

"Here you will stay," she murmured to herself as she paced along. Sweet music played, barely audible. The air was scented. Plants twined under UV lights, coiling among the rafters, tracing through the tubing and wires, camouflaging them. The beds the patients lay on were a peak of technology: tilted, ergonomic, their cargo was swaddled in silk and sheepskin. The nurses spoke gently to them. They massaged them, they coaxed fluids into them. They bathed their limbs as tenderly as any mother ever bathed her child.

Each of the new patients was wheeled to a waiting bay, where they were met by a dedicated team of attendants. While Cleo oversaw they were washed, dried, anointed. Their feeding tubes, IV lines, and catheters were meticulously installed. The attendants had gentle, efficient hands, not that any of the patients were conscious enough to feel. Finally, they were dressed in sleek, utilitarian garments.

A man with a silver tray approached Cleo, bearing bowls bored from massive bones, long, long ago. A bone-handled brush. Pure spring water. Ochre.

Cleo dipped and mixed with a practised hand. She stirred the ruddy, purplish ochre into a thick, satisfying paste.

"We'll start with you, Tomas," she said as she leaned over the young man's inert form.

On his forehead she used the brush to weave a circle, with an equal-armed cross inside. She bowed her head, briefly saying silent words. And when she was done with each one, all around her, attendants broke into spontaneous, quietly gloved but enthusiastic applause.

Chapter 55

RENARD

Martin was thinking. He was flipping through the things he could still remember in order to stay alive, if this place of lying in a bed and forever looking at ceilings could be called alive.

If he could have, he would have shouted or moved.

Failing that, if he could have, he would have found a way to swim way down and stay down and let the lights go out forever, because this halfway existence was just shit.

Josée. Whom I loved.

Rimouski. Where I lived.

My parents, gone.

Army.

Bosnia.

Red Cross.

Switzerland.

Hospital.

Since Switzerland he'd taken in a dizzying amount of information. The hum of the flight. The changes in air pressure. It had gotten so that swimming up to the surface of thought was more challenging. Some days, he wondered if he had enough stamina to keep trying. After the long flight, at last a destination. Canadian border guards — Canadian … that sounded like something. Like home? Toronto was so much nearer to Rimouski. The idea made something stir, deep within, it swirled the dark waters he swam in. But Rimouski might as well have been on the moon to him. Or at the top of a mountain to a fish in the sea.

After the helicopters and the enclosure of the elevator, the golden double doors and the high, high ceiling were a shift. What a welcome sight; the gilding and the arches and the paintings on the ceiling. He could see dancing deer, flowing brooks, waving wheat, cup bearers, stylized suns and moons. Maidens danced, men brandished weapons. He could almost feel his synapses regrouping and growing just to wander through those images.

But his view of the ceiling was soon obscured by attendants wearing dark scrubs. He caught glimpses of tubing and sponges, salves, and bandages as they worked on him. He was aware of the pressure but had no feeling when he was transferred to a table and thoroughly hosed off, blotted, soaped, dried, oiled. They shaved him, trimmed his nails, oiled his cuticles, working silently, working reverentially.

When he was dressed, he saw her again, the blond. He remembered the *K* sound but not her whole name.

"I think it fitting that we start with you, Tomas."

That name again, which was not his. It still irked him. But it filled him with bliss, just to see her.

"You'll remember me, I'm Cleo, from the Swiss clinic," she murmured to him, conversationally. She had always spoken to him as though he were awake and alert. Others tended to speak in monosyllables and broken sentences as if he were an idiot, not locked inside.

"This is ochre, Tomas. I wonder if you can feel the sensation of it as I paint it on your forehead?"

He could not, but he paid attention as her hand swivelled, holding the brush.

"Ochre is an ancient pigment, Tomas, rich in iron and found all over the world. Archeologists have found evidence of it being used *ceremonially* by hominids for nearly four hundred thousand years. The red, Tomas, the red is the thing. It's like the colour of blood. It signifies creation. Life. Sustenance." She traced his jaw. "The red was something new, once upon a time. Those of us who went on two legs could see it. It became a way for us to recognize who among us was conscious. Who had the gift of sight. Who had the gift of thought. We saw you. Long, long ago, in some forest or field. Painted with red, making sounds that bonded your group, bright eyes full of curiosity and wariness."

Tomas watched her as she painted, half in love with her. He knew how much she treasured him.

"This ochre I am using has been ritually heated and processed and transformed into hematite, which we Sanguin prize for its transformation from yellow to deep red, the same way the sun transforms energy into plants, plants into animals, animals into man, man into blood. This is an ancient chain of activity, Tomas, which we are binding you to. And we thank you for your sacrifice, for the gift of red that you give to us."

He hoped that she understood, though he could not speak, that he did want her to have his complete sacrifice.

"The image I paint for you is a token of the gift we gave to you, in return for your sacrifice. Your blood, our letters. The cross is nothing one sees in nature; two straight lines, intersected together — it's unnatural. It is a sign, as sure as ochre, that says 'We were here. We made our mark.' You are key to us as sun on leaf and wheat in field and water in stream. You are our dear lamb."

Here she paused and he saw her hold up a big needle. He could not feel the prick as she found a good, thick vein.

"Good. Good, Tomas. The blood in your veins is your gift to us. If we draw in small, regular doses, the body hardly notices the difference. By regularly releasing blood, the body is purified and strengthened. In the raw times of old, our dear lambs were utterly drained, and we wept to see our favourites make the ultimate sacrifice so that we could live. But no more. I have made this place where we can live symbiotically with our flocks."

She kissed Martin upon the lips, and he thought he could perhaps feel the pressure. "Thank you, Tomas," he heard her say from a great, great distance.

I am not Tomas, he thought, petulantly. He wanted her to know who he was, since he was to give everything to her.

There was a steady beep of a machine nearby. His breathing steadied, mechanically assisted. Cleo smoothed a hand down along his cheek, down his arm, down along his flank, lingeringly, but he did not note it.

And at that moment, Martin, once known as *Le Renard*, thought no more.

Chapter 56

LUKE

"I didn't figure you to be a smoker."

"Oh, I'm not." Dean smiled. He took one more drag, inhaled deeply, coughed a little, and tossed it, half-smoked, to the ground. "I wanted to try it, just once. Impulse thing."

"I got a little package from your girlfriend," Luke told him.

"Hmm." Dean nodded and smiled, in a friendly but distant kind of way.

"You know all about that?"

"Sure, sure. She keeps me up on just about everything." Dean seemed distracted while speaking.

"Well, I kinda thought stuff over," Luke said, running his finger over the steering wheel. "She filled me in on a bunch of stuff, and let's just say, I'm reconsidering my whole relationship thing."

"Yeah!" Dean smiled again, really broadly. Was he high? There was something odd about his enthusiastic, distant warmth.

"Are you okay?"

"Yeah, sure." Dean kept up the doltish smile and bobbed his head in a kind of groove.

"You think I could see Cleo?"

"See her. Wow. Okay. Yeah. I guess. I guess yeah."

"You're sure you're okay?"

"It's, um, it's a really interesting day, man." He put his two hands out as though that explained it. He stepped back from the vehicle as Luke got out. "Did you get your car fixed?"

"What? Oh, right. Yeah. Loaner. Can we go in?"

Dean nodded again, and Luke thought he seemed more and more out of it all the time. He walked ably enough across the street, but jaywalked into traffic that just barely stopped for him. Luke supposed people as good-looking as him were used to traffic stopping. Before they went in, Dean paused with his hand on the door handle and looked up at the sky. The rain had passed and the clouds had parted, like massive curtains. Bright blue shone through, piercing and brilliant, as though the rain had scrubbed the sky.

"The light, man. So beautiful." His face was almost beatific. Luke glanced at him surreptitiously. For sure the guy was high.

"Yeah. It's something."

Dean took them to the elevator in the lobby and used his fob. Something chimed as he waved it over a reader. The doors closed. Luke watched with interest as they went down. Dean leaned on the railing with his doltish smile still pasted on, gazing up at the ceiling as though he was still looking at that blue sky. Luke took out his phone. He watched the floors count down on the display. Mezzanine, Concourse, LL1 LL2, P1, P2 … P2 was the last floor a person could select, but Dean hadn't selected a floor. He'd just waved a fob. Luke felt them still descending even when the lowest floor had pinged and gone.

At Medspa. Bay Street. There's a sub-basement. Just in case someone needs to know.

He considered sending this as a text to Beatrice, but hesitated and sent it to Harry instead. He could still feel the floor of the elevator vibrating as they descended.

The text lagged on his screen and a progress bar showed up. Luke wasn't sure the text would even send, now.

The doors opened with a muted ping. Luke was greeted by a sumptuous hallway, carpet. It looked like a luxury hotel more than an office building basement. The hallway curved gently, punctuated at long intervals with low doorways. It reminded him of the sweep of a stadium, or auditorium.

He checked his phone. No bars. He pocketed it as he followed Dean as he loped down the hallway.

He could hear a slight drone of voices, and for a moment the drone became a hushed swell. It was the sound of many voices, responding in union.

"Oh, hey, man." Dean chuckled and rubbed the long hair on his head, absently. "I totally forgot. I gotta be in a different place. Can you just wait here? I'll tell someone to come get you."

Luke watched him disappear around the bend in the hall, walking strangely on the toes of his feet, almost bouncing.

The sound of the voices rose again, and fell, indistinct.

His head tilted toward the sound, Luke walked slowly forward, down to the source of the voices. He approached an opening in the wall, which led to a short, darkened hallway. He walked through the darkness toward a door. This led to a second door. He understood now: it was like double doors leading to a movie theatre.

He pushed through and found himself on the narrow balcony of a large auditorium. He felt the door click behind him as he went through. On instinct he turned and tried it. The handle was stiff and locked. He turned and moved forward toward the light but hugged the wall.

The balcony overlooked a high, hushed clamshell auditorium. The lower section featured desks, like a council chamber. They were ornate wood desks, with tiny brass lamps, and tall leather chairs, each one occupied by a woman. Dozens of them faced a deep red curtain and a golden podium. The room was almost tear-drop-shaped; velvety ochre walls and the crimson curtain fluted upward to a lofty point. It was a large, cocooned room with the hushed vibe of a lecture hall, the gravitas of a business meeting, and the hushed crackle of a religious ceremony.

The women present looked well-heeled, impeccably dressed, as though for church or a business meeting.

There was a swell of sombre music, a baroque trill of strings and woodwinds. It came from a small group of live musicians, near the front. All the players were women. Everyone down there, all women. From the level below, someone was approaching the podium along a central aisle and the standing women bowed their heads solemnly to the approaching figure.

Chapter 57

LUKE

It was Cleo, dressed in simple white, who came down the aisle toward the front of the room. She mounted the steps fluidly, barefoot and silent on the thick carpet. She reached the podium just as the music came to a climax and ceased. She held her hands out, and looked as though she might deliver a sermon. Instead, she stood, palms up, and bowed her head. The women did likewise, and the quiet room became even stiller.

Moments ticked by. Looking about, Luke realized there was a faint mural splashed out along the rough reddish walls, featuring black stick figures. Stylized figures of men chased small four-legged dashes — deer? sheep? The men ran after the animals, encircled them, surrounded them with sharp spears, carried the felled ones, dripping lifeblood, and gathered around them. They were watched over by crowned and robed figures.

On the other wall, those crowned figures were the hunters, herding their prey into group. But their prey was men. In a series of vignettes, they ran, were encircled, felled, shed lifeblood, and were surrounded.

"Welcome." Cleo's voice was warm and honeyed and resonant. Luke felt it warm him, from within, unreasonably. *This is why people join cults*, he thought, *this warmth in her voice.*

"Welcome to all of you, the elect."

"We are thankful for sacrifice," came their voices in unison.

"We are mindful of sacrifice," Cleo replied. She lifted her head after a pause. "We are come to remember one of our elect, who has passed on. We pause to reflect on that which joins us — the blood connecting us, woman to woman, sister to sister, mother to daughter, in an eternal chain of life. Today, we remember, and we celebrate Heloise. Our sister, and my beloved niece."

This brought Luke up short.

So that explained the connection. But why the subterfuge? Why the misdirects? He pulled out his cellphone and typed notes into it, capturing what he was seeing, and what he was wondering.

When he looked up, they were projecting images on a screen. Here was his Jane Doe, Heloise, alive. Even shown sitting at a luncheon or at a conference table, she looked powerful, with a coiled athleticism. She was radiant. Breathtakingly beautiful. The slide show revealed her at parties, rock climbing, finishing marathons, by luxurious pools, volunteering with animals, sitting behind power desks, signing contracts with gold pens, her grad photos. Her many, many grad photos — and as the film stock and grain changed over the years, Luke realized with an unsteadiness inside his head, he was looking at images of Heloise across a wide variety of times, which was impossible. The black-and-white and her flared dress, nipped at the waist, suggested the 1950s. The '70s were evoked with red-tinged film, bell bottoms, and ass-brushing long hair. The '80s arrived and with them a tightly crimped fringe along with gargantuan shoulder pads.

Interspersed among them, Heloise, holding various frilly-swathed babies — other people's babies, many of them in this very room he stood in. Some of the photos looked staged and posed professionally. Others were candid. She cuddled babies, kissed them, and appeared ecstatic holding them. The more he saw the more puzzled he grew.

"Let us state our Creed."

There was a rustling sound that rippled through the lowest level, where the women in desks pulled out thick leather-bound books and opened them. Together, they recited what they read, and the words ran together like watercolours, a muddle of sounds to Luke's ears. Until Luke realized they spoke in a language he didn't know.

After the reading Cleo relaxed her stance somewhat.

"My dear Sisters, we all know that there is a bitter joy when one of the elect passes. We mark their sacrifices, their service to their family. Heloise never got to make the mark on society the way she was intended to. She was not only a member of our group; to me, she was my kin. I raised and schooled Heloise across every continent. Parents always worry if their child is warm enough. Imagine *my* surprise when Heloise told me that she was taking a science gap year in Antarctica!" She paused for polite laughter. It was the kind of laugh a tense audience makes when their leader has allowed them a moment of relief.

"It is a tragedy that Heloise never birthed the daughter she wanted to give back to us. She tried everything she could to give us a daughter of the elect, but her wild heart somehow never found a nest with the right man. She denied herself the opportunity to try IVF, though we have programs to help each of our sisters achieve the healthy pregnancies we need. In the end, as a cautionary tale to us all, Heloise turned her back on us, on the safety of our group, and chose to become … savage."

There was a rustle in the room at the utterance of that word. Cleo raised her head, acknowledging it.

"It is a loaded word. I refer to the atavistic state of an unsocialized, wild animal. The state of hunters who need prey to hunt, who require life to feed upon. No one likes to think of themselves as stealing the life of another in order to live, yet isn't that what we all do, when we win a career out over another, buy the home that someone else covets, land the place in university and earn the degree that another yearns for? We are not savage. We follow rules. We pay taxes. We abide by laws. We do not simply eat one another. My goal here, in our spiritual home, has always been to temper and civilize the savagery. Life still requires life, but we need not be cruel. To survive, in a world populated by sheep, those ambling, propagating hominids, we must bend like reeds, we must blend as invisible as a breeze. We must continually adapt, embracing that which has always made us the apex: our minds. Fuelled by iron, fuelled by blood, ever more complex, ever expanding in capacity. We are here for a purpose. We shepherd the earth. It is our birthright." She paused.

"To continue that birthright, we add to our number when one is gone. Today we collect ballots to determine the next of our elect. Today we select a sister from among many candidates. Each one of our candidates here today carry girl children. To our great sorrow, only one of them will be permitted to carry that girl child to term."

Cleo lowered her gaze and her voice.

"We know that every one of the hopeful candidates who join us today must terminate the lives they carry. This is our tragic burden. This is our collective curse, our covenant, our sorrow. We have come to understand that our number must forever remain few or else we flirt with hunting the lifeblood we need into extinction. Only our daughters need the sacrifice of blood to bear and nurse the next generation of Sanguin, and to that end, only the chosen elect may bear daughters to term. This has been our way since we became enlightened. So, I urge you: choose carefully among the candidates. The future of our kind rests on your decision."

Cleo sat while the women at the tables took out sheaves of paper. As they did, a line of a few dozen women filtered in, robed with concealing hoods. The seated women read through the sheaves while the robed candidates stood with clasped hands. When they were done, each one held a sheaf aloft, and a young girl darted about the room collecting them in a basket.

The papers were taken off to a side room.

And then a girl in a long pale shift holding aloft a single sheaf of paper stood at the front of the room. She stood frozen while the room grew quiet again. She handed the sheaf to Cleo who read it, nodded, and stood at the podium.

"We remember to wish each other well, to wish each other kindness and help. We offer our greatest sympathy and support to our sisters here today, who carry unborn girl children. We weep that those mothers are not yet accepted within the select. We weep that they must destroy their girls — but we understand: we do this to keep our numbers down. We cannot have too many wolves feeding on the flock. We accept this. Though we also mourn losing Heloise, I know she would feel her heart gladden to know her passing has made a place for someone new. Her death, so painful to us, will nevertheless make room for a new life."

The room stilled to a complete, heavy silence.

"Welcome, our new sister." Cleo pointed to one of the other hooded women, who pushed back her hood.

Almost instantly there were cries from some of the hooded women. Stricken cries. Two of them were suddenly crying, shrieking, "No no no!" Not everyone welcomed the news or agreed with the vote. They were taken forcibly in arms by other women who shushed them, wrapping them, huddling around them with tight, grim faces.

"Sssshhhh!" Cleo silenced them, and the panicked women were muffled. Someone had come to join Cleo on the dais: it was Dean.

Chapter 58

LUKE

Dean stood near Cleo on the stage, which Luke realized looked like beaten copper. He wore a long tunic and had bare feet. His hands were lightly clasped, and he still wore the same doltish expression. From where he was, Luke could hear Cleo ask him if he was sure about his actions. He smiled at her with the most open of expressions and clearly answered her.

"I am."

She ran her hands up along his arms and held his face in them. She kissed him, deeply. They put their heads together and exchanged whispers no one but them heard. She kissed him again, and their ardour was apparent to everyone watching. But she stepped away and took her seat near the dais.

Dean was trembling slightly. The movement showed in the ripples of the long garment he wore. He was taking long, unsteady breaths in through his nose and letting them out with an audible "Haaaaaaa." At this point one of the women from the floor approached and went straight up to him. She put both her hands against his chest. A few inches taller, he inclined toward her and now they kissed one another, clingingly. Luke grimaced, wondering if he was about to observe some bizarre sex cult activity.

As they kissed he made a sound, into her mouth, a strangled sound. His body twitched. At his sides his hands flailed, but he didn't pull away. Cleo continued to watch, with a mild, vacant expression. Finally, the woman drew away from him and Dean staggered forward a little. They both had bloodied mouths.

Luke stepped forward, heedless now of anyone seeing him. All eyes were on the copper stage anyway, which Luke realized slanted down, focused on a central point, like a drain. Dean was looking around, a little wild-eyed. He certainly wasn't smiling now. But neither was he trying to leave. Before Dean could stagger any farther, another woman came up and clamped her mouth onto his. Dean was choking, convulsing, and his hands were pushing her off, but she had him gripped. The first woman had her hands clamped to him as well. Now it was clear this was something beyond fucked up and could only be considered assault.

"Stop!" Luke called out from the balcony. Heads everywhere turned to look at him. Cleo stood but didn't look particularly distressed. "Stop what you're doing. I'm a police officer and this man has been assaulted."

But rather than stop, the second woman grabbed Dean afresh and this time took him down to the stage, down to the floor, on his knees. Another woman had approached and now three of them surrounded him, pinning his arms. It was a mess of gore, blood splattered on the pale garment Dean wore. Luke realized that he was going to see the man die in front of his eyes.

"I said *stop*!" Luke shouted. In his own ears, his voice felt puny. His words were eaten up by the hushed space, like light sucked into a black hole. And then he felt many hands on his own arms. He looked over the balcony and considered the drop. Enough to break a leg. But likely worth it. Fighting off several sets of hands, he threw a leg up over the high railing and would have vaulted over had they not caught him by his arm, his shirt, his hair even. He dangled there for a moment.

Down below, the cloaked applicant they'd chosen was being led up to the stage toward Dean. She looked back, face eerily pale, eyes wide. Just as he was being hauled up from the edge of the balcony, he saw her. He tried to reach for her, and call to her. To try to stop her if he could. But their hands overcame him.

Beatrice.

They'd chosen Beatrice.

Chapter 59

LUKE

Luke landed face-first on the oatmeal-coloured carpet in a windowless room furnished with a large desk. He was still getting to his feet when the door opened noiselessly. He saw Cleo's bare feet peeping out from the hem of her garment before he was up.

"So, you found our inner sanctum."

"What *the fuck* is going on here?"

"Please, Luke, sit."

"What the fuck were you doing, were they doing to Dean? Why didn't he fight?"

He bristled at her from a few feet away, feeling like he was constructed entirely from anger and disbelief and gritted teeth and muscles twisted into ropes.

"Sit. Please." Her voice was calm, soothing, honeyed.

Reluctantly, he sat, but remained bolt upright, hands on knees, legs at right angles, barely supported by the lip of the chair he took.

"Very few men have witnessed that ceremony."

He pointed a stiff finger at her, a little dismayed that it shook slightly. "You have a lot to answer for. This ends with me arresting you."

She folded herself easily into a chair opposite him.

"Hmm." She laughed, and it was odd to see her do something involuntary. "I think you're well aware that there's evidence, hard evidence of your own missteps. Police are keen to observe protocols. Protocols such as not getting involved personally with suspects. So, an arrest might be some distance off, yet. But I am quite happy to talk. I enjoy our time together, Luke."

Luke felt himself being manipulated by her. He could tell she was working him with her body positioned sideways to him, with her smooth voice, her unchallenging tone. He felt like a child being schooled by a patient but cross mother.

"We lost Heloise, because of her spectacular misadventures. Her actions would make no sense to any homicide detective or profiler known to people. But she was acting entirely on old instinct. The instinct of the hunter. She knew the grooves of an old, ancient ritual of procreation and celebration and sacrifice. And in that ritual, the first and most potent sacrifice is the father. Whose very lifeblood helps nourish the life to come. It's always a bittersweet event because the father must be remarkable. Intelligent, strong, hardy, the soul of a poet or painter or builder or ruler. And sadly, he must give his life for his child to live. Dean always wanted to be a father one day. His sacrifice benefitted him too, you see?"

"So, is that what I was seeing there? You murdering a man because you have some twisted religion that says that will bring about new life?" But he stopped his outburst. Luke put both hands on his face, fingers digging into his own temples. He was stuck in a windowless room, several levels underground, with many hostile people who were quite willing to murder a man. And he was alone. The only thing he could do to survive this moment was maintain calm.

When he looked up, Cleo's chair was empty.

And before he could even rise from his seat, before he could prepare, she was on him. Hadn't even see her move … She seized him by the neck and shoulders and hauled him out of his chair. As it happened, chief in his mind was his amazement at her strength. And right after that, the awareness that her unmovable fingers were digging into his carotid arteries on both sides of his neck. And while he looked into her unblinking eyes, a percolation of nerves pinpricked him, and the room shrank into darkness.

†

In the darkness Luke saw that kid. The one with the freckles. He was sleeping on a bench where just anyone could come along and take him. Then he was Beatrice standing nearby. Why hadn't she helped the kid? She was standing there, naked and still dripping wet from the bath. She dripped on the ground, great drops of water that fell in plush globes and shattered against fallen leaves. The fallen leaves that lay crisp and curled on top, slimy, dark, mushy, and fetid on the bottom. She was naked but she wore her Keds. She looked down at the freckled boy, smoothed his brow. She was putting an IV into her arm and Luke knew she shouldn't do that. But she persisted and for some reason Luke was powerless to do anything but watch. She hooked an IV in her arm directly to the boy who was suddenly a nest of wires and cables and tubes and springs and cogs. She kept dripping on the leaves, and on the tops of her shoes that stayed gleamingly white, despite the black layer of putrid leaves turning to a sludge under her feet.

She looked at Luke and he could tell she was disappointed in him.

†

Luke came to with a sharp intake of his breath. He was lying on something, but he had the sensation he was still falling. He moved his head from side to side, trying to get rid of feeling seasick.

He could tell he was in a huge space, but he couldn't get his eyes to focus, and his head felt full of straw. He realized as he blinked away blurriness that he was looking at murals on a ceiling. When he lifted his head and peered around, it looked improbably like a convention space or a carpeted airplane hangar.

Nothing he saw made any sense. Banks of machines lined the wall to one side like something out of a 1950s Cape Canaveral rocket launch. Tubing, climbing plants, classical music? Placid workers in maroon scrubs tended to people who lay inert in cubicles … he tried to struggle up to his elbow to see around him better. A nurse approached with sincere concern on her face.

"Relax, relax! You're fine, sweetheart. Don't worry." She smoothed him back down. "Keep your legs up. That way your circulation will improve. You've had a real shock to your system." Her hand kept smoothing his arm. He felt something on his other arm and saw another girl in scrubs, with a similarly sweet expression. She stroked him on the other side and gazed down at him with all the care of a new mother.

"I'm going to get you started on some fluids," said the first woman. He felt her stroking along the direction of his arm hairs and then the small shock of a cold swab. "Just a little alcohol here. Now just a little prick here …" The sweet-faced woman gripped his left forearm as the needle, sharp and cold and relentless, drove into his flesh on the right.

"Hey, I don't want any —"

"Sh-sh-sh," said the first woman. "Don't worry." She was very encouraging.

"I don't consent!" Luke managed to blurt out. She shook her head a little vacantly at him.

"All done! All done. You're just fine." She smoothed him again, her hand bumping a little against the plastic tubing that wound up along his arm away from the IV she'd given him. And when he looked to the other side, he saw he was tethered on both sides. One side was a clear liquid dripping from an unmarked clear bag. The other was a long tube, coloured dark red. His blood. Going out.

He tried valiantly to sit up. To rip the damn things out. But he realized he'd been tethered completely; webbing strips held down his wrists and his ankles. And that was when he truly started to panic. His chest heaved, trying to draw air deep, all the way down to the bottom of his lungs, but his throat closed in on his breaths. It seemed like he wasn't getting any oxygen. He felt like vomiting. He felt like screaming. He felt his forehead prickle and the slightest stir nearby made tiny gusts of air make him realize he was bathed in sweat. The woman dabbed at his forehead and stroked his hair.

"All right. All right. Try to calm down your breathing ..."

"Nearly there." Cleo came into his narrowed field of vision, dark at the edges. "We are so thankful you decided to come to us, Luke." The sight of her filled Luke with another wave of nausea.

As Cleo approached they wheeled a small silver tray over.

"You'll be just fine. We take the greatest care of those who come here to us. We are ever mindful of the bond we share. Ever thankful." She spoke to the nurse. "You have it?" The nurse handed Cleo a tiny vial. Cleo picked up a small syringe. With an expert hand, she inserted the needle, drew out the fluid.

"What is that?"

"Don't worry, Luke. This is very safe. An active but safe sedative. After this is administered, you'll be given something much stronger, which is going to allow you to drop down into a completely inert state. Past care. Past any effort. Past longing or pain. Can you imagine, never again having to struggle, to yearn pointlessly?" She was stroking him, even as he pulled at his restraints. Her voice was soothing, lulling. "They say all those who come to us get to live in a dream state, a pleasant half world where nothing can harm them, bathed in a golden glow. Sleep now, my dear. Fear no more."

With an expert hand, she tapped the syringe, dislodging air pockets. She inserted the tip straight into the IV where it met his arm while he stared at her with wild, bulging eyes. And after a few seconds, he felt the grip of paranoia and terror subside. Even as his mind fought to cling to the sharp edge of conscious, fearful awareness, it slipped from him, and he felt an overwhelming sense of heaviness. He just barely felt the sensation of tape adhering to his eyelids and he fought momentarily against the glue to attempt to flicker them.

But soon he quit even that effort. He even had a sense of not feeling as though the urge to get up and leave was perhaps necessary. A lot of fuss …

Next, he heard rough shouting from all sides. Many, many people shouting and screaming words he swam toward but couldn't grasp onto. He heard furniture being tossed around. He was aware that he was being shaken. More shouting.

"Go, go, go! Get out! Now!" Luke thought that sounded like Cleo.

"Stop them!" someone else was shouting. Did he know them? It sounded like a little stampede. And then it was quiet.

"Over here!"

"Another one."

"Are these people alive?"

He was aware of light, and he remembered his eyes were taped shut. Nevertheless, he strained, feeling the pathetic muscles that moved them straining against the grip of the tape.

"Luke! *LUKE!* Hold on!"

Hold on? That was a strange thing to be told. Hold on to what?

"Luke! Can you hear me?"

Come to think of it, he did know that voice. He was just having a rough time connecting what he knew to what he could articulate.

Bumping. Rough bumping.

The tape came off, and with it his eyelids were torn open, and he was glad of the bracing feeling, the stinging bite of it tearing off a few layers of skin cells. He was looking straight into a penlight held by someone who seemed intent on slicing open his brain with it. Next to him was someone holding his hand and leaning over him.

That person was not Beatrice.

"Harry?"

Harry.

"Hey, Luke. Just hold on."

"Where's Beatrice?"

"Luke, just hold on."

Chapter 60

LUKE

"All right, we have returned from lunch break, and we are continuing with the testimony. Can you describe what you saw after you continued down the hall, please?"

Luke had waited through lunch, and almost a whole year before that, to come to this moment, when the wheels of justice would try to make some sense of everything that had happened. *Good luck* was all he could think.

"I was concerned about Luke's welfare, due to several alarming texts I'd received. The last of those was a location for where he was, which I understood to be letting me know where to find him in case he was in danger. I immediately alerted authorities who attended the scene shortly after I did. After a cursory pass of the auditorium in the Medspa basement, several officers and first responders ascertained that the male on the stage was deceased. We continued going from room to room." Harry was giving testimony, the last of many called over the course of several weeks to do so. "Farther down the hall, we noticed people coming and going from a set of double doors, people wearing what looked like hospital scrubs. My first thought was to get some first aid for the man in the auditorium."

Harry sat a little to one side, legs crossed easily. He wore one of his nicer grey suits with a blindingly crisp white shirt that picked up light slanting in from the pebble-glass windows. Luke watched him from near the back where he sat with one hand gripping each knee. Luke jumped a little at a brush along his ropey forearm. But turning to his left, he saw it was Beatrice.

She looked steadily at him, trying to catch his eye. "You'll be fine. Keep breathing. We can leave if you want."

"No," he whispered fiercely.

"Were there doctors or nurses there?" The lawyer continued grilling Harry.

"No. Or if they were, they weren't there to help that man. We thought they were nurses, orderlies, something, by the way they were dressed. But the minute we walked in, everyone stopped and froze."

"Can you describe the room?"

"Sure. A big space. Carpeted, no windows, tall ceilings. Lots of equipment, but sort of, well, formal. Almost religious. It felt like walking into one of those megachurches they've got. And spread out everywhere in the room these kind of space-age beds, each one with a person hooked up to all kinds of equipment. Lots of lights and beeping instruments, monitors. A hum throughout the room. One of the other guys I was with said there was music, but I didn't notice it at the time. Some of the people looked rough — waxy, emaciated, larval, all curled up. I think there were maybe thirty or forty of them? But I was looking for one particular person."

"And that was?"

"My good friend. Luke Stockton."

Luke, who had been studying his knuckles looked up at this. The qualifier "good." The warmth with which he said it. That was unexpected.

"And almost right away, we spotted him. He was strapped down to this table, with bonds, ankles, wrists. And having seen a dead man only a few moments earlier, I had to assume that something bad was going on."

"What did you do at that point?"

"I pointed him out to one of the two officers who were there with me. They drew weapons at this point, and we directed the people around Detective Stockton to step away. And then … all hell broke loose."

"All hell?"

"The lights were killed, and for a few moments it was pitch-black. People were running, knocking things over, lots of crashing. We were trying to get someone; I remember grabbing a woman by the arm, but she broke away. People were yelling go, go, go! And as much as I wanted to grab someone to find out what the hell was going on, my main concern was to know how Luke was — was he breathing? Was he all right? I know that one of the other officers was trying to put a call out to EMS, but the reception down there was nil."

"You were unable to apprehend any of the ambulatory healthy people who were down there."

"Not a one. And they seemed hell-bent on a scorched-earth policy. When the lights went down, I think that was someone throwing a kill switch for all the power. During the blackout we think the women, the accomplices or whatever, left via hidden doorways. Tunnels. I heard they never figured it out." Harry took a breath. He may have been a hardened cop once, and a practised television host, but remembering what he saw was taking a toll. "The silence when everything went dark was intense. No more beeping. Some of those people had machines to breathe for them, so you could hear … choking and rattling. People taking their final breaths. Whatever they gave to Luke, he was out, but not all the way under, you know? I stayed with him while one of the other guys got up to a level where he could call EMS."

"You indicated in your written statement that one person, sorry, one conscious person did remain after everyone else stampeded out."

"That's correct."

"Can you identify that person, please?"

"Right there." Harry pointed decisively at Cleo, who sat in the prisoner's box, hands on her lap. She inclined her head, as though in greeting.

The sound of the lawyer talking became a harsh buzz in Luke's head. He was gripping his knees harder than he realized and relaxed only when he felt Beatrice's cool fingers prying them gently off.

After Harry's testimony they were supposed to go out for drinks. *Get comatose* was how Harry indelicately put it. But Luke had had quite enough of that. And besides, he didn't drink anymore. And Harry had a plane to catch, which meant he was going to miss some of the other testimony.

"I wanna read the transcripts," Harry had urged. "Especially from that crazy bitch we found there."

EMS responders had found forty-two coma victims, most of whom had ceased all functions by the time they'd arrived. Luke was one of the first attended to, at Harry's insistence — officer down, line of duty, even if where the line was had become murky. Several vegetative patients survived, only to be transferred to other facilities, nameless unknowns.

They were never able to figure out where in the world most of them were from, or who in the hell they were. Cleo had created long chains of false identity papers. Some of that paperwork was digital and reduced to defragged garbage on hard drives that had been smashed and torched. For some, DNA helped, and they were able to match these people with families. Families were denied a reunion since the patients remained profoundly comatose. Whether they were claimed or not, those who had lived on breathing without assistance were warehoused in understaffed facilities across southern Ontario. Inquests were held. Articles were written. Hands were wrung. Files were closed.

One victim, found near Luke, had functions independent of assisted breathing. He surprised everyone at the hospital by regaining consciousness on a Wednesday morning. He revived sufficiently that he was able to take the stand, albeit with attendants, in a motorized wheelchair. There had been much conjecture in the media and the legal team as to whether he could physically take the stand or withstand cross. Or, since he was puckish at times, and incomprehensible at others, what he might even say under oath.

The man in the wheelchair appeared shrunken, a result of his long sleep. Muscles had atrophied. And it appeared that he had some cognitive deficits, which doctors assumed came from a head injury at some point. He spoke with an accent no one could make sense of. He knew nothing of himself, but that he went by the name Tomas. All that the court examination could get from him was that Cleo was his angel. His guardian angel who had saved him. He'd known her for as long as he could remember, and he knew that she wanted to take care of him. Cleo looked down, a little overcome, when, from the stand, Tomas declared his love for her and his vow that he would do anything to serve her, in thanks for his life.

His bizarre character testimony put holes into the Crown's side. But more serious loopholes than that lay ahead for the lawyers attempting to convict Cleo for conspiracy to mass murder.

Luke's own testimony took several days. Harry had gotten to Luke before Cleo had the chance to administer something permanent. But only just. He'd taken a big dose of sedative, and he was kept in hospital, under observation long past really needing to be kept. There were orders from the top to take the best care of him, lest they be seen doing less than they should. Luke's brush with death had led him to bump directly into monsters that couldn't be named or understood or known.

But in time, Luke was too healthy and restless to hold on to. Panels of doctors and teams of nurses had to agree — he was using more resources than he needed. He was discharged.

The first time he saw Beatrice was in his room. She gripped his wrist with both hands. When he tried to say something, she stopped him.

"Please. No. Just, let's be. Okay?"

He nodded and she kissed him, and he couldn't believe how warm her lips felt on his forehead.

After his discharge they began talking again. There were tears. There were expressions of disbelief and fear and distrust. There were, nonetheless, assurances of loyalty. There were recommitments.

She gave birth in a normal hospital, naturally. She insisted on keeping the baby in the room and sending him home that night. They actually got into a little fight about it. He was just happy to have her back in his life. By the next day, she was home with a seven-pound newborn who demanded everything and more from her and received everything and more from her and Luke.

The baby's tiny fingers needed only to ball up slightly, or her cheeks crease into the slightest expression of want or need or discomfort before they went running to see to her. She was their welcome despot. They were her willing adherents.

Hildy, they called her. Short for Hildegaard, which was Beatrice's choice. He was more than fine with it.

Luke was let go from the force.

It was a mostly welcome transition. Though he fell into bed exhausted most nights, punished by the baby's schedule, he could not sleep. Each day that passed, when he could touch the baby's doughy little arms or cup her fragile little head, he felt a deeper stab for each of those boys — some mother's child, given the greatest insult possible by that woman.

At the station he went through the formalities of handing in items, though he was spared clearing out a desk and a locker: they had already handed it over to new blood. He was advised to avoid the newspapers and, really, all media for a while, and he took that advice to heart. It helped him focus on the baby anyway. He discovered various uses for a retired homicide detective. Harry was surprisingly useful and available at all hours to spitball, be it career paths or late-night feeding patterns. Luke was more likely to turn to Harry than the internet in those days, when seeking information.

Days blurred into weeks and months. He was surprised when the court date arrived. He was surprised to even be called in to testify. But then, even if all his evidence had been compromised, sullied by actions he couldn't justify to anyone, he had still been a witness to things that had happened to him. His testimony was far from the only thing needed to close the case on Cleo and her outlandish operation. They'd found her, syringe in hand, ready to dispatch an officer, surrounded by the bodies of dozens of inert victims harvested from who knows where. They discovered women drinking blood from a dead man, for Chrissakes. They'd found murals depicting groups of maniacal women drinking blood … It all beggared belief.

Luke came to court, along with Beatrice and the baby, who was fussy. They did the full dog-and-pony show for the courts, the media. Suit for him. Suit for her. White frills on the baby who had leg rolls like the Pillsbury Doughboy. The picture of propriety. Even if the black-and-white glossy pictures that came out later in court made Beatrice look aside and suck on her bottom lip.

The details Beatrice herself had to share about changing doctors, considering abortions, repeatedly and willingly going to the Medspa to attend meetings with those people looked unpalatable as well. There was the weird business about what she was planning to do with the placenta, which she pronounced even as she held her child on her lap. At this point it was several good citizens' turns to turn their heads away, while Luke just focused on a point on the tip of his shoe.

He nevertheless took the stand, day after day. Tied the ties. Took the oaths. Looked into Cleo's eyes, unflinchingly. Said what needed to be said.

Beatrice was one of the star witnesses. Her involvement with the Medspa Vamps, as the media had started branding them, was spun into a lurid tale of kidnapping and brainwashing. The Crown made a case for Cleo to be considered a cult leader.

Wearing trembling pale-coloured crepe, which was messy when tearstained, Beatrice's testimony was difficult to hear. It was scathing. Lovingly drawn court images of her bent and weeping, delicately etched in chalk and oil was perfect fuel for the media machine.

Except for the botching of his evidence and the impropriety and the fire at that club and the missing body of Jane Doe and the breaching of the Medspa without cause, there was still mountainous evidence. Monstrous evidence. A conspiracy to commit premeditated murder, across borders, across time. It was mind-boggling how deep it went and for how long. It was a matter of time until other evidence was laid out, heard, judged, and she was put far away from people.

Yet Cleo sat there, day after day, in one cream or white suit after another. Legs crossed or neatly side by side, not a hair out of place, not an expression out of whack, more like a member of a royal family than a murder suspect. A constant look of curiosity glazed her expression. Never a sneer, never an unpleasant expression.

When she herself took the stand, and a kind of hush came over the room, she walked upright, graceful in the glare of scrutiny. Like a deposed queen mounting a scaffold.

There was some business with her oath. She would not use the Bible, she explained with a dazzling smile to the court officer. She ultimately said an "utterance of life" over a cloth symbol. The media got hold of it later and reproduced it for headline news: it was a mysterious circle with a cross inside, embroidered on an aged piece of leather.

When she sat she was nevertheless tall in her bearing. And she looked out over the courtroom, scanning from her left to her right, inspecting the face of each person who had come to witness her testimony, as though she herself were the judge.

She denied nothing. She answered cleanly, clearly, and levelly each mad claim, each criminal act that seemed to beg that new laws be struck.

All the pieces of evidence were brought out from their bags, their folders, their digital files and trotted out. The Crown conducted itself with aplomb. The defence likewise. But when the gavel fell and a judgment was pronounced, it caused a stir in the courtroom and a flurry of press:

Not criminally responsible.

Cleo, found brandishing syringes in the midst of a den of bloodsuckers, corpses, and coma victims, was not criminally responsible.

Despite massive outcry Cleo was placed under the authority of the Ontario Review Board, designated not criminally responsible. She was deemed to be a significant threat to the public if released and was to remain under the authority of the ORB with no set release date.

It was one of the most unpalatable pronouncements possible. One that mocked the idea that bad things had happened. That evil had happened. But the individual on trial for its execution was beyond any doubt: Not. Criminally. Responsible.

"How the fuck can that be?"

Luke and Harry met with their own lawyer whom they had retained for various reasons.

"DNA," he told them, and he seemed to revel in it, a little. "It's fucking brilliant. Masterful defence. Slam dunk. There's something wrong with her DNA."

"That doesn't make sense," Luke had yelled.

"It's brilliant, is what it is. And I think it will hold all the way up to the Supreme Court and back. Don't worry." His last two words came out, probably just in time to stop Luke from damaging property and his own knuckles. "She won't ever get out to see the light of day again. That bitch is some kind of psycho-socio-I-don't-fucking-know-what. She's gonna get the Bernardo treatment and worse. She fucked up a *lot* of people. They're going to change the law because of that one."

Luke sat down long enough to hear the explanation. She didn't possess what was considered human DNA. Or at least not enough of it. They'd brought in specialists to test it, then testify, then specialists to testify about them. They'd taken enough blood over the course of a few months to fill a proper human with blood and the results matched and were conclusive. Inhuman DNA coursed through her veins. The defence case was legendary. Certain rights and responsibilities flow from being human. These build the social construct. The law steps in when humans harm humans. The law has no purview over non-humans.

"So, someone could cook up a person with chimp DNA in them and get *them* to commit crimes!" Luke had exploded.

Harry had nodded. "Hypothetically, yeah. The law hasn't caught up to that shit yet."

They were never able to track down the many women who had worked at the Medspa. They evaporated into the ether — a miasma of fake names and identities. They left behind burned files and destroyed hard drives. Only Cleo could be connected to the people in the facility with the plastic tubes in their arms. Only Cleo could be linked to the stainless-steel canisters they sold from the front desk. The women in the files and receipts they sold them to were fabrications. They disappeared and faded as ink fades on thermal paper.

"There's more of them. They're a family. Cleo said so," Luke growled.

"Show me the bodies. Show me the relatives. She said she had no kids. No living relatives. It was a metaphor, the family business stuff. So she said," Harry countered by cell, on a break between scenes.

"She was lying," Luke spat.

Harry shrugged. "Point is, she's locked up."

Chapter 61

LUKE

Cleo was placed in the Oak Ridge Division of the Penetanguishene Mental Health Centre. The vast yellow brick building was situated on acres of rolling green grass about as far away from civilization as it could be. No one roamed the acres of land around the place except a lone gardener who spent days upon days on a riding lawn mower.

For weeks after the trial, there was public outcry. Social media screeds, opinion pieces, and demonstrations. There were full-throated demands to more fully investigate Cleo and her inconceivable designation: *not human*, at least not technically speaking. But over time, gasoline prices, droughts, floods, wars, celebrity divorces, and rising taxes wormed their way to the top of the headlines, and she was relegated to Wikipedia and corners on the dark web, fan sites, and memory.

Luke did not forget.

He was enthusiastically welcomed to visit Cleo by her keepers, as connection with the outside world was considered an important part of her progress. Not that progress would ever lead to being released. Even so, Cleo was a model patient.

In the beginning she spent entire days in a light-blue cinder-block room, seventy-five feet square. She was eternally patient and suffered all manner of questions and answered them with eternally good humour, with empathy, with intelligence. In time she earned more freedom. Hallways. Common areas. There was no maximum-security area to put her in: there weren't enough female NCR patients to merit it. She made crafts with other patients during long quiet mornings as thin light seeped through reinforced glass. The other patients fumbled and often got glue and cotton balls stuck to themselves. Cleo made haunting sculptures, unreasonably intricate, any of which could have become museum pieces. She cleaned hallways, both hands grasping the long handle with grace as if she were a dancer. She found dirt that no custodian ever did. Staff had to admit she made the place look better. She made her pastel jumpsuit look like it was cut to fit her alone. She composed thoughtful gift cards for her keepers and her fellow detainees. She knew every person on the ward by first name.

Luke was shocked that she was allowed to meet with him in an open space, which doubled as a lunchroom. It was populated by other patients who murmured to themselves or sang or rocked or sat still. She waited for him, seated in a moulded plastic chair, under flickering fluorescents at melamine tables — calm, legs crossed, hands folded as if she were any person, any human. He chose a seat with its back against a corner. One that provided long sightlines.

"They tell me there is a man here who once beheaded someone on a bus with a penknife," she told Luke as he sat. "But I haven't had the 'pleasure' of meeting him." The air quotes were meant to be a comfort, Luke figured. He did not feel comforted.

"It's weird you're housed here, mixing freely with humans," he said. He hoped she would notice the way he stressed "humans."

"You mustn't worry. I have no need of blood. I never took it myself. What's more, I have no need to harm any of these people here, or you. As far as you are concerned, I'm quite harmless. How is your child? Does it thrive?"

Luke wasn't sure how to respond. He'd thought she might ask. He'd thought of many things she might ask about, during the trip up here. He'd driven alone. He hadn't even told Beatrice about the trip. He told Beatrice less and less these days. They lived a comfortable, almost wordless life, focused on the baby, on runs to the drugstore, on the baby's coughs, her breaths, her fat rolls, her intake, her output, her minutes slept, her gross motor skills. These things consumed the two of them. Each night they fell asleep exhausted, smelling slightly of baby powder.

"The child is fine."

"Hmm. I thought you might say something like that. I rehearsed what I might ask and what you might answer. But there's nothing I can do to her, or Beatrice. Or you. So, you might as well tell me. It is a great favour to me, and it costs you so little."

"She's eleven months old. Still scooting. Never crawled. We thought she was going to walk sooner but she hasn't. Pulls herself up to standing with a toy. Almost says words, but who can tell? Pretty sure she once said 'egg' to me. Satisfied?"

"Is she weaned or is she still nursing?" Cleo asked it a little too eagerly.

"Not … fully." Luke answered, warily. Cleo closed her eyes and for a moment seemed to revel in this partial fact. Luke scanned the room while she sat there, stiffly upright, hands loose on her knees, chin up, eyes closed. "Look. I came here for one reason. I want to know. I want to hear it from you. I want you to tell me what the hell you are."

Cleo's eyes flicked open. She leaned in toward him, with a curve at the edge of her lips. Like a Madonna. Or a cat.

"You ever wonder where fairy tales come from, Luke? When you tell them to your baby at night? Princesses in slippers that wear out? Dogs with big round eyes like teacups? Stepmothers who cut off their children's fingers? Mothers who stab their breasts with needles and drop their blood in the snow? Humans tell stories about monsters so their children know the monsters get destroyed. Good wins in the end. Sleep tight. What about your ghoulish stories about the walking dead who suck the blood and the life force out of people? Or vicious sirens who use sex to lure helpless men only to lead them to death. Where *do* they come from?" She leaned in toward him.

He felt repelled and drawn at the same time.

"Well, since you've come this far, and since you're professionally discredited, I don't mind telling you. We've been here much, much longer than you. And we hunted you before you humans organized yourselves enough to have coherent thought or language or writing. We've been in your consciousness since before your consciousness developed. We were in the shadows that gathered around your campfires and caves. We were the sounds in the night. We were the cunning while you were the standing flocks … Isn't it interesting, how the blood suckers in the myths and stories are beautiful, cunning, and noble? You were always aware that we were greater than you, more advanced. Without us, you'd still be knocking rocks together to make arrows. We are ancient. And as your kind spread … you put us at risk. You multiply so quickly and you're such dangerous, arrogant beasts. It's a question of conservation, you see. Nature strives for a balance between the wolves and the deer." Cleo smiled at him with an indulgent smile. "I'm very fond of you, Luke. I feel a kind of bond with you."

Her look was dazzling. He blinked. She turned her body away from him, crossed one leg over the other. Elegant despite the scrubs, despite the melamine, despite the fluorescents that should have made her pallor green and sickly. But she looked at him, aside.

"In the end you're all sheep, Luke. Sweet little lambs. Ready for sacrifice. Without the yoke of sacrifice to guide you, I wonder if your species would even know what to do with itself?"

With this she turned away, slightly. It was just an angle of her head. She appeared extremely fascinated with the cinder block of the opposite wall, and no question, regardless of the urgency of his need or the volume of his voice, would get her to turn her head. When he did get loud enough, attendants came for him.

She was placid and quiet and kind and spoke softly while he yelled and knocked over several chairs and needed to be dragged out. She sat there in her chair, with an innocent shocked expression.

It went in her file that she was receptive and polite and social and that she would continue to be allowed visits going forward. It was noted that Cleo had expressed a feeling of discomfort and fear when her visitor came. She talked about it with an extremely empathetic counsellor, later on. Luke was escorted out by several guards. He was shown the door, he was given his coat, and was told he wasn't allowed to return to see her for some time and until he was fully cleared by a therapist.

Chapter 62

LUKE

Iain Burns was laid to rest in a massive funeral in Chicago. They held it at Graceland where weeping willows were reflected in the water. You had to be rich to get into Graceland. But no amount of worldly wealth would get you back out. All the city's legal and political luminaries came to pay respects. The funeral gathering was huge, black limos lining the winding paths. The casket was massive, thick, and heavy, borne by six hearty fellows. One of the pallbearers was Iain Burns's eldest son, Hunter, who walked stiff and strong under that weight while his own child and wife looked on.

Only the immediate family knew how little of their patriarch Burns had been left to place in that closed casket. And only the immediate family knew about the assailant or her motives.

The wife had known. She'd met Heloise at many events. Shook her hand. Cut ribbons at openings with her. And after the separation, knew that Heloise had carried on with Iain. There was the initial burst of lurid gossip about inter-office impropriety and rampant sex, which had given way to lurid gossip about the sensational murder. It livened up many a golf match and board meeting. In time it gave way to sober appreciation for a man with a storied career. It became a salty detail in an otherwise remarkable life of service and excellence. The lurid talk dissipated. They laid the man and his accomplishments to rest, and their world continued on without him.

Hundreds of kilometres away, an OPP officer made the long drive from Toronto to Montreal. He attended Rich Beauville's parents to break the news of their son's demise. They rushed a cremation, family only, no service. An obit ran in the paper with his high school photo and his beaming, cocky, take-on-the-world smile. In the photo he was wearing the same shirt police had found him wearing at Club Nausea.

Luke was the one who'd connected with the next of kin for the boy in the alley and the boy in the park. The boy in the alley turned out to be Liam Siskind. Nice family. No problems. No abuse. No weirdness. Possibly some schizophrenia on the dad's side. And very likely Liam had found himself deeply alienated by divergent sexuality from his sober family. He'd ghosted away from them, cut himself off. Never got to find out that his parents knew all along which way he swung and couldn't have cared less who he wanted to kiss. It was one of those follies of adolescence: high passions, a dramatic breaking off, a feeling of deep alienation on the kid's side when in reality they couldn't give the kid enough. A big misunderstanding that would have smoothed out in time, had the kid been given the opportunity to even out. But Heloise and wrong time and wrong place had conspired to rob him of the chance.

Mr. Marathon, the jogger from Rosedale was identified but had no other family. He rested in Mount Pleasant Cemetery. His home sat on a side street, the envy of real estate speculators for miles around, but there was no one to claim it. The weeds grew up around the front windows and a pile of tax bills collected in the foyer.

The hardest one was the kid from the park. The kid with the freckles. He passed away in hospital. The mother disappeared. They eventually figured out next of kin and Luke had attended a squat brick square in deep Scarborough, hidden behind a rampant threadbare mass of bridal wreath hedge. He had to step over weeds and recycling bins and milk crates full of empty paint cans. A brand new, bare MDF door and crowbar marks on the trim told the story of break-and-enters. Or maybe forced police entry.

The gruff man at the door had nodded when the photo was shown.

"Not my kid. Stepkid. No blood relation."

"Do you know where his mother is?"

"Mother's dead."

"So, no next of kin."

"Nope."

"Sir, this boy died. Alone. He was living on the street. Someone attacked him."

The man looked him dead in the eye and shot back, "Had it comin'." Right before he slammed the MDF door shut.

There was still that one more kid. Not Luke's, per se … Down a forested embankment up north. That runaway in the forest when he and Beatrice had tried spicing things up at that spa. Luke had tried to connect with the local detectives again, but the wheels moved slowly on the case outside his jurisdiction. By the time the court case had happened, and Luke was on leave, it was still grinding along. He lay awake sometimes, wondering about that kid, and the others. And felt a bottomless sense of unfinished business with some mothers' sons. It was Beatrice who had pointed out the wavy interlocking pattern of the shoe prints to him when he'd peered at crime scene prints in bed.

"They're Keds. Just like those." She'd pointed them out, in her closet on her way to brush her teeth. "Like about one hundred million suburban moms have. Don't you have a media thing tomorrow?" she called to him through a mouth full of toothpaste.

"Yeah. Same one Harry's on."

"No kidding! You're giving him a run for his money now." She spat, rinsed.

She came out, dressed in her bathrobe.

"You'd better wear that nice suit we got for the trial. The blue one. With the brown shoes," she said as she crawled up to him from the foot of the bed.

"No one's gonna see the shoes." He was surprised she laid herself lengthways against him, pressing. Her inner thigh hooked over his knee.

"I will."

With a shock, he recognized her tone of voice. Flirtation. He could feel his veins open up, and his blood rush. He turned to her and found the side of her cheek, her earlobe. Her mouth found his.

"Isn't it close to feeding time?" They listened. But the baby monitor was quiet. The hall was quiet. There was only the still of the house and them together in bed.

"I don't hear anybody complaining."

They both shut up and kissed and Luke told himself repeatedly inside his head to be cool, though neither of their bodies were. She broke against him like storm waves. She initiated it all, she saw it through. At one point he tried to grab her waist, her ass, but she had him pinned and he thought it was weird how immobilized he was by her and wondered when she'd gotten so strong — but her tongue in his mouth wiped his mind clean. He was almost disappointed when, straddling him, she reached behind and cupped his balls because then it was immediately and enthusiastically over.

She got up when he was still trembling, spread-eagled and breathless and huffing out simple words like "Wow" and "My God." She found her dressing gown discarded at the foot of the bed.

"Hey! Where are you going?" he complained good-naturedly. "Who said I was done with you?"

"I'll be right back. Feeding time." He let his head fall back hard onto the pillows.

"I don't hear anything yet …" He reached a hand toward her.

She tossed a hand towel at him.

As she went silently down the carpeted hall, he turned onto his side. Sleep began to overtake him, numbing his thoughts and his body. As his eyes started to close, he was looking through the half-open closet door at her Keds, trying to remember a half-thought he'd had. The thought dissipated like a puff of air.

Chapter 63

BEATRICE

He lay sprawled on the bed, his chest hairs plastered down with sweat. He had that goofball look of post-sex glow. That exact moment when a man could be told to do practically anything. She looked away. She felt for him. Warmth. Affection. Truly. He'd provided for her and the baby. But it irritated her to see him so vulnerable.

"I think you're going to need to clean up a little." She winked.

"Oh man, that wink kills me." He surveyed the damage. "Clean up a little? Whoa."

But instead of stirring, he let his head drop back down on the pillows, carried away by endorphins.

She walked down the hall, carpet thick underfoot, muffling her steps. She glided down the steps of the staircase. She walked past the double-door kitchen fridge where the baby formula was kept.

Though things were ultimately working out for the best, she couldn't help but feel sad. She loved her little girl, and thank god she'd been allowed to keep her in the end. If she'd been forced to abort the baby because of what the others told her to do ...? She likely would have chosen to end her own life, out of grief. It pained her as well, that if she'd only had a little boy instead, everything in her life with Luke could have gone on, as normal. No Medspa. No Cleo. No choices to make. But fate had spoken and given her a girl. And the women had spoken, and allowed that girl to live. Soon everything in their little family would change. She needed to prepare for Hildy's future.

She passed through the kitchen, down the four steps to the garage.

In the garage, over in the corner, was the ratty back-up fridge. Inside the fridge sodas, soup stock, leftovers. And at the back, all the way at the back, a nylon cooler. One that she kept closed. And from inside the cooler, she withdrew a stainless-steel canister, with the Medspa logo on the side. Standing in the light of the fridge door, one foot balanced on the other, she threw back her head and drank deeply. From her pocket the baby monitor picked up a hungry baby cry.

"In a minute, baby," Beatrice said, dabbing red from the corner of her lips. "Mommy needs to eat so you can too."

Acknowledgements

To readers everywhere who gave me such encouragement while touring my debut book, *Autokrator*, and hinting about the story to come with *Hemo Sapiens*. Thank you so much, Russell, my acquiring editor, for believing in the power of a story to entertain and thrill and in Luke as a character, and for adroit guidance through the edit. Thank you to Jennifer Hale for her encouraging copy edits deployed with sharp eyes. Thank you to Willem, who was there when it was first conceived and there when it was picked up and there for all the juicy conversations in between. Thank you to Ginger for many interesting conversations. Thank you to Ed Kay for being an early reader. Thank you to Sam Hiyate for submitting *Hemo* and to Kat Foxx, my agent, for notes and bringing her home with enthusiasm and hard work. To Erin Pinksen for steering me through production. To Laura Boyle for hard and delicious work on a great book cover. For horrific writing life inspiration: Andrew Robertson and Tim McGregor. Thanks to Wayne the EMS worker and Barbra Gousvaris, the nicest nurse I have ever met! Additional thanks to Sgt. Chris Beattie for his police work insights. Thank you to Madeleine Fyles, Ph.D. candidate in archaeology, for a thoughtful read and notes. An enormous and warm thanks to Doug

McCaw and Carol McCaw who read early versions of the book. A fellow Coe Hill "graduate," Doug gave me so much insight into procedures and practices of police work to give my crazy made-up world of anthropological vampires a backbone of plausible reality, not to mention thrilling horse visits (hello to Invictus and Bunny and the rest … I owe you more carrots).

About the Author

Emily A. Weedon is the CSA award–winning screenwriter of *Chateau Laurier* and *Red Ketchup*, and the author of the epic dystopia *Autokrator.* She enjoys cooking, film, and reading, with a love for nonfiction that has been neglected of late. She has Ehlers-Danlos, a very weird syndrome that early on compelled her to ignore her body in favour of her brain, which, to her, only proves the Adlerian idea that our so-called weaknesses can become the basis for our strength. She grew up in a small town and probably checked out *Dracula* and other vampire books more than anyone else in the Coe Hill library. She played Lucy in two separate productions of *Dracula*. Her first screenplay was called *The Carpathian* and won her the prestigious Doodle of a Vampire Frog, drawn by her creative writing teacher, and an A++ — an honour yet to be surpassed. She lived for a year in Budapest, which is pretty close to Transylvania. Given all that, it was probably inevitable that she would write a novel about vampires. She endures Toronto and wonders if small towns might not be the way to go. *Hemo Sapiens* is her second novel.